WREN JANE BEACON

THE BRILLIANT AND THE BAD

BOOK FIVE

A NOVEL BY

DJ Lindsay

See also:
Book One: 'Wren Jane Beacon Goes to War'
Book Two: 'Wren Jane Beacon at War'
Book Three 'Wren Jane Beacon Runs the Tideway'
Book Four 'Wren Jane Beacon On the Cut'

www.wrenjaneb.co.uk

© D J Lindsay July 2021

All rights reserved.
The principal characters in this story are all fictitious. In a story set at a particular time and following closely the actual events of that time, major figures inevitably enter the story. The real people are portrayed in this book in the actual roles they had. So far as one can tell from the written record, I have shown them as they were, and have stuck to my basic rule of only showing them in a good light. Where less attractive personalities have intruded, they are fictitious.

A CIP catalogue record for this book is available from the British Library.

Design: Alan Cooper, www.alancooperdesign.co.uk

Acknowledgements

Above all, my thanks are due to Jeff Blackett, recently retired Judge Advocate General who gave unstintingly of his time and expertise to work on the Court Martial sequence. Taking my dramatic but legally inaccurate portrayal of a court martial and turning it into an approximation of what would actually have transpired, was fundamental to making the sequence legally sound. For this I am profoundly thankful.

As always, my beta readers have kept my efforts clear and to the point. They know who they are.

Thanks also to my editor Hazel Reid and designer Alan Cooper for turning my raw ideas into a polished final book.

Dedication

To the Authorities for good and bad.

Contents

PART ONE: THE SUNLIT UPLANDS 9
    CHAPTER ONE: The Meaning of Whore 11
    CHAPTER TWO: Wedding Day 18
    CHAPTER THREE: Something Different 27
    CHAPTER FOUR: Mother 39
    CHAPTER FIVE: Training Course 48
    CHAPTER SIX: Losing Them 56

PART TWO: THE DESCENT INTO HADES 63
    CHAPTER SEVEN: Moving On 65
    CHAPTER EIGHT: Preparations 74
    CHAPTER NINE: Into the Jaws 82
    CHAPTER TEN: The Defence 92
    CHAPTER ELEVEN: The Processing Continues 103
    CHAPTER TWELVE: Correction 110

PART THREE: SAPHO'S SONG 117
    CHAPTER THIRTEEN: The Slow Road Back 119
    CHAPTER FOURTEEN: Closer 127
    CHAPTER FIFTEEN: Moving On 136

PART FOUR: BEYOND THE STYX 143
    CHAPTER SIXTEEN: A Little Excursion 145
    CHAPTER SEVENTEEN: On Taking a Deep Breath 154

PART FIVE: BEYOND SURVIVAL 163
    CHAPTER EIGHTEEN: Eastward Ho! 165
    CHAPTER NINETEEN: Going Close 172
    CHAPTER TWENTY: Recognition 179
    CHAPTER TWENTY-ONE: Lunch: Trial or Pleasure? 188

BIBLIOGRAPHY 194

WREN JANE BEACON
THE BRILLIANT AND THE BAD

PART ONE:
THE SUNLIT UPLANDS

CHAPTER ONE:
The Meaning of Whore

She rolled over and languorously looked around the suite. "Just think, David, in a couple of weeks we'll be together like this as a right, mister and missus. Have you any thoughts on a honeymoon?"

"Not really. Town or country? Any preferences? And what's this mister and missus? You will be Lady David Daubeny-Fowkes y'know."

"Oh I do know, David, but that is so unimportant compared with our being married and together whenever we can. Let's hope our leaves work out."

He reached out and gently stroked her scarred cheek. "I suppose we have to survive this stupid war first, but there is so much to look forward to."

Jane smiled and eased out of bed. Stark naked she was ambling towards the bathroom when there was the rasp of a key in the lock and the hall door was flung open. "Good God!" An elegant blonde woman stood in the doorway, big eyed and startled. Jane wailed "David!" and shot into the bathroom slamming the door behind her. David emerged, pulling on his dressing gown. "Arabella! What on earth are you doing here? I thought you were in New York and only arriving a day or two before the wedding."

"Yes, well I was coming over for my brother's wedding and was offered a seat on the flying boat to Foynes. That was too good a chance to miss so here I am. But I am utterly shocked to find said brother amusing himself with a whore just weeks before he gets married. Getting in some practice, are we?"

"That's no whore, that's Jane, my fiancée."

"Ah, so she's been acting the whore to entrap you. I knew you were a green innocent but really David even you should be able to see through that one."

"Arabella, it's not like that. We love each other and Jane is the most important thing in my life to me. Remember she's a fighting Wren who rescued me at Dunkirk."

"And has been trading on it ever since."

"No, no, that's just not true. Our time together is magical and makes me feel good in a way I've never felt before."

"Hah! Been well despunked, have you?"

This fierce exchange was interrupted by a loud banging on the bathroom door. "David, would you fetch my dressing gown, please."

Dutifully he did so, passing it in through the barely opened door.

Then Jane emerged, the light of battle in her eyes. Struggling to control her temper she drew herself up to her full five foot ten and looked down on the rather smaller blonde in front of her. "Our first meeting might be a bit unfortunate but I'll thank you not to talk about me like that. How d'you do." And she held out her hand.

"Whore! I wouldn't contaminate my hand by touching yours. The thought that some cheap tart is worming her way into my family horrifies me. If I didn't have business here, I'd turn round and go straight back to New York now."

Jane had stepped forward, shaking with rage, and had to resist a strong urge to slap the girl's face. She lowered her head to be eyeball to eyeball. "Damn you, I will not be called a cheap tart. You heard David; we love each other and this marriage is about our love which we show in bed as well."

Arabella sneered at this. "Which is just what every tart does to catch a man. I wondered why reception was a bit unwilling to give me a key to the family suite. Now I know. I think I'll take myself off to the Ritz."

"How dare you!" Rage overtook the embarrassment Jane was feeling. "How dare you! I will not have our beautiful love muddied like this." She was damned if she would be called a whore just because she'd been caught naked. David just looked distraught.

By now the red mist was up. She poked the girl in the chest with a stiffened finger, still struggling with the urge to do something much more violent. "Listen you. I gather you're David's sister? It's all right for you safely tucked away in New York, but for those of us caught up in real war, every day you're alive is precious and to be made the most of. I would have been very happy to be David's blushing virgin bride but knowing that either of us could be dead before we ever got to the altar changes how you see things. I'll not have you calling me a whore just because we wanted to make our love as complete as possible."

"That doesn't make you any less of a hooker, trading your ass for a ring on your finger. Don't talk to me about love; I know your sort of love and it has a dollar sign on it."

The two women were now standing just inches apart. Jane drew herself up to her full height again, forcing the smaller woman to look up to her and hissed, "You filthy-minded nasty little bitch; I'll not have this. You obviously don't want to understand the ties between David and me so there's no point in arguing about it. Now clear off out of here and take your dark insinuations with you."

"Don't you go ordering me around, little girl. If I chose to come into the family suite I will do so and you are the interloper, not me. Now get dressed and you clear off."

David had been listening to this with open-mouthed horror and shook himself out of a trance-like state. "Arabella! You will not order my fiancée out. She is here to be with me and is staying."

CHAPTER ONE: The Meaning of Whore

Arabella curled her lip at that. "White knight riding to the rescue, is he? How brave of you, or is it just besotted? Either way I'm not impressed. If I have anything to do with it you are finished at Hemel Towers."

Jane interrupted. "We have already decided that if need be we will just live for each other in a garret somewhere. Your threat is empty because we love each other and being chucked out of Hemel Towers would not stop us wanting to be married and with each other. Now stop this; accept me for what I am or get out."

"I don't think I want to stay in this filthy atmosphere for a minute longer. But don't think that I am accepting you because I have walked out."

"Y'know, the Admiralty said something like that about me after Dunkirk. Fortunately, there were others more friendly and I'm still a Wren and still knocking about. It seems I am a survivor so your bile doesn't bother me. Now clear off."

"Bah!" And with that Arabella turned and stamped out of the room.

Jane and David looked at each other with dismay. "Well, that was a bit unfortunate. I hope she hasn't hurt you too deeply."

"Jane, that sister of mine has been cruel to me from the day I was born. She delighted in sneakily pinching me when I was little. Nanny couldn't understand why I spent so much of my time in tears and I couldn't explain it. Going away to school didn't make her any better. Yes, this is unfortunate but she'd have found some other way of being nasty if we hadn't had this scene. I can't say I like it but I don't let her sway me. Is there any truth in what she was saying about you?"

'Oh dear' thought Jane 'and thank you dear sister for putting doubt in his mind'. She had already had to wrestle with her own doubts after the canal trip, and even now that lingering longing for the open spaces and a free simple life had not entirely gone away. But getting together with David again had brought her love for him to the top and it squashed those other hankerings down into a deep place.

"No David, there isn't. Or at least, perhaps there's a grain of truth mixed in with the nastiness. Yes, I am keen to go to bed with you but that is one way of showing my love for you and the love comes first. If having you happily in love with me follows, we are both winners. But if we hadn't had that part to our relationship, I'd still love you and want to marry you. I meant it when I said I would have been happy to be your blushing virgin bride. But that's gone thanks to the war and our need for the deepest possible involvement means making love as well."

"I'd never thought of it that way. Our being together has seemed like a miracle to me from the start and this physical part of it has just made it even more wonderful. Did you really make love with me deliberately so I would be utterly tied to you?"

"David there was nothing deliberate about it. You knew that I had done it before so I wasn't losing anything by making love with you, and I just wanted to show you how much I loved you. Please David, forget that horrid bitch and concentrate on us."

"All right. It is sad because our love was such a beautiful pure thing in its way and now it has a slightly sordid edge to it. Damn that sister of mine. Shall we get dressed and go out?" But a lingering coolness lay over them for the rest of the day.

That night as they lay in bed together but hardly touching, Jane found herself thinking idly about recent times. Returning to her family home for the first time in nine months had been very pleasant and nice to see everyone but again she had had that feeling that it was no longer her home. It had been strange to find the place overrun with other people's children plus a couple of mothers. Her father had managed to arrange it that they got children of hospital staff which meant that they were a reasonably decent lot but were still young children, full of energy and noise with seemingly the run of the house. Her mother had a worn-out look to her, trying to keep her home together under the onslaught.

Jane found her mother was still deeply dubious about marriage to an aristocrat – in her eyes not people to be trusted – and she had harped on about it. Younger sister Sarah, growing up rapidly and now to be a bridesmaid, had tried to be loving but again there was a gap which they found it difficult to bridge. But arrangements had been made for the family to come to Hemel Towers for the wedding, packing up all Jane's things and bringing them to her. After her flying visit home it had been back to London, a couple of nights with David then head north for the signals course which headquarters seemed to think was essential. It had been a packed month which had her thinking in Morse and flag hoists before she was finished but it had kept her mind off her doubts about getting hitched to David. She was still struggling with the conflict between the freedoms of life on the narrow boats and the constraints of life as a Naval officer's wife; the thought that it was too late to change did little to comfort her. As she lay next to him listening to his slightly snorty breathing, she wished she could get her reservations out of her head and just commit totally to him. They were now due to head up to Hemel Towers and finalise the wedding arrangements. Invitations to over a hundred people had been sent, she had selected which one of the three heirloom wedding dresses his family could offer, and the special license had been issued.

Her mind then drifted over the previous day's altercation with Arabella. Thinking about it now, there was something odd about it all. Over breakfast she raised these doubts with her fiancé. "Did it strike you, David, that she knew an awful lot about our situation? Y'know, the language she used spoke of understanding what we were doing? I've met a lot of totally green innocents among the Wrens and they don't even have a vocabulary for sex, let alone any knowledge of it. Arabella did, and knew just what the score was in a cynical sort of way. Makes you wonder a bit."

"Really? That hadn't occurred to me but perhaps you are right. But so what?"

"I just don't trust her; she's the sort to go spreading mucky stories about us and I'd rather not have them. I think I'll make some enquiries."

By convenient chance, the Naval attaché to the British Consulate in New York was an old family friend, and a lengthy cable was sent to him that day. The reply the next day was very interesting, to the point that Jane cabled again asking him to rush a photograph by express air mail to her at Hemel Towers.

That photograph arrived the day before the wedding and confirmed Jane's suspicions. Although she was intensely busy with last minute arrangements, she caught Arabella in the morning room and said, "I need to talk to you, can we find somewhere private?"

"I'm not sure I want to talk to you, whore."

"I'm not asking you I'm telling you and the sooner you come the better."

"Really? This is interesting. Let's try the library."

With Arabella in front of her Jane produced a long cable from New York and a photograph of one Lady Arabella Flower. "I'll read this cable to you, as I thought you might be interested in it. It says '*In New York Lady Arabella Daubeny-Fowkes calls herself Lady Arabella Flower stop She is well known as the highest-class call girl in the city stop Charges several thousand dollars for a night and only the wealthiest can afford her stop Quite a celebrity stop*'"

Jane then produced the photograph – a copy of a New York newspaper article which showed the same person as was in front of Jane, being called Lady Arabella Flower. "So, whore, what have you got to say to that? You must be a wealthy woman by now."

Arabella had gone deathly pale and was trembling. Slowly she tried to speak. "Wha – wha –what do you want?"

"Oh, nothing much. Just you to stop your hypocritical nonsense about me. At least I only bed my own man and my ass is not for sale. Providing you shut up about me and my presence as David's wife, I will keep quiet. But the slightest hint of your poisonous nastiness being produced against me and some people will get an interesting surprise. And no, David does not know about this although he will be the first, but not the last, to hear about it if I have to let it out. Now you tell me how you are going to behave."

The shocked terror in Arabella's eyes had been replaced with a fierce hatred. "I suppose it takes one to know one. You'll not be forgiven for this. Don't ever come to New York because your life might be quite short. But round here I'll say nothing. Will that do?"

"Dear me, aggressive to the last, eh? That's an empty threat. The originals of these are locked away safely where you can't get at them with instructions to release them if you do anything to me. Our more scandalous newspapers would love a story like this. So unless you want to be ruined you will say and do nothing hurtful to me. Would you like to end up selling your ass on a street corner?"

Arabella was shaking, with rage as much as fear, but had a cornered look. "How on earth did you get suspicious enough to make enquiries in New York? I never thought you'd go that far."

"The way you spoke on our first encounter showed you knew the score very well already. It wasn't how an innocent offended young lady would. So I smelt a rat and decided to see if there was anything known about you in New York; fortunately, I have contacts there. But I have to say I didn't expect anything as lurid as came back in the cable. Can you really charge several thousand dollars a night? I've heard a little about that sort of thing in London but a hundred pounds a night was considered wildly expensive."

"I am the only one who can and it's because those dumb Yanks just love the thought of bedding an English aristo. And that price keeps the riff-raff away."

"A life like that must be hard work. How do you manage?"

"For me it's not every night, y'know, and it's only the threesomes that are serious hard work. Married couples are not so bad but dealing with three excited men in one session can be exhausting; it's the six thousand dollars that makes a bit of sore tiredness worth it."

"Three at once? My goodness you are a professional."

Arabella curled a lip. "You catch on pretty quickly."

Jane couldn't help laughing. "Really you and I should be on the same side."

"You've no idea how much I hate being blackmailed but let's call it a truce. Enjoy your wedding, whore."

"All right, whore, I will." And they both laughed. There was no warmth between them but the parting was amicable. Even so, Jane was surprised to find that she was trembling too. She had a feeling of having come a long way from rescuing sailors off a burning ship at Dunkirk.

There were twenty people to dinner that night, one advantage of a large country house. Jane's parents with brother David and sister Sarah represented her family. Lady Ormond was in fine form and actually met the Beacon family for the first time after a good deal of long-distance contact in quietly looking after Jane's interests. The Earl was there, resplendent in the uniform of a major in the Household Cavalry. He had the same little mannerisms as Arthur and her David and although he was shorter the family resemblance was strong. Arabella was at the far end of the table entertaining some Colonel and avoided Jane who was seated next to the Marquis.

She was starting to get a little connection with him and found him easy company so long as she stuck to his topics. The ladies withdrew and drank coffee with their brandies over domestic chatter.

Later, alone in the bed for the last time, Jane reflected on the power sex had to shape lives. The conversation with Arabella had given a glimpse into a quite different world she knew virtually nothing about. And what was it Sparrer had said? "That's a valuable thing you've got there between your legs an' if men want it, they have to pay for it one way or another." At the time Jane had just seen the comment as the practical attitude of a person from a poorer background. Now she sensed a wider dimension to it, Bermondsey's version of Arabella's exhaustion. Did this commodified view of relationships really have any bearing on her own position? Surely, she loved her husband-to-be and was just showing it bodily as well as emotionally? Well perhaps but there was no denying that David was as keen on what her body could do as on the rest of their relationship. It had not occurred to Jane to see herself as a temptress and there had not been anything calculated about her bedding David but the result was the same, wasn't it?

Oh, this was silly and the sooner she got back to seeing her impending marriage as a love match the better, she decided, rolling over and trying to go to sleep.

CHAPTER TWO:
Wedding Day

Between nervousness and narrow boat habits, Jane was wide awake by six in the morning. She eyed the wedding dress hung up waiting for her; it seemed to say, "I am the garment in which you bid farewell to your free and easy life. Good luck." Shuddering gently, she rolled over and tried to go back to sleep but lay wide awake. Giving up and getting up, she pulled on a dressing gown and was buffing her nails when her lady's maid brought in early morning tea. Jane's hands were just about restored to some elegance after the battering they had received on the narrow boats but she meditated dreamily for a little on the life which had caused the damage. Even now the tug of that lifestyle was close to the surface but this was the day she conclusively closed that door.

With a little sigh she went for a bath; by the time she emerged both her maid and her mother were in the room. "Good morning Jane. Ready for your big day?"

"I suppose so mummy."

"Good heavens. Are you not sure?"

"Oh I'm sure enough of my love for David. He's who I want for my life partner and that bit of it is fine. It's all the Hemel Towers stuff that bothers me. Look at that wedding dress. It is absolutely beautiful but it's not me. When I put it on it will take hold of me like a straitjacket and carry me into a new world."

"Well, that is what marriage is about, dear."

"Oh, I know but it's more than just getting married. To David all this stuff is natural and he won't see how Hemel Towers wraps a kind of net round you; casual freedom to live just as you'd like is lost in the formality and expectations. But too late now. I just hope David and I can find some space for a life of our own."

"Well you know that you can always fall back on the Old Grange as some sort of retreat. We've thrown out your childhood bed and installed a nice new double bed for you both which we hope you will be coming to quite soon. Have you arranged a honeymoon?"

"David's got some ploy on but is being mysterious about it. Whether that will take us into the West Country I have no idea."

At this stage the maid re-appeared with breakfast, stopping the conversation. Jane struggled to eat anything but managed some toast. Her mother had a heartier meal then said, "Well, I'll go and see how Sarah is getting on. Her bridesmaid's dress is very beautiful but awkward to get into."

CHAPTER TWO: Wedding Day

Jane, wrapped up in her own confusions, had quite forgotten her bridesmaid younger sister.

The hairdresser came and coaxed Jane's mop into a rather elegant style with flowers through it. She had decided against any sort of hat, settling for an Alice band with a veil on it. Then it was time to put the dress on. This felt like going through some great one-way gate but with assistance from her maid she was eased into the dress, a beautiful concoction of silk and lace in the fashion of 1901. From then the room filled with people. Her mother returned with Sarah, tall and slender like Jane but fairer, suddenly a butterfly emerging from the chrysalis of childhood, beautiful in an ankle length pale lavender oyster satin sheath. Then with half an hour to go her father arrived in full morning suit. "Well, young lady, ready to go? The guests are filling the chapel nicely."

"Yes, father I'm as ready as I will ever be."

He gave her a puzzled look but said nothing and with ten minutes to go quietly tucked her hand under his arm, saw that Sarah was in place right behind with Jane's train in hand and they set off. They waited two minutes at the chapel door and then swept up the aisle. David was waiting for her in his best uniform and smiled as she arrived. Suddenly all the doubts faded into the background and solid before her stood the reason for her being there, dressed up like a Christmas tree fairy. Sarah arranged the train round the steps of the altar and the rector stepped forward. "Dearly beloved, we are gathered here today in the sight of God to witness the marriage of............"

After that it was all a blur. They spoke their lines, made their vows, the ring was slipped onto her finger and suddenly she was being guided into the vestry, a married woman.

There was a champagne reception before the wedding breakfast during which Jane and David circulated as a pair, meeting more elements of David's spreading clan. Jane had spotted the Wrens' uniforms and was delighted to catch up with Punch and Suki from *Kittiwake*, Suki at her ease and Punch looking distinctly discomfited. The Honourable Alicia, now a petty officer and Third Officer Merle Baker, both relaxed and comfortable, completed the Wren contingent, clumping together for security. "Hello, you lot, how is life on a launch these days?"

"Oh, we're going along pretty well. It's no surprise that Punch has proved to be a good skipper and we're more of a co-operative since you left, with each of us doing a bit of the admin as well as our operational jobs. Makes life easier. They decided we didn't need another hand after you left so we get along perfectly well with four, although it can be a bit tight when someone goes on leave and there's only three of us on board. But we manage. And would you believe it, Evadne has got herself a boyfriend and suddenly our tough girl has gone all dreamy. He's a reserve lieutenant

19

from a farming family so they are well suited. But tell us about this canal boat you went on. That sounds to have been a bit different."

"You can say that again. Absolutely fascinating and utterly different." And Jane spent five minutes telling them about motorboats and horse boats and the joys of the cut until David dragged her away to meet yet another distant cousin. Jane was then interested to find her father deep in conversation with the Marquis's brother. Like her father, he had been injured at Jutland and they were energetically swapping tales about who they knew and who did what.

The wedding breakfast was as sumptuous a feast as the Hemel estate could provide with French onion soup, pheasant with all the trimmings then roast beef; this last the product of one of the estate's cows being sacrificed in the cause. Sherry trifle finished this repast and the cake cutting went well with David's sword making short work of it. The Earl, as best man, proposed the toasts and David gave a typical wardroom-trained response full of glowing references to his new wife.

There followed a general retiring for a break and a change of clothing before the ball started. The Earl's regiment of Household Cavalry was due to go abroad with their light tanks and scout cars; the Ball was a farewell to them as well as the final celebration of the wedding. It was a white tie and medals occasion which Jane had prepared for by having her green shot silk taffeta ball-gown brought up from the Old Grange. She was sitting in it when her parents swept into her room, each bearing a box. First, her mother produced the Russian necklace which she carefully arranged round Jane's neck; its sparkle transformed the ball gown. Then her father opened the other box; in it lay a set of miniature medals. "I got these made for you for occasions like this. Presumably, you'll do a fair bit of society entertaining now, so you will need them. If you are given any more medals, I'll arrange for those too." She had taken in her father's rows of similar miniatures but was startled to see a row of five on her mother's gown. "Mummy! I knew you'd been awarded something but had no idea it was such a collection."

"Yes, well dear one was called on to work under tricky conditions at times and being able to keep going was seen as a plus point which was recognised."

"Very impressive." Jane's set was pinned to the bolero top she had had made from the stole of the same material as the dress. Jane had decided that the hole in her shoulder plus other sundry scars would be better covered up and the dress's bodice was much too low-cut for that. "I'm meeting David at the top of the stairs at 1930 sharp. After that I suppose the transfer from family to husband will be complete. Shall we go?"

The Ball Room at Hemel Towers was a separate wing, high-ceilinged and glittering with a huge chandelier and blaze of wall lights. A multi-coloured throng made a

CHAPTER TWO: Wedding Day

kaleidoscope with the first few couples taking to the floor. The Household Cavalry officers were magnificent in their ornate mess dress uniforms, in many ways more brilliant than the ladies' gowns and even the naval officers looked splendid in their mess dress, the more senior ones with gold stripes down their trousers. Jane's Wrens were in evening dress, Suki wearing what looked suspiciously like one of Jane's white dresses. 'How on earth had she got hold of that?' pondered Jane. The one exception was Punch, still in her Wren's uniform but even she had made the small change to a black bow tie, probably not official uniform but a gesture in the right direction. It was interesting, Jane thought, that as the evening went on Punch did not lack for dance partners and seemed to be thoroughly enjoying herself. Sarah, attending her first such event and still in her bridesmaid's dress, seemed to be getting on effortlessly well with the august company. Later, she confessed that she just chattered to her dance partners and drank rather too much of the excellent punch which flowed freely.

The Cavalry officers were all tall and stiff, frightfully well-bred but somehow remote in their social contacts. Jane found them all excellent dancers who held her firmly but carefully as they waltzed round the room to the twenty-piece orchestra drawn from the Household Cavalry's own band. She waved to David in passing; they both seemed busy with the social whirl. A good few well-bred girls had been invited and mostly they seemed as stiff as the officers with whom they appeared able to converse most easily. Things changed for Jane when it came Arthur's turn to dance with her. Now there were no polite distances, he held her up close and a hand dropped to her backside, firmly grasping her buttocks to pull them close. The dance was a quickstep which allowed for close-up rubbing and suggestive little jerks. Jane eyed him frostily. "Arthur, you just behave yourself."

"Oh I am, really, but enjoying being close to you for a minute or two. It is rather fun, isn't it?"

"Not really, no, but I suppose I have to tolerate you briefly. Kindly lift your right hand a bit." So he did, but just by an inch or so. Jane wasn't sorry when the dance finished.

Carriages were for 0100 and for the first time Jane and her new husband retired to their own bedroom to consummate their marriage. Breakfast the next morning drew the odd ironic glance but Jane was content to stay in her own gently dazey world. "Where now, David?"

He grinned. "Let's get packed."

In short order she found herself easing into a rather fine Sunbeam two-seater. "We've managed to get the petrol and coupons together for a trip, so we're going to Poole."

"Poole? Why Poole?"

"You'll see. I don't think you will be disappointed."

Driving south on a mild autumn day with the hood down was fun and they laughed a lot along the way. They drew up alongside a large, elegant motor yacht, a little faded but her pedigree unmistakeable. "Here we are. Welcome to the Daubeny-Fowkes yacht. We'll stay here for five days then have a weekend with your family before heading back to Hemel Towers."

"She is rather nice, isn't she? She must have been closed up for some time, I would imagine?"

"Yes, but I got our people to open her up and make everything ready so I think you'll find her nice and comfy. I've arranged a cook to come in morning and evening to make meals for us. You don't cook, do you?"

"No, I'm afraid not. Just never been something I've had to do. I suppose I ought to learn one of these days but it hasn't been high on the priorities so far."

He laughed and escorted her up the gangway. "We've got the Master suite all ready. It's tucked under the bridge."

A deckhand and cook welcomed them. "Everything is ready, m'lady. Dinner in half an hour."

'Being Ma'am-ed was bad enough; it was going to take a good deal longer to get used to being m'lady', reflected Jane.

But dinner was excellent, so far as rationing would allow, and a mellow evening with a decanter of a rather fine port saw them in a relaxed glow of love and contentment.

Next morning tea in bed was welcome and from somewhere the cook had obtained a couple of fresh eggs which made a pleasant breakfast change. The morning was taken up with a tour of the boat.

"She is rather nice, isn't she? But she could do with some upkeep. Shall we do some cleaning and painting?"

"Do you mean us? That's not what we do. We have crew for that. Tell them what you want done and they will organise it."

"What, even in a war you have crew sitting around? I'm surprised the boat hasn't been taken for naval duties, let alone having crew for her."

"Well, so far pater has managed to resist attempts to take her and the crew are all working in the boatyard, just looking after us as and when. It works pretty well on the whole although I suspect the navy will get *Hemel Lady* eventually."

All this seemed a bit too high-nosed for Jane's tastes. "So what is your family contributing to the war effort?"

"Quite a lot actually. We're down to twenty staff and servants now and all three boys are doing their bit. Remember the Earl is about to go abroad on war duties and

CHAPTER TWO: Wedding Day

Arthur contributes in his own way. The produce from the estate very largely goes into the market and even Arabella does her bit for good relations."

"Yes, she does, doesn't she?" Jane was about to enlarge on this sharp comment but remembered that she was not supposed to be sharing her knowledge, so bridled her tongue. "Does the Earl have a girlfriend?"

"The Earl? Good heavens no. He prefers boys although he knows he will have to do his duty by the family line at some stage. It's not a thought that warms him. "

"And Arthur?"

"Oh, he's still playing the field and with this war on he has plenty of choice. He's actually pretty well known as a rake in social circles."

"Yes, I've rather got that impression of him. Anything female will do, without any moral scruples to hinder him."

"Yes, that's Arthur all over. He's got himself into a lot of scrapes along the way."

"I can believe it. He's even made a pass at me."

"Oh, nothing strange about that. You have no idea how lucky I think I am, being the one that actually got you."

"David, really. If anyone is lucky round here, it has to be me."

"If we both think that we'll make a good team, won't we?"

She smiled. "Too right." And they laughed happily into each other's eyes.

"The way they talk of them, your brothers and sister are pretty knowing about sex and relationships. How come you were so naive, with almost no experience or understanding? You can't blame it all on the Navy."

"I don't know, Nanny treated me as her baby and kept me fairly secluded until I went away to school. A boy's boarding school might have been full of wet dreams but actual doing anything was almost zero apart from some bum boys. In the Navy there was a lot of enthusiasm but if, like me, you didn't really want just to grab whatever was passing there wasn't much scope for anything more meaningful. It's always been a real relationship that I wanted but somehow that passed me by until I met you. Now it's all quite different."

At breakfast next day she casually enquired "Are we doing anything while we're here? Beyond more of the obvious, that is."

"I have arranged for the launch to be fuelled and available so we can take a few trips round the harbour. I thought you would appreciate being on a boat again. I hope I'm right?"

"Oh yes please, that would be fun."

"And you can tell the yard what work is needed on *Hemel Lady*. It will be good practise for when you are being Lady David at Hemel Towers."

"Well fine, I can see what needs doing fairly obviously. Do I have authority to put them to work?"

"Yes of course."

So she spent a pleasant morning with the yard foreman agreeing what needed done to keep the boat in reasonable shape. But something was tugging at the back of her mind and that evening she casually asked "David, what did you mean when you said instructing the yard foreman would be good practise for living at Hemel Towers? We're not staying there, are we?"

"Well, why not? Now you are married you will be leaving the Wrens, won't you?"

"You what? Why on earth would I be leaving the Wrens?"

He looked puzzled. "That's what married women do, isn't it? Set up home and wait for their husbands?"

"David really. Are you suggesting that I give up my job to go and sit around at Hemel Towers waiting for you? Are you mad? There's a war on and every female in the country is being called on to do their bit. And my bit happens to be an important job."

"Yes, but . . . Daubeny-Fowkes wives don't have to work, and there is so much to do at Hemel Towers. Surely that can keep you occupied? And what about children?"

"Right now children are the last thing on my mind and fortunately that is up to me. Let's be clear about this, David. The Wrens are expecting me to turn up in Guzz in early October to be part of the training staff for the first Wrens boat crew training course and are counting on me being an important part of an important development. I am not giving that up just to sit around at Hemel Towers on the off-chance that you might turn up."

"Yes, but Jane I was hoping to see a son, something of me being carried on."

"And so you will as soon as this stupid war is over. Believe me, nothing will please me more than to give you your son, or half a dozen of them once other things are not getting in the way. Would you give up the Navy to stay around trying to impregnate me? I think not and that cuts both ways. "

"Yes, but Jane, I am a man and that means I do the man things, like having a career and being out there making things happen. Surely you can see that."

"Well, yes of course but that doesn't mean the reverse is your wife being a drone and not pulling her weight. You have seen what I can do, including saving your life. Do you really think that I should cease being that person just because I've married you?"

David shook his head in bewilderment. "I just don't know. I thought it was the normal thing for a woman to give up her job and make a home once she married. I hadn't thought of it any other way."

"A fat chance I'd have of making a separate home for you at Hemel Towers. Do

CHAPTER TWO: Wedding Day

you really think your mother is going to give up her position to let me take over? I don't, not for a minute. All that would happen would be that I was under her thumb and another minor cog in the estate. No thank you, David."

"But what happens when I come home on leave? If you are away somewhere, we might miss each other and I wouldn't like that at all. Do you remember the first time we made love, how you said you would be my safe haven, away from the stresses of the war? How can you possibly be that if you are somewhere else driving a boat? I've seen how the other married men on my ship behave, longing for home and wife with the two all tangled together. Now you're saying I won't get that because you are pursuing your commitment to the Wrens. It's not fair, you know."

"Well, maybe David but that's the chance you take in wartime. With any luck we can make our leaves co-incide, or at least manage to get together while I am doing a day job. "

"That's a poor substitute for knowing you will be there waiting for me. Can we really manage to get together like that?"

Jane looked at him, sympathetic to his difficulties but determined not to give in. Then she compounded his problems. "There's one other thing I might as well get out now while we're on this sort of subject. I have decided that in the Wrens, and for war work, I will keep my well-known maiden name and remain plain Jane Beacon. My new name is such a handle that I suspect it will get in the way of my relating to ordinary girls to an extent that I'd rather not have. So, I will be plain Petty Officer Jane Beacon in the service. I'm sorry if this bothers you but I think it will be better this way. Of course, I'll be Lady David etc for official and social purposes. I've had Merle, who is a solicitor, remember, investigate it and there is no legal requirement that I must be Lady David so I think it will be better to stay Jane Beacon."

David had gone white-faced during this little speech. "Jane, Jane, that means we are hardly married at all. I can't say I like this one little bit. I really want my wife to be a part of me, not a separate person with an identity of her own. How can you be my wife when you have a different name?" He shook his head slowly, sadly. "I don't know, everything I thought I knew about marriage has just been turned upside down."

Jane crossed the cabin, sat on his knee, smiled at him, and kissed his forehead gently. "Not everything, David. There are still bits that apply and we do rather well. Think of this as a long game, being subject to peculiar variations just now but with the same prospects out there. We will sort it out, my love, and be the better for it in the long run. I'll be your Lady David when we have done with war work and can be a fully married family without all these outside demands. "

He smiled, cautiously, and murmured, 'All right then, let's enjoy the bits we do have."

Later, sated and gently cuddling, Jane remarked, "They do say you should never go to bed on a quarrel. We've just had our first and I'm glad we've managed to be friends again after it."

He now had a sad lopsided smile, recognising defeat. "Let's hope that is how things are going to be, that our love can overcome the problems. But I still think it is a funny way to conduct a marriage."

CHAPTER THREE:
Something Different

Next morning, they were in the launch by 1000. "I presume you will want to drive?"

"Well, that would be nice David. It seems like ages since I did and I do miss it. Let's go."

She took the little boat away from the yacht's side with her usual neat competence then asked, "Where are we going?"

"I thought we'd just have a look around. A lot of it is off-limits for military purposes just now but it is a big harbour so we'll potter round in it. Let's get out into the main part."

They were quietly heading down the harbour when a fast launch swung alongside them. Its skipper called, "Keep away from here. A flying boat is about to take off and you are close to the flight path."

"Can we just stop here and watch?"

"Yes, but don't go any further to the east."

A short while later the bellow of multiple large engines came across the water as a huge looking aircraft coasted gently over the town end of the harbour, turned to point south and opened up its four engines. With a deafening roar it gathered speed, got up on the hull step then lifted off, the spray it was spreading round itself ceasing abruptly.

"Well, that was something I didn't expect. I wonder if there is much of that round here. I suppose Poole would be a good place for them, with lots of sheltered water."

The range safety boat came back to them. "Thanks for waiting. Are you just sightseeing? We don't get much of that nowadays."

"I suppose you could call it that. We're both Navy and having a short break here. Are there other flying boats here?"

"Lots of 'em. Can't say more than that; security y'know."

"But presumably we can come and look at them?"

"Don't get close. That is not allowed."

"All right, we understand."

The range launch went roaring off. Jane and David started in the same direction at a more modest pace. Rounding Brownsea Island they saw other flying boats in the distance. "Funny how we didn't notice them earlier."

As they got closer, they could see boats fussing round the aircraft, running between shore and moorings. Passenger boats transferring people; open boats with piles of goods mailbags and stores; several of the aircraft with gantry frames round engines and mechanics working on them; one of these giants being hauled up a slipway with temporary wheels fitted under it. Apparently in charge of all this was a smart launch flying flags which meant nothing to Jane and David. They stopped alongside it and David hailed "Is it all right if we stop and watch? We're both Navy and haven't seen anything like this before."

"Don't get any closer but you can stay here if you like. You say you're Navy? What sort of?"

"Well I'm in destroyers and my wife here is boat crew. We're having a short break."

"Has the Navy got girls on its boats now? I presume you are a Wren?"

Jane answered direct. "That's right. We are still a very few and considered experimental but shortly there will be a lot more. So far so good."

"Now that is interesting. I'm the marine superintendent here and finding enough crew is always a problem. Can girls really handle boats?"

"Most certainly. Do you want a demonstration?"

"Sure. Come on board."

This posed a small problem for Jane, who had been thinking of twirling *Hemel Lady's* boat in a couple of circuits just to show off. But too late to back out now. She boarded the superintendent's boat, saw a neat wheelhouse with direct control of two engines, and asked, "Have you much power?"

"She's good for twenty knots if opened right up. That should be enough. Take me to that big American boat over there." And he pointed at quite the largest aircraft in the moorings. "You call these giant things boats?" Jane asked.

"Well, it is a convenient shorthand and yes we do fairly universally."

Jane pushed the boat ahead and spun it towards this American 'boat'. 'Yet another way of speaking to learn,' she thought.

As they got close to it the superintendent cautioned, "These things might look impressive but they are actually quite fragile with very thin skins. Take it dead slow going alongside."

Jane nodded acknowledgement and concentrated on the job in hand, coming alongside smoothly. Four technicians in strange uniforms climbed on board with their tool kits and at the nod Jane eased away again. "Where to now?"

"We'll go ashore at that jetty," and a waft of an arm showed the way. Pushing the launch up to full power was exhilarating for a few minutes before easing down and berthing neatly alongside the jetty.

"Hmm. Very impressive. You do a lot of this?"

"Oh yes. It's my full-time job in the Wrens."

CHAPTER THREE: Something Different

"Would you mind waiting a few minutes? I think our station manager might be extremely interested in you." And with that the superintendent disappeared ashore. He was back five minutes later. "He's busy just now but says, would you like to come to lunch tomorrow? Bring your colleague too."

"Yes, I'm sure we would love to. My colleague, incidentally, is my husband. We're on our honeymoon, y'see, and staying aboard *Hemel Lady*. "

"Good heavens. I didn't realise I was interrupting such precious time together." The superintendent turned to David who had caught up with them. "Are you friends with *Hemel Lady's* owners, then?"

"Well actually, my family are the owners so no problem. Here's my card."

The superintendent looked at the card and his eyebrows went up.

"Indeed. You are an impressive pair. I shall look forward to meeting you again tomorrow. Just come to the pier here for midday and I'll escort you."

As they pulled away from the jetty Jane giggled, "Do you like being 'an impressive pair', David?"

He laughed ruefully. "I'm not sure that it's me who was impressive but never mind. Where shall we go for lunch today?"

They had a leisurely start next morning. and dressed in their best uniforms they set off in good time for their lunch appointment. As promised, the marine superintendent was on the jetty to meet them and ran an appraising eye over them, looking somewhat smarter. He looked startled on taking in Jane's medal ribbons but said nothing. Taken into the station manager's office, they were introduced to him plus the station superintendent and an obvious pilot who turned out to be a senior flight captain. From there they were escorted into the on-site restaurant. The station manager explained "Strictly it is for passengers but we have arrangements to use it when the occasion justifies. I believe that you two do that."

The flight captain looked closely at Jane's face then her medal ribbons. "By Jove, you've been in the wars. I didn't think girls got that close to the action. What on earth were you doing?"

Jane smiled, used to this reaction. As casually as she could manage, she remarked "Oh, at Dunkirk. It got quite hot at times."

"You were at Dunkirk? I say, that's something."

Jane smiled, taking David's arm, "Yes, and met my husband there too."

The attention turned to David. "A DSC and bar suggest you have been pretty active as well, sir. What did you do?"

"Well, apart from being rescued from a burning ship by Jane, I was on convoy duty and rammed a U-Boat which sank it."

There was a general murmur of appreciation at this and they settled to lunch.

The assembly was treated to her well-polished twenty-minute routine of the beaches and soldiers and a donkey; then the discussion turned to Wrens in boats. There was a slight lack of belief about girls being able to work on boats so Jane told them about *Kittiwake* and her all-Wren crew. This was followed by the marine superintendent being emphatic that Jane was highly skilled and competent. "And where I go there is no reason why other women cannot go just as well. Training may be needed but a fundamental capacity to do the job is well within women's abilities."

The station manager looked at his staff. "This is something to keep in mind. We are all right for now but I can see the day coming when we may be short of crew for our boats." He turned to Jane. "You are an interesting young woman. Would you be able to come and train them?"

"Being in uniform means that I don't decide for myself what I do. You'd have to ask the Wren HQ but I'll let them know about this discussion. Speak to Third Officer Merle Baker and ask about Petty Officer Wren Jane Beacon."

"But I would expect you to be known by your married name? Why aren't you Lady Daubeny-Fowkes?"

"Well I am but within the Wrens and for practical purposes I've chosen to retain my maiden name. Petty Officer Wren Lady David Daubeny-Fowkes really is a bit of a mouthful. It's a potential barrier and I prefer to stay closer to my people. And to imitate what the Navy does, only ratings are boat's crew. Therefore I cannot be an officer if I want to stay in the boats and I know which is the more important to me."

While this was going on the waitresses had been M'Lady-ing Jane, so clearly word had been passed before they came into the restaurant. Again Jane had a feeling that it would take some time to get used to this change in status.

The pilot captain was looking thoughtful. "Would you two like to come for a little spin? We've got a crate going up for an hour this afternoon for testing. You could come along if you liked."

Jane's eyes gleamed. "What you mean go for a flight? I've never been in an aeroplane. That would be fun; what do you think, David?"

"Oh, I'm all for it. Yes please. Do we go now?"

"Very shortly."

And half an hour later they found themselves in the cabin of one of the BOAC flying boats as it started its engines. It roared across the water, bumping a bit then lifted off. Once airborne one of the crew came into the cabin and said, "One at a time you can go up to the flight deck and see what is going on." Jane smiled, "You go first, David."

When her turn came, she was fascinated by the way the cockpit was neatly laid out so that everything was to hand. 'We need launches like that,' she thought. Even

CHAPTER THREE: Something Different

a couple of thousand feet up, the view was magnificent with the whole of the Solent and Isle of Wight laid out below them. 'No wonder they use planes for reconnaissance,' she thought. The pilot said, "We've nearly finished the testing. If you like to strap yourself into that seat behind me you can stay there while we touch down."

She was fascinated by the way the water slowly seemed to come up to them and by the cool way the captain eased the aircraft down, making it all look very simple. Thank-yous said and safely back on dry land David said, "Well, that was an unexpected bonus. It's a shame we have to leave tomorrow. I'd like to look into flying; might be something I could do."

"David, you just stick with your nice safe destroyer. I don't want you doing anything dangerous."

"You're a fine one to talk, taking your boat into all sorts of dodgy situations. I think I'll make some enquiries."

"Well, all right but if you're going to do anything daft, think of me then think again, please."

He smiled and took her hand. "For you, anything, my dear."

"I'll take you at your word on that." And that night his education was taken a step further with an introduction to the last secret of her anatomy. Although she deeply loved their close bodily contact, she had been getting highly frustrated sexually and decided it was time to do something about it. Once over his surprise and with some guidance David worked it out sufficiently to give Jane her first climax in a long time. The pent-up drive was explosive, startling David with the sheer force of it. And the coupling which followed was their best yet; one way and another they fell asleep deeply contented.

The drive down into the West Country was spoiled by a steady drizzle but under the car's slightly inadequate cover they were warm and content. Arriving at the Old Grange, David was somewhat startled to be formally introduced to Eunice the cook as well but politely took it in his stride. The home of a well-to-do middle-class family was going to be different in many ways. But Eunice had excelled herself and dinner that night was well up to Hemel Towers standards. Over dinner David fell to chatting with Jane's mother and the two of them found that they got on really well. Something about her motherly warmth appealed to him, such a contrast with his own remote mater. And he utterly charmed her, allaying her suspicions about an aristo being aloof and chilly. So for two days the newlyweds tested the new double bed, established a mature but warm relationship between the generations, and explored the area. They even visiting the *Dolphin;* Jane took her accordion so for the first time David saw - and heard – what a musical wife he had acquired. Somehow Hemel Towers had not seemed an appropriate place to be playing an accordion.

A letter addressed to Jane from a Plymouth solicitor had been waiting for her when they arrived at the Old Grange, giving Jane a major jolt. This letter advised that Rear-Admiral Rodmayne having been declared dead missing in action, his heritable property was being distributed according to the instructions in his will. This provided that his yacht *Osprey* was bequeathed to Jane. It would be necessary for her to formally purchase it for one pound, and if she would complete the attached Bill of Sale and enclose a cheque for one pound the formalities could be finalised. Jane was totally taken aback. "Why on earth leave it to me? Surely G as his son should be the person to inherit it? It doesn't make sense."

Her father responded. "I knew this was coming and discussed it with Mrs Rodmayne. It seems your Godfather felt you were the person most likely to look after it and to make good use of it, so you should have it. He knew there would be nothing to do with it until the end of the war but after that a new world would allow you to take it to sea again, so you should have it."

"That's all very well but I have a full-time job myself. How on earth am I to look after her just now?"

David joined in. "We can always appoint someone to do any running maintenance. Can we take a look at her?

"Yes of course. I'll row you up there this afternoon."

A small warning that she was a bit out of condition came: her shoulder and stomach muscles were sore by the time they got there. But *Osprey* sat as quietly as ever, looking faded and seagull be-spattered but sound beneath the canopy. They pumped her out, re-spliced a few lashings and checked round below decks, David approving of what he saw. "I'll really look forward to taking her to sea," was his main comment. 'Hang on a minute,' thought Jane, 'she's my boat now and I will take her to sea.' But she chose not to make an issue of it. David rowed them back to the Beacon boathouse. Returning to the Old Grange, a formal letter was waiting for David, forwarded from his home. It advised that his ship was now repaired and dock trials were being carried out. Re-commissioning was planned for fifth October and his presence was required as soon as possible. Kindly advise by return when they could expect him. "Oh dear, I didn't expect that for another week. I wonder why they have brought it forward?" Agitation gripped him and he paced up and down for five minutes before asking to use the phone. The result of half an hour's anxious long-distance discussion was that repairs were complete, testing the new boilers had gone exceptionally well and they would be ready for sea trials within a week. It was time to re-commission the ship. "I'm afraid I have to go in the morning. Sorry to lose a day but I can't afford to be late getting back." Jane sensed the difference which had come over his demeanour. His ship, always at the back of his mind, was now

CHAPTER THREE: Something Different

central again and that night at dinner he seemed distracted and far away.

The drive back to Hemel Towers was a drag after the fun of the previous trips, with each of them wrapped in their own thoughts. For a last night together they cuddled close but there was no lovemaking. The outside world and their duty commitments were pressing too close for anything more than clinging to each other. David was up early next morning and by 0900 was busy packing for sea while Jane gathered up her clothes including her more formal garments. She had decided that Lady Ormond's flat was a better place to keep them, suspecting that her welcome would be less kind at Hemel Towers when she was on her own. By mid-afternoon David was on his way, leaving Jane to have a last night at the place before she too went back to 'doing her bit'. Dinner was as formal as ever; the Marchioness was noticeably less forthcoming now Jane was there as of right but on her own. The new wife retired early, intending a good night's sleep with the bed to herself before getting on her way to an exciting new job.

Jane was peacefully sound asleep on her side, curled up as always, and still wearing the short frilly nightie she had acquired for her honeymoon. Slowly she drifted towards the surface, warm hazy thoughts of her husband making love to her spreading through her as she jigged up and down to his movements. Then it hit 'Hang on, David has gone back to his ship. Was this a dream?' No, it was real and it exploded in her mind that someone else was pleasuring themself in her from behind. As she jerked with the realisation, a strong hand clamped over her mouth, the other arm pulled tightly round her waist, holding her tight. Her assailant had some ferocious final spasms and climaxed. They lay locked together for a minute or so then he sighed and rolled back from her. Jane twisted round. "Arthur! You filthy shit! What are you doing here?"

"What does it look like, Jane? That was the most heavenly thirty minutes of my life. I can die happy now."

"You bloody well will die if I have anything to do with it." Rage and humiliation and despair all coursed through her. "Get out!" She gave him an almighty push and heaved him out of the bed. "If you have got me pregnant you'll pay for this in a big way, Arthur Daubeny-Fowkes. Now get out of here before I make a scene that will cause you trouble for the next twenty years." Totally losing her temper she kicked him in the face, knocking him flat again. Hastily he scrambled to his feet, grabbed a dressing gown and headed to the door. "Don't worry, that won't be the last time we do it. Enjoy your self-righteous rage in the meantime, my lovely."

On her own, Jane shambled into the bathroom and douched as thoroughly as she could, acutely aware of his sperm in her at her fertile time of month. She lay in bed for a long time weeping, thinking of her mother's warning about the aristocracy being either snobs or degenerates. They were even worse when they were both, she thought bitterly. Mulling it over, she decided not to make a fuss about Arthur's nocturnal visit but to make quite sure he couldn't do it again. Was she right to put a sense of family solidarity before her own well-being?

In the morning, puffy of face from the weeping, she went down to breakfast to find Arthur there already looking very sparky despite a growing black eye. "Hello Jane. Been crying for your husband gone away? Never mind, you'll be comforted again soon enough."

Jane curled a silent snarl at him and managed to force some cereal down to stop her tummy rumbling. She was just finishing her coffee when she was summoned to the phone. "Hello Jane, David here. Listen, it's all go here and we are re-commissioning day after tomorrow. To celebrate the wardroom is having a lunch for all my ship's officers and partners tomorrow and they have invited you and me as well. Can you be at Chatham station by ten o'clock tomorrow morning ready to stay for a couple of days? I will meet you there. Come in your best uniform."

"Yes David, I can be there but surely as a rating I can't go into the wardroom in uniform?"

"Oh, we'll overlook that one for once. Just be there."

She had a busy day, too busy to dwell on Arthur's nocturnal visit. Lady Ormond was as graciously friendly as ever, waving the stump of her left arm about. Having stowed her clothes, Jane spent a cheerful evening regaling the Lady with tales of flights in flying boats and similar doings. An early start saw her at Chatham station for 1006 the next morning and relief washed through her on seeing David waiting with a car complete with Wren driver. This young lady started noticeably on seeing Jane in her best uniform and her hands trembled on holding the door but she carried out her duties efficiently and dropped them at the foot of the gangway of HMS *Bowman*. As they came over the brow Jane automatically faced aft and saluted to the surprise of the duty quartermaster. What on earth was happening that the ratings she was encountering were all being startled by her? Had word gone round about her in some way? She knew how efficient the galley wireless could be.

For the moment there was no time to dwell on this; David ensconced her in his day cabin (with the door open) waiting for the summons to the wardroom. This was not long in coming and as she came in the eight officers and six wives gathered there all stood up. David introduced her to his officers who in turn introduced their wives or sweethearts. This distaff group proved somewhat mixed with a couple of very young ones and the engineer's wife a plump middle-aged housewife. With gin in hand Jane circulated, trying to have a few minutes with everyone before the summons for lunch. Again, there was this sense of nervousness in the air; although Mrs

CHAPTER THREE: Something Different

Engineer took it all in her stride and was clearly a seasoned naval wife, the young ones were very cautious and monosyllabic. Jane was finding this heavy going and was relieved when lunch was called. She was seated at the opposite side of the table from her husband and had to remind herself that she and David were guests here. As principal guest she was placed on the right hand of the first lieutenant who as mess president had her and the youngest member of the mess, a blushing midshipman, on either hand. Her first attempts at conversation with this young man just left him tongue-tied, but the first lieutenant proved more self-assured. Like most of the officers he had two wavy stripes on his sleeve but seemed to have been in the Navy for long enough to have become a seasoned sailor. "Were you with the ship before the ramming?" Jane enquired.

"Oh yes, I've been with your husband for two years now and latterly as his first lieutenant. It is good to be sailing with him again; there will be no lack of action while he is around."

Jane smiled. "Oh really? He's always a little bit cautious about telling me much but I gather he has been pretty active. You must have been with him at Dunkirk but abandoned ship earlier than my arrival?"

"Most of us who survived had managed to get away in a boat which was alongside when we were bombed. The foc'sle party were stranded and but for your intervention I doubt if they would have survived. We are all in your debt for what you did that morning."

Jane looked slowly into some distant flame and had a gentle reminiscent smile. "Is there anyone else in this ship's company who was there then?"

"Yes, our upper deck buffer was one of the injured ones you took off. I know he is hoping to meet you and thank you for what you did that day. It really was quite exceptional."

Jane decided it was time to change the subject. "Anyone else here from before the ramming?"

"Lieutenant Johnson, our engineer; he has been standing by the ship while it was rebuilt and if the machinery works it'll be down to his supervision and taking no nonsense from the dockyard mateys. And young Kennedy who has used the time since we got in to take a course in navigation and is now our pilot. The rest are fresh out of the box."

"So you'll have a job on your hands getting them worked up to full readiness?"

"Well yes but that husband of yours will have them whipped into shape in no time. No-one stands in his way for long."

Not for the first time Jane was struck by the contrast between the fierce martinet David apparently was in his command, with the scared bottom-of-the-heap runt he

35

had had to emerge from being in the Daubeney-Fowkes clan.

The chat flowed more freely and by dessert time she had even managed to get her tongue-tied midshipman to speak. Martin was his name; he was nineteen and had been briefly a bookkeeper before joining the Navy. This was his first full sea-going appointment and he hoped it might lead to great things, like being able to make a career in the Navy. So far, he was loving it. It struck Jane that he was only two years younger than her yet seemed a lifetime greener.

With coffee served, George the first lieutenant rapped on his cup and called for attention. "Ladies and gentlemen, as we stand here on the brink of going back to doing our bit to defeat Hitler, there are a few things I'd like to say. First, I would like to say how delighted we all are to have our well-tested commanding officer leading us again. For those of us who have sailed with him before it is an honour and a comfort to know that he is here. And a warm hello again to our engineer, Lieutenant Johnson. I am quite sure our engines won't let us down while he is with us. And it is nice to welcome his wife today; we had heard about her and her fondness for knitting pullovers. Now we have a face and a person to put to the stories. And by no means least, welcome to Maryanne. We knew our young pilot would put his course time to good use but had not expected it to be quite so useful and it pleases me to be the one to break the news that last night young Kennedy got down on one knee and popped the question. The answer being 'yes', welcome Maryanne to our little society. I hope you manage to find some happiness in becoming a Naval wife." The mess president turned to the commanding officer, "Over to you, sir."

David smiled, demurred and said, "I will be saying my piece about our ship and what I expect of you at the commissioning tomorrow. On this occasion I feel something a little less military is called for and invite my nice new wife to say a few words." There was a cheer and a beating the table to welcome her.

Jane gave him an appraising look. "Well thank you, sir. I could have done with a little warning of this." She stood up and looked round the company, some anxious, some relaxed and putting their worries out of mind for a few minutes.

"When I rescued a bedraggled and scorched group of sailors from their burning ship at Dunkirk, I had no idea who they were nor what the consequences would be. Yet here I am today, newly married to one of that group and waving him off to the war again. Life plays some funny tricks on us and never more so than in the middle of a fierce war. All you men will be putting yourselves in harm's way again very soon while we wives can only go about our lives, doing our bit for the greater good and hoping, hoping that you come through safely. Ladies, in being married to a Naval person you are accepting that your husband can never be wholly yours, for you have a rival. There's an old saying about a sailor having a girl in every port. That isn't what

CHAPTER THREE: Something Different

troubles us though, for we know where your hearts lie. The greater rival has a flag flying and that white and red-crossed flag represents where their greater loyalty lies. There is no point in trying to fight it as all that does is put unfair pressures on your other half which he can never get beyond. Better by far to accept it and through your support for your husband also give your loyalty to that flag, the ship and its people, and the cause we are all fighting for. That way while we wives are doing our own bit, we can also do our bit to make our husbands' lives more bearable and enable them to give their all in the cause." Jane turned to the new fiancée. "Maryanne, I hope we will very soon be welcoming you as a full member of the most exclusive club there is, the wives of *HMS Bowman*. I hope it makes for a happy life for you both."

With that she sat down to a round of applause and, "Well said".

After lunch Jane acquired a signal pad and pen and set about recording the wives' names and addresses. Eight copies of this were made so that each had one. "In this uncertain world you never know when it might come in handy to be able to speak to other members of our little club. Ladies, let's keep in touch and be ready to help each other." For an hour they discussed this, Mrs Johnson commenting that in twenty-five years of Naval life she had never seen a support group spring up like this quite so quickly. It was plain that some of the younger women responded to her mother hen presence and already were looking to her for advice. Jane, they treated with cautious respect, falling silent whenever she spoke.

David had booked a hotel for them for the night, making it clear that he wanted her to be there the next day for the actual commissioning ceremony. "But David, I am due in Guzz tomorrow. I can probably get away with being an odd day late but no more."

"And that is why I wanted you to give up the Wrens. I'll be in and out of Chatham for a week or two yet before we go north to work up and we could have had some more time together."

"Tell that to Hitler, David. By relative standards we've done well for togetherness lately and it really is high time I went back to work. There are sixty keen young Wrens arriving in Guzz in a few weeks' time to be turned into boats' crew and we don't want to disappoint them, do we? And just think what that means. All the effort I've put into succeeding as the pioneer boat crew Wren is coming to fruition now and to suit your convenience, you'd like me to resign at this critical moment? I'm sorry David but that just isn't on." David just shook his head slowly, acknowledging the inevitable.

It was the first time Jane had witnessed a commissioning ceremony and the crew, lined up on the quay in their best uniforms, made a fine sight. The white ensign was broken out, Lieutenant-commander Lord Daubeny-Fowkes addressed his ship's company making it plain that they were about to be worked very hard indeed. He would seek a happy ship but one that achieved happiness by being efficient and well-run. They were all in the enterprise together and the more they saw success coming from being mutually supportive the better all their lives would be. A padre, imported for the occasion, blessed the ship and company then led them in singing 'Abide with me'. As required, David then read the Articles of War to them before calling them round in an informal circle to lay down his expectations in more detail. Ceremony complete they were dismissed and returned to their duties.

Jane had watched all this from the bridge, a stray Wren not being any part of it, and was still there when the first lieutenant appeared with a matelot in tow. They exchanged salutes in proper Naval fashion then introductions were made. "Lady Daubeny-Fowkes, this is Leading Seaman Robertson who you rescued at Dunkirk. He wants to say thank you."

Jane took advantage of her fellow rating status to dispense with formality and shook his hand warmly. "How nice to see you under pleasanter circumstances. I hope your wounds healed up all right?"

"Oh yes ma'am. Took a little while but all well now. I've never had a chance before to thank you for what you did that morning. I was convinced I was a-gonner then you miraculously appeared through the flames. I've never seen anything like it and how you got that boat out again beats me. Lying in the bottom of the boat like I was, the flames looked twenty feet high. Thank you and thank you again for what you did."

Jane smiled that gentle reminiscent smile. "Oh yes, they were certainly ten feet high and must have looked worse from lying on the bottom boards. I just charged the flame wall and hoped for the best. We were all a bit singed and the Navy wasn't impressed by the state of the boat when I brought it back but we survived that. How did you get back to Blighty?"

"D'you know, there were some crushers there that wanted to leave wounded people behind. But my messmates weren't having that and made sure I was carried with them onto a destroyer on the East Mole. We were bombed on the way over but luckily they missed and I've never been so happy to see Blighty."

"And now you're going back into the thick of it again. I'll be thinking of you and your messmates while I'm running round Guzz. Good luck and have a tot for me."

He laughed; "I certainly will, ma'am." They shook hands again and suddenly Jane's time was up. She took her farewells of David in his day cabin, the same Wren driver – a bit calmer this time – took her to Chatham station and as the train pulled out she had a tremendous feeling of changing skins, going from one life to another with a huge, exciting challenge in front of her. She just hoped she was up to it.

CHAPTER FOUR:
Mother

There was something comfortingly familiar about her mother waiting at the station with the Austin Ruby. Even the train being an hour late seemed normal. The run home was equally familiar, with Jane putting snippets of news into the conversation while her mother went on at great length about the difficulty of getting petrol these days. The Old Grange establishment was unchanged with Eunice the cook admitting to increasing pains in the hips and finding she lacked the stamina to go a full day on her feet without a break. The house was overrun with evacuee children, only now most of them seemed to have a foreign accent. "Dutch and Belgian" explained her mother, "from a refugee ship." Jane was delighted to find some of them were French speaking and drew on her by now rusty French to chat to them. They seemed to have had a tough time getting from Belgium through France to Spain then finally Portugal before being put on an elderly Irish cargo ship which lowered a boat to land the children, on their own, off Plymouth. They were cheerfully unconcerned about the lack of adults other than Jane's mother who did her best to keep these boisterous youngsters under control. But the strain was showing in her careworn face.

Jane had telegrammed Superintendent Welby that she would be a day late for her appointment. Her orders letter had been quite clear: "*Report to Devonport dockyard, with an appointment to see Superintendent Welby at 0930 before reporting to the Boats Officer to join the boats crew training team.*" A day late, she got her father to drop her at the dockyard gate in good time and made her way to the Wren office. Second Officer Jones was still in post as Mrs Welby's secretary and greeted Jane in familiar fashion. The superintendent herself was less impressed. "Well, Beacon, still doing things your own way, I see. You do not disobey clear orders and send me a telegram to say you are doing so. Here we are, on the brink of achieving what you and I have been working towards for two years, and you are incapable of carrying out a simple order in the preparation. I am not impressed, and you will get out of your head now any idea that your position allows you to flout clear orders to suit your own convenience."

"I am very sorry Ma'am, but my husband was most insistent that I attend his ship's re-commissioning before I came here. He felt it was really important that I should be there."

"Ah yes, your husband. This latest development has not appeared on your documents yet. Who is this blessed gentleman?"

"Lieutenant-Commander Lord David Daubeney-Fowkes, ma'am. He's in command of a destroyer which had just completed major repairs after he rammed a U-boat with it. We met at Dunkirk and one way and another he wanted me to be there before he took his ship to sea again."

"Which is all very well but someone like that should know that individuals do not change their orders to suit themselves. It is clear that marrying has not made you any more amenable to keeping within the system. I suppose you have a fancy surname now?"

"Well yes ma'am I am now Lady David Daubeney-Fowkes, but I have made a deliberate decision not to use it and to remain plain Jane Beacon as far as the Wrens are concerned. I have checked and it's perfectly legal to do so."

"I suppose I have to congratulate you on making such an exalted union. But do not let that give you ideas above your station, either. You are still a rating under orders and discipline so you will do what you are told whenever it is necessary to tell you. Now, let us move to the business in hand. I have followed your career in the boats with close interest and have been delighted with how you have managed to show up so outstandingly. Your time on the Thames has been well spent and you appear to have left a very well-trained crew to carry on the good work after you were moved to special projects. Therefore, we are expecting a lot from you as part of the training staff here. This is the opportunity we have been working towards from the time you were first sent to *Amaryllis* and it marks a tremendous step forward. It is essential that you do not go and mess it up in some way. Is that clear? I do not want you going off on some approach of your own and leading the trainees astray in any way."

"Ma'am, one of the features of being married is being faithful to my husband. There will be no dodgy shenanigans from me and if that causes me to set a good example, so much the better."

"I suppose I should be thankful for small mercies, then. But I was thinking more of the technical training you will be giving them; they will receive the same six-week course as would naval ratings converting to the boats and you will be expected to remain within that syllabus. Your approach to administration while on the Thames was downright uncooperative and we don't want any of that attitude here."

"But ma'am, that's…"

Mrs Welby cut across her, "There you go again, Beacon. Do you know that you have a reputation as being the most argumentative Wren in the Service?"

"But ma'am, that's seriously unfair. I had no idea what being a detached unit meant and all I got was a pile of forms and left to get on with it. A little bit of in-

CHAPTER FOUR: Mother

struction would have helped a lot. I know I am being used as a pioneer but surely that means cutting me a little slack to find out about new things."

"Ah, but if you had been a little more receptive, I suspect you could have had some guidance at least. Anyway, that is not the main point of your being here. Soon we will have sixty keen Wrens all raring to go and you will be setting an example to them all. Kindly remember that in your dealings with them. Now I think it is time for you to go and see Boats Officer so you can make a start. Good luck and remember that I shall be watching this course very closely. It is hugely important that we make a success of it. Goodbye for now."

Jane saluted and marched out giving Mrs Jones a friendly wave in passing. She made her way to Flagstaff Steps and found the Boats Officer's office quite unchanged. She took some pride in marching in, saluting and reporting in correct form. "1095 Petty Officer Wren Beacon, sir."

The commander returned the salute, sat down, and gestured to Jane to sit opposite him. "A bit better than last time you were here, though you did try. Hello Beacon, and nice to see you again. We've come a long way since those early days in *Amaryllis*. I must say I am impressed by your medal haul which I knew about but hadn't really grasped until I saw the ribbons."

Jane smiled. "That was Dunkirk, sir. "

"Quite so. I hope you are not planning any such wild disobedience here."

"No sir, there's no obvious reason to go running off on my own here. We have a job to do and I am so pleased to be a part of it."

"I gather you are married now to young Daubeney-Fowkes. Congratulations, that is quite a match. Where is David now?"

"He's at sea, sir. His ship recommissioned last week and they are about to go north for work-up."

"So you will be able to devote yourself to the job in hand here?"

"Yes, indeed sir. This is such an opportunity for us and I certainly don't want to be the one to mess it up. I gather we have a keen group of girls for this first course. Do I understand it correctly that I will be instructing them in boat handling and the likes?"

"Well, certainly instructing them in working on the boats. There will be two launches with three Chief Petty Officers who are experienced cox'ns plus you. The plan is that after some whole course teaching ashore, groups of around half a dozen trainees at a time will go on the launches while the rest are in the classroom. How the instructors divide that up is being left to them. You will fit in with that arrangement."

"That is fine, sir. Where do I find these gentlemen?"

"Two huts along the quay here. That is where you will be based too. Good luck."

Jane came to attention and exited left. She found the relevant hut, pushed the door open and cautiously looked round it. Three very senior chief petty officers were sitting by the stove, discussing the contents of a piece of paper, and did not look up as Jane came in. "Good morning, gentlemen." This produced that Naval look, up and down, without visible enthusiasm.

"You must be Beacon. What's the lanyard for?"

"My knife. I found working on the beaches at Dunkirk that looping it round my neck was a convenient way to wear it and it has become a bit of a badge of office."

"Are you planning to wear it like that here?"

"Well I do everywhere else so why not?"

"It's not uniform."

"It is when I wear it. Senior officers don't seem to mind it so there's no reason why you gentlemen should have any problems with it."

"All right. Do you know what you are doing here?"

"Working on the training staff. What that involves I don't know."

"Right, the plan is that you should have one of the boats assigned for training and teach these recruits how to do it. Can you do that?"

"Yes of course. I'm told we are following the same course as matelots would when converting to the boats. Do we have a copy of the syllabus?"

"Here." And it was handed to her.

"I'll take some time and study it."

This discussion was interrupted by another very senior chief stumping into the shed. Jane jumped up. "Stan! By all that's wonderful, what are you doing here?"

He came in, his wooden peg leg plainly visible. "I'm in charge of the boat office for this course. They said my experience training you would be useful in keeping order among this lot."

"That would be right, I should think. Will you be in charge of the boats' daily orders?"

"Yes lass, all the organising admin."

"Oh, that will be good. What is first up?"

"The trainees are mustering on the last Sunday of this month, coming from all over the Wrens. There will be a meeting on the Sunday evening for general introduction and assigning training groups. We'll be working it with some in the classroom, some on shore-side training and some on the boats with swapping round each week. You will be in D45 taking groups on the water. We cannot afford for the boats simply to be training Wrens so a lot of the time they will be running live errands which hopefully will make it all more real for them. The time until they arrive here will be spent on routine boat work plus planning sessions. Will that do you?"

CHAPTER FOUR: Mother

"It sounds great, Stan. Do you know if there is a Wren officer looking after them?"

"PO Wren Welby will be looking after them for general organisation."

"PO Wren Welby? Any relation of our superintendent?"

"Yes lass, her daughter. You are not the only well-known Wren round here. But you will be afloat so you'll each have your own area of responsibility."

"Well well, this should be interesting. Am I needed today? If not, I'll find the PO Wrens' quarters and get settled in."

"No, on you go. Be here 0800 in the morning."

"0800? We've got it easy, then."

"For now, yes. That will change when the course starts. They must get used to scrub out at 0630 every day and guess who will be showing them how? Enjoy the easy life while you can."

Next day she went with one of the Chief Petty Officer trainers plus two unenthusiastic matelots to collect D 45, one of the larger diesel-engined harbour boats and found herself in charge of it from the start. It had never occurred to her that she might be on test herself and got quite irritated as they fetched and carried through the day with the Chief looking over her shoulder and quite obviously marking her card. 'Even now, here, these old relics don't really believe girls can do it, do they?' she thought. She decided the best way of dealing with this was to perform exceptionally well and by the end of the day the Chief had lost interest in watching what she did.

For the next couple of weeks Jane settled into this routine very happily. Although D 45 was a single screw, single rudder boat it handled well and she quickly got a working relationship going with the two matelots and engine room tiffy assigned to her. She met Petty Officer Wren Welby who was a bit stiff and formal, but they dealt with Wren issues amicably enough and with planning meetings from time to time the rest of the month flew by.

With just four days to go she was summoned to the boats officer's office. 'What have I done wrong now?' she wondered but could not think of anything. Reporting in due form she was told to sit and wait. Boats officer got connected to Jane's father and passed the phone over. "He wants to tell you himself," was the gnomic comment.

"Hello father, what's up? We are awfully busy here."

Her father sounded deeply distressed. "Oh Jane, Jane, I'm glad to get hold of you. Are you sitting down? It is bad news I am afraid. You know there was an air raid last night?"

"Oh yes, I spent it in the air raid shelter in the basement."

"Well, I'm afraid our home was bombed and your mother was killed."

43

"What! How could that be? We were strict about blackout and isolated in the country."

"It seems likely that one of the refugee children was shining a light upwards through a skylight and one of the bombers seized on it. The Old Grange is a burnt-out shell and everyone in it was killed. All those little refugees were finally got by the Boche."

"Oh my God, what a tragedy. Where are you staying?"

"At the hospital for now and I'll move into our boathouse temporarily."

"Listen, father. I'll try to get a forty-eight and join you there but it's only four days till the course starts and we are awfully pushed for time. How are you?"

"I just don't know, Jane. I relied on her totally."

"I'll see you in the morning, I hope."

With their three minutes up the line was disconnected. After some hasty re-organisation Jane secured her forty-eight hours leave pass and caught a bus to their road end. She was appalled at the state of the place which had been her home, with jagged bits of wall sticking up amid the blackened ruins. She found her father wandering disconsolately around the garden, with Eunice and Gladys trailing behind him. She gave him a hug and sensed that he was far from his usual self-contained self. "Here was the centre of my life, Jane."

"But you always seemed so wrapped up in your patients."

"Yes, but my self is here – your mother, the place, my books, my children; they were the centre of me as a person. And now it's all gone." And to Jane's alarm he sat on a surviving piece of wall and started to weep; slow, silent tears running down his cheeks and dripping into the charred remnants under his feet. To Jane's surprise it was Eunice who put an arm round him, cradled his head in her ample bosom and made soothing noises. His response was close and affectionate, wrapping his arms round her and hugging tightly. Jane picked up Eunice calling her father Johnny, which was new. By the time they disentangled, her white apron was soaked but he had found some equilibrium again. Jane, a silent spectator to this, moved off and wandered round the ruins. "How long have you got, Jane?"

"I really should be back in quarters by tomorrow night. I presume I can stay at the boathouse as well tonight?"

"No reason why not. The boat bedding is stored there and you can manage something from that."

"Oh, I've slept in worse than that. Meantime what are we going to do?"

"I have arranged for the bodies to be removed this afternoon. There is a heap of formalities which I will have to sort out but I am hoping that you can deal with your siblings. I don't think we want them home until the funeral and goodness knows when that will be. But they will have to be told now."

CHAPTER FOUR: Mother

"Well, all right but where will I find a phone?"

"There's an extension in the boathouse which seems to be working. Try that first."

Deeply distressed Jane trailed down to the boathouse and one by one called her brothers and sister. David and Sarah were both shocked and dismayed by the news. The twins took it all quite calmly and seemed more bothered by the destruction of their bedroom and their little treasures than by the loss of their mother. Jane was not long finished with this tricky task when her father arrived at the boathouse, closely followed by Eunice who bustled round and made a pot of tea then a light meal; this seemed to help her father a little. It occurred to Jane that she had no way of thinking of him except as 'father'. 'Johnny' had never been a name used by his children and the small barrier this produced made it difficult for Jane to get closer to him now.

Early in the evening, with practical matters dealt with, Eunice withdrew to Gladys's cottage where she had been staying for some time, and left Jane alone with her father.

Sitting at the boathouse entrance watching the sun go down over the river mouth, Jane could see that her father was struggling with something on his mind. 'Maybe not surprising,' she thought 'this must have been a terrible blow to him'.

"Jane, with this disaster on us there's something I must tell you. I would not be bothering you with it but with your mother's death it is important that someone else in the immediate family should know. You may have noticed that Eunice and I are friendlier than would normally be suitable for a master and servant relationship even after the years we have all lived together. This goes back to the First War and the Gallipoli campaign. Eunice was engaged to my marine orderly. He and I went everywhere together and when we had to go ashore under a dropping fire, I promised that if anything happened to him, I would make sure Eunice was all right. Well, he was killed by a bullet through the heart - they were accurate, those Turkish snipers - and when Eunice was pushed off the farm she had grown up on, we took her in. She suggested that she should become our cook/housekeeper and your mother liked the idea. So it was arranged. Our household settled for a long time then, but your mother struggled to give birth safely and she had a terrible time with Sarah. We were advised that another pregnancy would kill her so we decided that abstinence was the only safe way of ensuring her survival. I loved her very much, y'know. But abstinence didn't suit me either; with Eunice still in her prime one thing led to another and with your mother's tacit agreement, Eunice took me into her bed. I am afraid we got a bit careless and Eunice fell pregnant. We looked after her, of course, and I was able to arrange for her to go away to a safe place for the births. Have you ever noticed that the twins are a shorter, stockier build than you three? They are

45

Eunice's children. Your mother agreed to adopt them as though they were hers and Eunice returned to her position in the household."

"Which means that really the twins are half-brothers to me?"

"That's right. There is no doubt I am their father but they have a different mother. I am telling you this now in case anything should happen to me. Your mother, of course, knew the whole story but with her death I felt it important that someone else should know to act as an extra witness should that ever be necessary."

"Do the twins know about this?"

"No, not yet. The plan was to tell them when they got to eighteen, but we may have to think again. I will discuss it with Eunice and see what she would like to do."

"What about David and Sarah?"

"We'll keep it quiet for now but they will have to be told at some stage, I suppose."

"So, what happens now? We have barely begun to think about where we go next. Will you try to have the Old Grange rebuilt? Will the twins go to live with their actual mother or remain in our family set-up? And where do David and Sarah go when not at school? There's so much to think of."

"Thanks Jane, I was hoping you would take a practical view of this story, being married yourself and that much more knowledgeable. You're not planning any children yourself, are you?"

Jane smiled. "Not yet, father. I have promised David a brood once the war is over but until then I have an important job to do. It disappoints him a bit but too bad."

Her father gave a little half laugh, looking out to the darkened horizon. "I think I can get a few weeks off now to deal with all the practical matters and try to find somewhere to live. It's all right for me here in the boathouse but hardly somewhere for all of you to stay."

"D'you know, father, I think we might quite like staying in the boathouse for a spell at least."

"I must say you are taking your mother's death very calmly. Are you not upset by it?"

"Yes father, terribly, but two years of war have left me a bit numb emotionally and I have discovered the hard way that I can stay calm at the time when trouble and trauma are all about me. The deep hurt only kicks in later on. I suppose it helps me to stay active and in charge of myself while things are going on. That's what war does to you."

"It saddens me beyond belief that my eldest child should have to go through the same cruel process."

"Believe me father, I will grieve quite enough when I have time to stop and think about it."

CHAPTER FOUR: Mother

And later, lying in a nest of boat blankets on one of the lumpy mattresses, the sudden loss of her mother caught up with Jane and she quietly cried for a long time before exhaustion overtook her. But next morning she woke to a bright Autumn day streaming in and Eunice cooking porridge, "Sorry Jane, this is all we've got." Refreshed, Jane went back to the remains of what had been her home and started poking about in the ashes. Something blue caught her eye. She picked it up and rushed to show her father. "Look, look, it's the Russian necklace." Its box was a bit singed round the edges but still sound. The necklace inside was totally undamaged.

"I was told in Russia that it was an omen of good coming from bad." Her father said. "Let's hope its survival means that that holds good. What should we do with it? It is quite valuable y'know."

"I suspected it must be the first time I wore it, going to that subbies' ball. Meantime, stick it in a bank vault, I rather think."

"You're probably right. One more thing to do." Her father looked so careworn and gloomy that she had to give him another hug and murmur "Come on, father, we'll survive it."

"Oh, I suppose we will but it won't be the same without her."

"Well that's true for all of us. You don't just pass off losing your mother as a minor irritant; David and Sarah were both dreadfully upset when I told them."

He nodded sadly and sighed. The next few hours passed poking about in the debris; a variety of scorched domestic objects were turned up and carefully put in a tea chest but really there was very little left. Always conscious of her work commitments Jane said farewell and left in good time to catch the last bus into Plymouth, leaving her father standing where his study had been and muttering, "My books, my books." One way and another she had a lot to think about, brooding on the bus.

CHAPTER FIVE:
Training Course

Jane couldn't help feeling a stirring of pride as she looked out over the rows of alert faces. Seeing all sixty trainees together emphasised how far the movement to accept boat crew Wrens had come. From one, to two, to five and now sixty, women were slowly but steadily creating the opening for them to be sailors too. 'If only Punch were here,' thought Jane, 'She would really appreciate this.' The faces were mixed. Some weathered brown ones among them suggesting previous experience afloat. Others were the palest of white: had they escaped from working in a tunnel somewhere? The instructors were lined up on the stage, along with the Welbys mother and daughter, plus boats officer Commander Burrell. Jane had elected to come to the meeting in trousers and with white lanyard prominent. This had drawn a sharp intake of breath and a pursing of the mouth from Mrs Welby, but nothing was said. 'Too bad,' thought Jane 'they might as well get used to this rig from the start'.

It had been a late decision to hold this Sunday evening introductory meeting but a good one. First, Superintendent Welby gave a five-minute pep talk about the importance of this course. "You are creating women's history in the uniformed services and a great deal is expected of you." She explained before introducing the training staff. When it came Jane's turn the introduction was fulsome. "Petty Officer Beacon has two years' experience as a boat crew Wren and has blazed a trail for you all to follow. Her outstanding performance has been a primary driver in persuading the Admiralty that Wrens can do the job at all and you can be thankful for her success. We are hoping that you learn enough from her to follow along the same path."

Then boats officer explained how the boats served the Navy and how, in driving the boats, their crews came under direct naval control. "When it was suggested in October 'thirty-nine that we experiment with a Wren as potential boats' crew, I was dubious but knowing of the manpower difficulties we would face I agreed that it was worth a try. Within a month of Beacon coming onto a boat, my doubts were evaporating and ever since she has demonstrated a hundred times over that women are well able to do the job. Now you have the opportunity and the responsibility of proving that what Beacon has pioneered, you can pick up and develop. I fervently hope that you can match up to the challenge."

CHAPTER FIVE: Training Course

Then it was Petty Officer Welby's turn. "You will all be kitted up tomorrow morning and given time to change into boat crew uniform. Monday and Tuesday there will be general instruction which you will all take part in, then from Wednesday onwards you will be split into small groups to rotate around detailed instruction sessions, including time on the boats learning the practicalities. There will be a test after three weeks to see how you are getting on, then a full exam at the end of the course which you will have to pass to become a fully-fledged boat crew Wren. I hope you succeed." There was then some general briefing about practical matters before the group dismissed.

First, there were two days of teaching and tying knots for everyone. Jane was impressed that well over half the course knew the basic knots already, and the newcomers were very willing to learn. Inevitably there were a few who struggled to get the reef knot tied correctly and one or two were still at the 'bunny out of its hole' stage of tying the bowline, but they grasped the flick of the wrist readily enough. Late on Tuesday afternoon the trainers, with PO Pat Welby, worked out the smaller groups which the trainees would stay in as they moved round the different training modules. Each group included a couple with boats experience, a couple of practical but less experienced girls and a couple who had already shown up as complete novices. It was hoped that within each group people would learn from each other as much as from the trainers.

Jane's first group were on board D45 by 0630 as instructed, clutching their packed lunches and oilskins but were crestfallen to find that this early start, still in semi-darkness, was to scrub the boat out. They were introduced to the naval scrubbing brush and mop and initial grumbling over, they set about cleaning the boat with some vigour. This brought back to her, Jane's introduction to cleaning the boat and Stan's tour of inspection on completion. Determined not to let anything slack pass by from the start, she found fault in various corners and had to be quite firm with a couple of the girls to achieve the standard she was looking for. Jane was aware of how far she had come in two years, now demanding total commitment even to a mundane task like cleaning the boat. Cleaning over, there was a short break before the first job of the day so Jane sorted them out. "Who knows about boats already?"

A lean dark girl held her hand up. "My dad's a fisherman and I've been on and off his boat all my life."

Jane didn't recognise the accent. "Where are you from?"

"Lyme Regis."

"Ah, mostly potting?"

"In season, yes."

"So you'll be used to handling the boat?"

"Oh yes, done plenty of that."

"Right, Colman, isn't it? You can be first on the helm here, then. Does anyone know pusser's boat hook drill?"

They collectively looked blank.

"Right, watch me." She seized a boathook and went through the motions a couple of times. They practised this for ten minutes then it was time to go, to collect mail and stores for an ack-ack battery on the detached mole. For this first trip she took the helm herself and had the group cluster round to watch as she laid the boat alongside. Then they loaded up and set off. Once under way she invited Colman to take the wheel while she introduced the rest of the group to their duties on the ends of the boat, on the fenders, and when to hook on rather than tie up. The fisherman's daughter made a neat, if slow, job of coming alongside the mole and Jane moved around the deck making sure each of the others was doing something useful.

She quickly established a rhythm to training so that they all got the beginnings of experience in every job.

Something else which became a regular part of the training was the quizzing she got during the lunch break. "You are the Wren who went to Dunkirk, aren't you?"

"Oh yes, that's where the medal collection came from." She had already decided that mock modesty would not serve in these circumstances and happily gave them a five-minute potted version of the Dunkirk tale. Even Colman, who was showing signs of being cynical about the whole process, seemed suitably impressed by tales of derring-do at Dunkirk. The white lanyard also had to be explained, how she put it round her neck to cut the propeller free from the dead soldier's greatcoat and had worn it there ever since as a sort of badge of office.

After lunch they had several short runs to *Defiance* with personnel; this gave useful practice in boat hook drill. After the second one they were ordered to lay off on the boat boom which gave her learners something new to cope with.

The boat boom is a standard fitting on all warships. It consists of a wooden boom, usually about twelve feet long, mounted on a swivel on the ship's side set at half the ship's freeboard above the water. At sea it is secured flat against the ship's side; in port it is swung out, hanging horizontal on a wire topping lift and with side guys to hold it in position at a right angle to the ship's side. Hanging down from it are pendants ('lizards' in naval terminology) for boats to secure to by the bow and jumping ladders – short wire Jacob's ladders with wooden rungs - to give access to the moored boats from the boom. There is a single back wire along the length of the boom about head height above it which is the sole handhold for boat crew personnel walking along the boom while transferring between ship and boat. From the boom to the ship's upper deck, a series of iron rungs attached to the ship's side provides a ladder. Using it is a gymnastic exercise which is considered an integral part of boat crews' skills. But at first sight it looks an airy and flimsy construction to be moving around on.

Colman, on the helm, needed three attempts to get the bow near enough the lizard for the bow girl to get her boathook onto it and was shaken to find there was more to naval boat handling than laying alongside. Once secured on the boom Jane mustered them and said, "Another part of boat crew life is boarding and leaving over the boom. I'll do it first so you can see what is involved then you can try it yourselves, one at a time." One of the more pale-faced girls looked very dubious about the process. "Do we really have to go up and down that thing?"

"Oh yes and climb a rope."

"Oh dear, I don't know if I can."

"Oh, you will manage. Just watch me."

Her Tiffy had emerged from his machinery and nudged the doubtful one. "Just you watch this."

Jane grabbed the jumping ladder, shinned up it, moved rapidly along the boom and up the ship's side rungs. Time from boat to deck, twenty-five seconds. She turned around and came back down in twenty seconds.

"That's how you do it. I want you to go more slowly until you are comfortable with it, but at work you are allowed thirty seconds to do it and will have to get used to this being an everyday part of your life as boat crew. We'll start with the jumping ladder today. Who's going first?" They looked at each other uncertainly. "How high is it?"

"I think about thirty feet to the ship's deck. The boom is about halfway. Does that bother you?"

"Not really but it looks a bit off-putting."

"Come on, Colman, let's see if the fishing life has equipped you for this."

"We don't get off the deck there but alright, I'll give it a go. You go up the side of the lower ladder – jumping ladder you call it?"

"Correct. That stops it from swinging out from under your feet."

Colman was anything but cynical now. Nervously she got hold of the side wires and started to work her way up. About halfway up she suddenly found her feet and started to move more easily. Even so, the transfer from ladder to boom almost defeated her. With nothing to hold onto above her, hauling up onto the boom then standing up with only a single back wire for stability was challenging. She managed it in the end but came back down the ladder looking distinctly white under the tan.

"Right, next?" One by one the others struggled up, balanced precariously on the boom, and returned to the boat with a sigh until there was just one left. She was a substantial lump of a girl whose weight was going to give her problems. "I really don't think I can do this," she muttered.

"Surely you're not going to give up on day one of the course, Walters? You can if you try, y'know."

"It's the transfer from the ladder to the boom I'm not sure about."

"All right, tell you what, I'll go up first and help you this time."

Jane waited patiently while Walters struggled up the jumping ladder. With her head level with the boom she was in tears and trembling all over. "I just can't go any further."

"Yes you can, come on and reach up so that you get an arm over the boom." Walters tried and got an arm over but just could not lift herself any further. At that point there was a bellow from the gangway. "D45 alongside now."

Jane called down for engines and for the other girls to stand by the mooring pennant. "Come on Walters, go back down for now. You've been let off for today but we'll try again another day. You need to build up your upper body strength for this job." The girl made her way slowly down the jumping ladder, followed by an impatient Jane and collapsed in a heap on the deck. Colman had been sensible enough to go to the wheel so that everything was ready as soon as Jane hit the deck. "Cast off forward. Colman, keep her head to the tide as you come along side." This was understood and acknowledged with a wave. The brow quartermaster was getting very impatient. "Come on, I need you five minutes ago. Now is too late."

"Sorry. These are first day trainees so it's all taking a while. You will have to put up with a bit of this for the next few weeks."

"That I will not. When I say now, I mean now. You've held up a whole team of dockyard mateys."

"My heart bleeds, you've no idea."

"It will when I put in a complaint."

In the meantime, the dockyard gang had come on board and disappeared into the forward cabin.

"Is that the lot?"

"Yes, get on with it."

The two upper deck matelots had stayed with the boat, under instructions to let the girls do the work but helping and demonstrating as necessary. With the need for haste, Jane signalled to the sailor supervising a girl on the bow boathook and stood by as Colman took the boat away, again making a neat job of it using the tidal flow. Whatever else might be new to her, this young lady could handle boats.

By the time the dockyard group had been landed it was 1700 and time to secure for the day. She gathered her little group round her and sorted out who would do

CHAPTER FIVE: Training Course

what the following day, then dismissed them to find their way back to their quarters.

Back in the trainers' hut she asked Stan "Do we have any way of building up their strength in some of this lot? I've got one who is so feeble she can't lift her own weight."

"I'll make enquiries – give these useless club throwers something to do."

The training process quickly settled into a regular pattern, with the group swapping jobs each day. Walters proved as uncertain on the steering wheel as she had been on the boom and despite close instruction from Jane, made a complete hash of coming alongside. On the Friday night she detained Jane after dismiss and said, "I'm not going to make it, am I?"

"Walters, there's no reason why you can't if you will only believe in yourself. Say to yourself, 'I can do this, I will do this, then apply what you're being shown here. I've arranged for some gym exercises for you to build up your strength then it will be a lot easier. I'm not going to mark you down as a failure yet. Do you want to be a boat crew Wren?"

"Oh yes, more than anything, but I hadn't realised how challenging it would be."

"If it is new to you, it is certainly a different world but you can adapt to it if you really want to. Keep trying."

Coming back into the petty officers' quarters there was a letter for her. It proved to be from her father. *"Funeral arranged for midday next Saturday. David and Sarah are coming home for the weekend. Can you get a day off?"* Well, she could try. Perhaps her mother's funeral would be counted sufficient for more time off but the grumbles over her previous forty-eight did not bode well. But she found authority surprisingly willing to help and got a forty-eight on the understanding that she would be there, ready to start again, at 0630 on Monday morning. Week two was very similar to that first week, with mixed abilities to deal with from another well practised boat driver to a couple of girls out of their depth and struggling with every job. The boom was proving a particular barrier and Jane suggested that a shoreside mock-up would allow them to practise and get used to this bit of equipment. By week three a boom was in place close to their quarters and one by one the trainees mustered the courage to master it.

On the Saturday Jane put on her best uniform, caught an early bus, and arrived in the remains of her home by 1015 to find her brother and sister there already. David, in his new Cadet's uniform, was a bit down but Sarah, still in her school uniform, was very woebegone. An hour later a taxi drew up at the remains and out stepped her David. Jane had telegrammed her husband but had not had a reply so assumed he was busy on work up. "David! Oh, how lovely to see you!" and she rushed into his arms.

53

"Yes well, I managed to bring our boiler clean forward by a few days which has given me just enough time to get here. But what a tragedy this is."

"And then some. I've been so busy it has barely had time to sink in yet but it does change everything down here."

Attendance at the service was larger than Jane expected, with a good number of her mother's relations there. Some she knew, others came from more distant parts of her mother's spreading Devon clan. A couple of older ladies proved to be nurses from her mother's service in the First War. Both wore impressive rows of medals showing that they had lived as her mother had, close to the front line and its dangers. The service ended with singing 'Abide with me' and virtually the whole congregation was in tears before its end.

Following her mother's wishes, her father had arranged for her to be buried in the Old Grange's grounds on a knoll with a clear view of the river mouth and the sea. A marquee had been set up near the bombed remains for the reception after the interment. Eunice and Gladys were in charge of the catering and impressed Jane with how at ease Eunice was, giving directions to a group of village women brought in to do the catering.

By early evening, the family was on its own again and retired to the boat house. A gloomy debate centred around what they were going to do now that the Old Grange was no longer available as a central point. Her father listened for a while then cleared his throat. "I don't think I want to see the Old Grange rebuilt and I am actually thinking of getting a new house built just above where we are now. Something modern positioned to take advantage of the view that we have from here. Whether I can get it built before the end of the war, I don't know, but it is worth a try. Meantime I think I have found a place to rent just East of Plymouth. We can all go and look at it tomorrow." The Old Grange's wine stocks having gone with the bombing, it was a fairly sober evening and there was a general move to turn in early. There being no privacy at the boathouse, Jane and her husband retired behind a pile of boat gear and snuggled down under boat blankets. Their lovemaking was restrained and silent but the close cuddling seemed more important and they fell asleep in each other's arms.

The proposed rental house was somewhat run down as the Army had been in occupation but it was felt that with some cleaning it could be acceptable. Both Jane's siblings had to catch a train in the afternoon and Jane was expecting to have to return on the Sunday evening but to her surprise her father offered to run her in early on the Monday morning then drop her husband at the station. This allowed the young couple another night together but the cloud of melancholy hanging over them meant that they settled for cuddling again. David was not optimistic about prospects. "We'll finish work-up in a few days now, then I suppose it will be back to the convoy routine again. But we are getting a hammering from the U-Boats just now so it is not going to be much fun. I think this is the first time I've ever not looked forward to going to sea but I suppose it's got to be done." At six o'clock in the morning they exchanged a hasty kiss at the Wrennery door then their working lives swallowed them.

CHAPTER SIX:
Losing Them

The course settled into a regular routine with Jane getting a new group on board D45 each week and trainees rotating round the various aspects of being a boat's crew. The mid-term exam was passed by everyone and all was going well with Jane being shown a lot of respect by her groups. Until week four, that is. That week's group included a tall fair-haired girl, well-spoken and behaving with a languorous ease. Her first greeting to Jane was "I've got an Ocean Yachtmaster's ticket, y'know."

"Oh really? That will be handy for helping you to work on the boat, then."

"Never mind handy, there's nothing you can show me here that I don't know already."

"Well now, that is interesting. Do you know boat hook drill yet?"

"You reach out and hang on, don't you?"

"Not entirely. I'll be giving a demonstration shortly. Kindly observe and learn."

"Yeah well, if you say so."

"I do. What is your name?"

"Cassandra, but you can call me Cassie."

"I most certainly cannot. You must be new. Surname?"

"Pitt-Thompson."

"Right, Pitt-Thompson, get this clear. You always address me as Petty Officer Beacon and you will pay close attention to everything that I show this group this week. I will not tolerate any hanging about at the back of the group thinking you know it all already. Can you quote the Collision Regulations?"

"Oh yes we did them for Yachtmaster so I know them already and we had classes on them last week. Easy stuff."

"Hmm, we'll see."

What was it about this girl's casual superiority that irritated Jane so much? She had known many girls like this at school without being troubled by them. Here it felt different and she was determined to crack the girl's lofty air.

But for a couple of days the group behaved well and Pitt-Thompson proved to be a competent boat handler. Then, as happened every week, they were sent to moor on the *Defiance* boat boom and Jane had a chance to introduce them to shinning up it. After giving a demonstration she was pleased to have a couple of the group go straight up it unhesitatingly, one of them even going straight on up and onto *Defiance's* deck. Another couple struggled but did it. Then it was Pitt-Thompson's turn.

CHAPTER SIX: Losing Them

"I've not got a head for heights, y'know."

"Well, this is an integral part of being boat crew and if you don't do it you will fail the course. Kindly get on with it."

"Oh please, you can't do this to me."

"Oh yes I can and will. If you like I'll go to the boom and help you first time. Now come on."

Suddenly the superior air had evaporated, and she looked close to tears. Looking up at the boom she shuddered. "It's all right for you. I just can't do it."

"I told you, you will have to. Have you tried the training boom set up near your quarters?"

"No, I didn't think it was important."

"Well as an everyday part of boat crew life you have to be able to do it."

Jane went up to the boom and called, "Come on, your turn now."

Shaking her head and trembling all over, Pitt-Thompson got hold of the jumping ladder and very hesitantly went a few steps up. She paused, took a deep breath, and struggled up to under the boom where again she got stuck.

"Now reach up and get an arm over the boom." The girl tried but missed and fell backwards. Fortunately she fell into the water so was unhurt but was panic-stricken. To Jane this was an opportunity for another bit of teaching. She grabbed a boathook, fished around and got hold of Pitt-Thompson's belt. To the rest of the group she said, "Right, when you are on liberty boats you will get lots of this, drunken Jacks missing their footing. You deal with it like this. Get hold of their belt with the boathook, pull them close alongside the boat and pull them up. They are usually sobered up smartish by the cold shock of the water so can pull themselves over the bulwark. Come on, Pitt-Thompson, reach up and grab the bulwark capping."

"I can 't, I just can't," she wailed. "Help me, I'm drowning."

"Oh rubbish, come here." Jane used the boathook to pull her close to the ship's side, reached down and grabbed a hand. She pulled hard on this and the half-drowned girl finally got hold of the bulwark cap and pulled herself up a bit. Jane reached own, grabbed her belt, and hoiked the girl onto the deck where she lay in a sobbing, wailing heap. "Right, Pitt-Thompson, are you hurt at all?"

The girl shook her head.

"Then the best thing for you is to go into the forward cabin, take off your outer clothes and wrap in a blanket beside the stove. Can I have a couple of volunteers to help her, please?" Th other members of the group had been watching this, wide-eyed with horror. They all put their hands up so Jane detailed the two closest ones.

At that point the brow quartermaster bellowed "D45 alongside now."

Jane's three matelots had kept in the background during the unfolding drama but now moved swiftly: engine on, two trainees taken forward to the lizard and Jane went to the wheel. Once alongside, she called up "Did you see our little drama just now? I'm afraid the forr'd cabin is out of use for a bit."

"That's all right. Just the mail to go ashore."

The day's work done, Jane saw to it that Pitt-Thompson was dressed again in her still damp uniform and although still very shaky was able to go ashore with some help from the other girls. "You'd better see the nurse when you get back to quarters, just checked over in case." Pitt-Thompson could only nod.

Inevitably this drama required a report and Jane spent an hour writing out the five-minute incident while it was still fresh in her mind. Coming in the next day she dropped it off with Stan, indulged in a few sharp comments about wimps, and picked up her orders for the day. Her trainee group were very subdued and Pitt-Thompson conspicuous by her absence but a perfectly good day's work was done. Coming into the Trainers' office Stan gave her a severe look. "Eeh lass, what have you been doing? Boats officer wants to see you right away about some complaint."

"Well, I can take a guess about what it is Stan, so I'll pop in now."

She entered Commander Burrell's lair calmly and reported in official form.

"Right Beacon, what have you been doing? We have a formal complaint today about your bullying behaviour which I have to investigate. I presume you know what I'm referring to?"

Jane could see her report on his desk along with another letter.

"Well sir, I see that you've got my report on your desk already so you know the story. Beneath her toplofty style Pitt-Thompson really is a bit pathetic."

"Yes, but it makes a claim that your bullying behaviour forced her to have an accident."

"That's entirely due to her own inadequacy and she's got to deal with this. I might not have pushed her so hard if she hadn't tried to be so superior with me earlier. Stupid girl said she had nothing to learn from me and rather implied that she was above me in some way. Well, now she knows she isn't but with a bit of everyday humility we can probably build her up again provided the boom isn't the end of her."

"Hmm. Have you had any other trouble like this?"

"Oh, there's been a few had difficulties with the boom which is why I recommended building the mock-up at their quarters. I gather it is being well used, except by Pitt-Thomson. But none of the others were giving themselves airs and graces about how wonderful they were already, so I was able to give them sympathetic encouragement and instruction. Will there be any trouble from this?"

"Well luckily she wasn't hurt so not really, but I do have to caution you to be a bit more thoughtful with these complete novices. You could easily have caused a

CHAPTER SIX: Losing Them

nasty accident there. Why were you so pushy with this girl?"

"Mainly because she had got right up my nose with her superior airs and I was determined to bring her down a peg."

"I rather think your emotional reaction has clouded your judgement here. To be a successful trainer you do have to be able to control your own feelings and take a cool view of your charges. You must remember that. This business will go through usual channels but I don't think we will be taking it further. We will make sure Pitt-Thompson is not placed with you again."

"Well that's fine. I presume I can go back to work now?"

Commander Burrell smiled broadly. "Yes Beacon, this is one you have been lucky to get away with but do be more careful."

And that was the end of the matter. But it did leave Jane with a wary sense of caution in her dealings with the rest of the trainees who mostly were so in awe of her that they did not offer any sort of challenge. Interestingly, with the help of a PTI, Pitt-Thompson did overcome her terror of the boom and completed the course successfully. But for the rest of her time in the Wrens, Pitt-Thompson referred to Jane as 'that dreadful Beacon'.

Week five whizzed past. By now the girls coming onto the boat had had a good deal of shore-side instruction already and were more knowledgeable in their performance. Which just left week six and the end of course exams. These apparently went well and all bar three of the course were passed fit to start work as boat crew. Superintendent Welby was seen to smile and look happy as she handed out the course certificates and her short speech of encouragement was well received. Jane met her father in his rented house on the Friday night and spent a somewhat gloomy weekend discussing plans and arrangements with him. Christmas was expected to be held as ever, even having a turkey which Doctor Beacon had managed to obtain from one of his patients.

On the Monday morning Jane was back at work filling in a gap in the rosters, with four of her newly fledged boat Wrens as crew. Her two upper deck matelots had been taken away and they were on their own. This did not bother Jane but she found she still had to keep a sharp eye on her inexperienced crew. She called in at the boats office for her orders. Instead of just giving them to her, Stan said, "Eeh Lass, have you heard? The Japs bombed the American fleet at Pearl Harbour yesterday and the Yanks have declared war on them. They were saying in the mess this morning that the Germans will declare war on America within a day or two now which has to be good news for us."

"Well I never. I don't see how either of them can hope to beat the dear old US-of-A but presumably that will take the pressure off us a bit?"

"Yes and no. It will probably help to have the Yanks on board here in Europe. But now we're probably in the Japanese sights as well which will give us another war to fight, as if we didn't have enough already."

"Oh well, Germans, Italians, Japanese, we've got 'em all to wrestle with now. I wonder if we'll see any Americans over here? That could be interesting."

But the immediate world had to go on and her orders promised something different; she gathered her crew round to explain. "Right, today we have to secure a frigate to a mooring buoy in mid-stream. I take it you haven't done that yet?" Shakes of the head all round. "Right, this involves climbing onto the buoy and passing a mooring wire rope through the ring, attaching it to the messenger rope and seeing it fed through without snagging while the messenger rope is hauled up by the ship's crew, dragging the mooring wire back to the ship to form a bight. These are passed down to you from the ship. At other times they hang off an anchor, taking it off its chain and using that chain to secure to the buoy. With that you have to shackle the chain's end to the buoy ring, which is hard and heavy work. These buoys are not easy; no hand holds, difficult footing and the bloody thing always ready to rotate and throw you into the oggin. But it's a regular part of boat crew work so we'll go and lie on the buoy until the frigate turns up, then you will see what is involved." It was mid-morning before the frigate arrived, approaching the buoy very cautiously. This ship was rusty and unkempt looking, her grubby crew hanging slack over the rails dressed in odd bits of uniform. The mooring wire that was passed down was equally dry and rusty. Jane was not impressed by what she saw but her job was to secure the ship to the buoy, not indulge her own opinions so she selected two of the more enterprising of the crew and said "Right, follow me onto the buoy and I'll show you how. The rest of you watch closely because you will all have to do it as a regular part of your work."

Being so dry and rusty, the mooring wire was stiff and difficult to feed through the buoy ring. But eventually they managed and secured it to the messenger line to haul back to the ship. On board the ship they heaved away on the messenger and it came tight, dragging the mooring wire through the buoy ring. But it jammed and the two new crew could not get it clear. Irritated, Jane took hold of the wire; like the others she was wearing heavy leather work gloves. Freeing the wire, she called on the ship to heave away. As they did so Jane's left glove caught on one of the many snags, bits of broken wire sticking up from the mooring line. She tugged but could not get the glove free. She tried pulling her hand out of the glove but because it was curled round the wire, she could not do that either. She screamed "vast heaving" but it kept moving and horrified, she watched as her hand was dragged into the ring under heavy pressure. A pain of a sort she'd never known before shot up

CHAPTER SIX: Losing Them

her arm and she screamed in agony, a howling yelp of a noise she didn't know she could make. On board the frigate they now saw what was happening and slacked back on the messenger which allowed the boat crew with Jane to lift the wire and pull her gloved hand off the wire. A steady trickle of blood was coming out the cuff of her glove. Struggling on the edge of passing out she scrambled back onto the boat and watched while the wire was pulled taut again and her two crew members climbed back onto the boat. Barely able to talk she mumbled, "Better get me to hospital quickly." By good fortune one of the experienced boat handlers was in this crew and took the helm, charging in to flagstaff steps as quickly as the boat would go. Rushing into his office Jane shouted "Stan, Stan, get me an ambulance at the double." He took one look at the bloodied arm and her contorted face and got on the phone. "Stonehouse for you, Jane."

In the hospital casualty department she showed them the damaged hand, still in its glove. Carefully they cut the glove away, challenging in itself as leather work gloves are tough, well beyond the ability of ordinary scissors to cut. But with clippers and a scalpel they got it off. Jane looked in horror at the bloody pulpy mass with bits of bone sticking out of it. "Hmm," said the Sister, "Straight to theatre for you." After that it was a bit of a blur before the chloroform mask was fitted over her face and it all went blank.

PART TWO:

THE DESCENT INTO HADES

CHAPTER SEVEN:
Moving On

After a hazy day while the anaesthetic wore off, Jane was awake and clear-eyed the next morning when the surgeon called by. "Right, young lady, you can't see anything under the bandages just now so let me tell you what has happened. There was nothing we could do for the crushed fingers except remove the remains and make a tidy job of the stump ends. You have lost your pinkie, ring finger, and half your long finger. By some miracle, your index finger escaped damage. What is left has been tidied up and you will have good use of the hand but inevitably with some limitations. You do seem to have been in the wars a bit, judging by the other scars you have dotted about your body but their condition tells me that you should heal up well and it won't be long before we can take the bandages off. Any questions?"

"What happened to my wedding ring?"

"It is bent and crushed too but was rescued and it is in your bedside locker drawer."

"Oh well, I suppose it is good that it survived at all. My husband will be concerned but I'll just have to have something on my right hand instead. How long do I have to stay in bed for?"

"You can get up and move around now if you want but keep the left hand well out of the way. It needs a week or two to heal up properly. Assuming all goes well we will think of discharging you in a few days and you can have the stitches out as an outpatient." And with that he moved off to his next patient.

Later in the day Commander Burrell called by and was a relaxed and chatty visitor. Stan was a bit tongue-tied with what by now was a familiar greeting "Eeh lass, you did this time," but reported that the newly passed out boat Wrens were showing up well in their first jobs. He sympathised with losing body parts but assured Jane that she would get over it soon enough. "Losing me leg was not nice but you get used to it not being there and can play up to having a wooden leg instead."

Superintendent Welby was sympathetic but brisk, discussing the practicalities of convalescent leave. "As Christmas is almost on us anyway, we'll leave you to heal until the new year then think about what you will do next. Apparently, headquarters has some ideas but is saying nothing just now."

The last visitor was her father who had already had a medical report from the surgeon but now enquired after her general wellbeing. "Well not too bad all things considered but it is going to take some adapting to not having fingers. What a stupid little accident to cause so much trouble. I will be let out in a few days. I presume I can come to your place as it looks like David will be at sea?"

"Yes of course. Your siblings will be pleased to see you. I still have Eunice and Gladys coming in each day, and what d'you think? It looks as though Papa Gianni will be coming back to UK early next year. We don't know yet whether he will be interned here or if he will be let out completely but I've written to the relevant authority and am standing guarantor for him. We can only hope."

"Oh, that will be good. It would be nice to see him again."

With her father departed she settled down and apart from pains in her left hand disturbing her at times, she had a good night's sleep. Next morning the young house doctor came to her bedside and after a quick check on her state said "Have you heard? The Japs have sunk the *Prince of Wales* and *Repulse*. It seems they were bombed and torpedoed by Japanese aircraft off the East coast of Malaya and were just smashed to bits. Bit of a tragedy all round."

"Dear me, the Japs are having a field day, aren't they? First Pearl Harbour and now our battlewagons, ancient and modern. How on earth are we going to stop them?"

"Who knows, it certainly doesn't look good just now. But we must not give up; we will win through in the end, especially with the Yanks now in the war as well." He sounded a bit as though he was trying to convince himself, thought Jane, but one way and another, prospects looked pretty bleak.

About ten o'clock in the morning the Sister came in with a telegram for Jane. She froze, as telegrams like this tended to be bad news, and it was. It read REGRET TO ADVISE THAT LIEUTENANT-COMMANDER DAVID DAUBENEY-FOWKES IS MISSING IN ACTION, PRESUMED KILLED. Jane just sat there motionless for some time, drained of any spirit. The Sister stopped at Jane's bed. "Bad news?"

Jane nodded. "My husband has been killed." Operating on autopilot she asked "Do we have a phone I could use? I'd like to try to find out more." She phoned the Marchioness at Hemel Towers who could only say that his ship had blown up, then tried Lady Ormond, explaining the story and asking if she could find out any more. Still totally frozen mentally she went back to bed, lay down and stared fixedly at the ceiling. Tears did not come; somehow this disaster was beyond ordinary grieving.

She lay there for several hours, her mind blank except for an awful feeling of overwhelming greyness. Then there was a commotion in the entrance and a Naval officer strode into the ward, escorted by a nurse. He pointed at Jane; "This the one?"

The nurse nodded; the ward sister had quietly come in as well. He stumped to the bottom of Jane's bed and without any preliminaries announced "I am the commanding officer of the ship you almost moored to a buoy a couple of days

CHAPTER SEVEN: Moving On

ago. I have lodged a complaint that you left your station before mooring up was completed. I knew it was going to be disastrous from the moment I saw females on the buoy trying to pretend that they could do a man's job." Jane drew breath to protest about this but the officer, a short fat red-faced lieutenant-commander, kept talking. "You really are a silly goose to be getting involved in stuff like that. A woman's place is in the kitchen, tending her babies, not trying to pretend that they can do a man's job. I was told I should be sympathetic to you but I don't feel in the least like that, just annoyed that a stupid woman like you got yourself where you shouldn't be and paid the price. You deserve whatever you got, and now perhaps you will just quietly go back to your kitchen and stop pretending you are good for anything else. I shall lodge a complaint every time I see one of you stupid ninnies in a boat. It really shouldn't be allowed." He paused to draw breath which gave Jane half a chance to get a word in edgeways. The red mist of her rage was rising rapidly. "How dare you! How dare you! It was because of the neglected state of your ship that this happened in the first place, you and your sloppy crew."

"Pah! You'll not pin the blame on me you stupid feeble girl."

This was too much for Jane. She hopped out of bed, marched up to this objectionable man, and towered over him. Looking into his eyes she saw nothing but contempt, and her whole mind went red. She snarled and quite out of control slapped him across the face. It was the snake strike again, with added ferocity; it knocked him over, his cap flying away under a bed. Puffing and panting he climbed onto his feet again; the nurse retrieved his cap and handed it to him, dusting it as she did so. "You'll pay for this, woman. Striking an officer is a serious offence and you'll not get away with it." And clapping his slightly battered cap on his head he rushed out of the ward grunting as he went.

As quiet descended the ward sister looked appraisingly at Jane. "He asked for it but it was probably a mistake to hit him. Good luck with the follow up."

Jane climbed into her bed again and suddenly the outburst of rage and physical action allowed the emotional dam to break. She howled with anguish, tears streaming down her face and the misery welling up inside her, overflowing. Several hours later she was still moaning and sobbing, "Gone. It's all gone. Good-bye." This last in a gentle singing tone. Her father called by and was dismayed by her condition. "What's wrong? Has something upset you?" Jane could not bring herself to give him the whole story but handed him the telegram. He shook his head slowly, sadly and for five minutes tried to comfort her but to little effect. In the end he gave up, said "I'll pick you up tomorrow afternoon," and left. Later she was given a sedative which, combined with an exhausted slump, put her to sleep for the night.

By the time her father called the next day, Jane had recovered her composure and

67

was ready to come with him. Somehow everything was on autopilot; constructive thought was beyond her but she went through the motions, answering in monosyllables and staring fixedly ahead. Coming into the place her father had rented really drove it home: her real home, her mother, now her husband, all gone. A stray bit of her brain thought 'well, that's my three. Perhaps the fates can leave me alone now.' Despite her father sitting next to her she felt very alone, bereft of anyone she could turn to. He tried to talk to her but got very little back: her siblings were due back towards the end of next week, the rented place was proving quite comfortable now it had been cleaned and patched up, her mother's will had left various items including the Russian necklace, to her; all this passed by and probably registered but did little to penetrate the grey fog which had enveloped her. Her left hand was still hurting and she found it easier to hold it up so she went along with her left arm in the air.

Eunice and Agnes were both on hand to greet them on arrival but took one look at Jane's strained, sad face and quietly made a cup of tea without comment. In this haven of sorts she settled down for a couple of days, then mail forwarded from the Petty Officers' mess started to catch up with her. The most important letter was from Lady Ormond:

Jane, my dear

I have been able to find out a little for you. It seems David's ship was on some special detached duty off the North of Norway on ninth December when it suddenly exploded with the loss of all hands. It must have been close to Russia when it happened for the limited information we have has come from them. They picked up some bodies but not David's. I was not able to find out what his ship was doing on its own off the North Cape, except 'special duties'. There was no explanation of why the ship blew up. My dear Jane, that is all I can get out of them so may I offer you my deepest condolences and remember you always have an alternative home with me.

There was more on the latest difficulties of living in London but Jane did not register the rest. She thought about the message from Lady Ormond's letter. Ninth December? That was the day she lost her fingers, so it was fingers and husband at the same time. The bent and crushed wedding ring, now on a fine chain round her neck, somehow seemed a symbol of the disaster which had overtaken her. But what was that symbolism? Was some malign force pursuing her? She shook her head, trying to clear the fog round her brain and think logically but she felt impelled away from any conclusions. Her husband had gone with her fingers and a stupid part of her mind thought 'perhaps he is holding them in Heaven, wanted them as a souvenir'. Much good that pulpy mess would do him. He was gone and now she had to face up to being a widow, aged just twenty-one. No doubt she wasn't the only young widow in this horrible war but that was scant comfort.

CHAPTER SEVEN: Moving On

The next day she received a letter from the Marquess. After some trite banalities it got down to business:

You may have the Daubeney-Fowkes name now and doubtless David's will has provided for you, but you are not welcome at Hemel Towers except on official business. You may call to collect any effects you still have here but we do not wish to see you here again and you will refrain from using Hemel Towers as any sort of an address. Any attempt to turn up uninvited will be treated as trespass. Our lawyers will contact you about David's will and make it clear to you, what you can and cannot do regarding your title. Kindly acknowledge receipt of this letter and that you fully understand its contents. Any attempt to go against it will be treated severely and possibly as a criminal act.

Jane sat for some time staring blankly out of the window. 'Well,' she thought, 'You certainly know how to twist the knife in the wound. Here we are, your youngest son and my husband, missing in action, and not a hint of feeling from you. I might as well be a miscreant servant you had turned out for all the humanity you show now. All right, Missus Marquess, I will remember this and not forgive you.' Her fighting spirit was up and helped to lift a little, the fog of misery which had enveloped her but it was a sour, acid sort of lift. There was a strong temptation to go 'the hell with them' and dismiss the Daubeny-Fowkes clan from her mind, but somehow she knew that she would not get away from the lingering effect of David's estate so easily.

Letters seemed to be coming in profusion and next day there was another important one from Wren HQ. It came from second officer Merle Baker and was official despite its informal tone.

Jane, what have you done? Today we have had notice served on us that you are to be court-martialled. This in itself startled us because Wrens are not subject to court-martial but because you committed an offence against an officer which is against an article of war, it seems you can be. Now that I am a qualified solicitor, I can take on a case like yours but we will need to know much more to be able to mount a good defence.

We are gathering evidence and the details of the prosecution case and will go through it with you very soon as they are talking of holding the court-martial in the middle of January which leaves us precious little time to get organised. I will plan to come and see you right after Christmas so we can go through the story and the documentation together. Meantime we have asked for all communication with you to go through our office so we can see exactly what is happening. Please write to me by return confirming that you are available and fit enough to meet me right after Christmas.

Yours truly,
Merle Baker (2/O, W.R.N.S)

This was getting to be too much and Jane sat quietly for some time trying to take it all in. That fat miserable little man must have made some sort of complaint about her slapping him and she had a strong spurt of rage that him and his rusty slovenly ship should be the cause of so much trouble. But doubtless the Navy would take a narrow view of her action, striking an officer being an absolute offence. She showed her father the collection of letters that evening, hoping for some words of wisdom, some relief from the pressures that seemed to be pressing in from every side. He sat in silence for some time after reading them. "Lady Ormond really is an exceptionally good friend to you. You could do worse than write and tell her about your problems. The Daubeney-Fowkes clan are simply behaving as one would expect, pushing out the interloper as soon as an opportunity presents itself. It is unlikely that you will get them to behave any other way. As for the court-martial, I'll make a few discreet enquiries myself but I will have to careful as the Navy doesn't like obvious string pulling. I have to say that calling a court-martial to deal with this case really is using a giant sledgehammer to crack an exceedingly small nut. If it happens you will find it an awesome event which you'll need to be well prepared for."

A letter was duly despatched to Lady Ormond laying out Jane's woes, without specifically asking her to do anything but doubtless questions would be asked. A brief note to Merle confirmed Jane's availability. With her siblings not due to arrive home for a few days yet, Jane found time hanging heavy in her grey, deeply miserable world. Her father had quite obviously still not recovered from the loss of his own life partner and was prone to long heavy silences which did nothing to improve Jane's depression. On the spur of the moment she decided to visit *Osprey*, now hers to look after. She got Eunice to make up a couple of cold meals; with a loaf of bread and some tea she was equipped to stay away for a day or two. Having found her way to the boathouse she decided to stay on board her yacht, so took some bedding, a lamp and a primus, piled them all into the dinghy and rowed up to the creek. *Osprey* was lying quietly, looking much more faded but still sound. And for a couple of days she found a measure of peace. She had always been comfortable with her own company and settled to doing little maintenance jobs about the boat. In the evening she wrote out a full description of the events leading to her finger loss and the captain's disastrous visit to her in hospital; she did not hold back with her opinions of the ship and commanding officer who had brought her so much trouble. She found getting it out and on to paper was cathartic in its way even if no-one ever read it. With her left hand still bandaged and distinctly tender to the touch she was limited in what could be done but she managed some one-handed splicing, scrubbed the topsides and cleaned the seagull droppings from the canvas

CHAPTER SEVEN: Moving On

cover. Then, with her siblings' arrival getting close, she gave the boat a final pump out, gathered up her bits and pieces and left *Osprey* to its rest. Looking at her as she rowed away, she still found it very strange to think that she owned it, that that beautiful old cutter was hers to do with or dispose of as she chose. As she went down the river, warm thoughts of what she could do with it after the war left her cheered up and ready to get on with her life. And at least there would not now be any argument about who would be taking the boat away. It was strange, she reflected, already David was starting to seem like a historical dream, crowded to the back of her memory by more pressing matters. 'What would he have made of having a wife being court-martialled,' she idly speculated. 'That certainly would not have done his career any good.' The couple of days, living quietly on her boat, had given her some peace of mind with which to face her very uncertain future.

The arrival home of her various siblings shattered that peace soon enough. Brother David, now full grown, stood well in his cadet's uniform; his obvious pride in getting close to being a working part of the Navy gently amused Jane. The twins, who she now saw through a different lens, were as cheerfully boisterous as ever but even they were showing obvious marks of maturity and of a cooler view of their world. And her sister Sarah: well, the last few times she and Jane had been together the underlying affection was still there but they had struggled to find much common ground. But Sarah's recent fifteenth birthday seemed to have given her a more sophisticated view of her world to go with the growth spurt she was showing, now only a couple of inches shorter than Jane. She was intensely curious about all things Wren, despite Jane's warning not to mention who her sister was if she really intended to join up as soon as she could. Another trend she was showing, following Jane, was her growth, now too tall and full bodied to aspire to ballerina status. Like Jane she had been good at it and loved the movement, the discipline, the grace of it all; but now she was having to put it aside. Here was something which Jane could empathise with directly through experience and it allowed her to draw closer to her young sister again.

Christmas day was a qualified success, with everyone in relaxed mood and putting their cares aside for a brief spell. But the lack of their mother hung heavy over the feast and when their father stood up and proposed a toast to her memory there was scarcely a dry eye round the table. Jane had thought, 'hang the expense' and bought her sister a small bottle of perfume and this acknowledgement of her rapidly developing maturity had been well received.

After that, Jane's attention was on the thirtieth and Merle's arrival to discuss the rapidly onrushing court-martial. Merle had seemed to think that one man's anger against her should not cause Jane too much trouble but the Navy is an unpredictable beast when irritated and there was sufficient risk to merit Merle and Jane giving it their close attention.

So, when Merle was collected from the station Jane was puzzled by her pre-occupied, worried state. Once in the house the reason why rapidly became clear. "Jane, yesterday we received a whole fresh batch of papers about your court-martial, and they are not good news. For whatever reasons of their own, the Admiralty has taken over your case and has decided to throw the book at you. Now, there are five charges against you, all of them based on an Article of War so the most serious type. The debate about whether you should be on a court-martial charge at all, is still raging but has been relegated to a minor consideration and they have come down heavily against you. You are aware that there are some admirals who have wanted to get you out ever since Dunkirk. Well, it looks as though they have come out on top in their admirals' politics and have seized this as an opportunity for revenge as much as anything. One particular Sea Lord has instructed the Navy legal department to handle the case. We will, of course, continue to dispute their interpretation of the Articles and whether you should be court-martialled in the first place but it looks as though we will have to be ready for a much tougher inquisition than we had expected. They are appointing a barrister member of their legal department to lead their case and act as prosecutor and the senior Deputy Judge Advocate will be in attendance. A lot will depend on which officers are appointed to sit on the court. You know that a Naval court-martial is made up of a Board of serving officers who act as judge, jury and sentencing authority? Given a group of hostile officers like your Gribben it could be very sticky indeed, as these officers all owe their careers to the semi-unseen forces at the Admiralty and will be over-ridingly conscious of what verdict they are expected to deliver. There's a serious chance we may not get a fair trial from a group of senior Naval officers protecting their own positions. Our Director is deeply worried about it all and is in discussion with several Sea Lords but is finding them a solid stone wall. For her, there are huge matters of principle at stake as until now we had thought Wrens, being civilians, could not be court-martialled but the Admiralty is trying to use some obscure part of the Naval Discipline Act which says that if they do something directly contrary to the Act in a Naval setting, civilians and hence Wrens, could be. She is hoping that at least we will get two senior Wren officers on the Board for a bit of balance. We are going to need to do a lot of fast footwork in the first few days of January to get a defence in order. I presume you can come up to Town for meetings with your defence team?"

Jane had sat silent through this flow from Merle, utterly stunned by what she was hearing. Now she nodded. "Yes Merle, I can come. Just let me know when. I presume I will be in uniform and technically on duty?"

CHAPTER SEVEN: Moving On

"Yes Jane, that is correct." Merle then took Jane through the five charges laid against her and the relative strength of each. The one unarguable fact was that she had struck a superior officer, contrary to Article 16 of the Articles of War and on that alone a major case could be built against her. The story behind the striking seemed to have been relegated to a minor point of mitigation. The other major matter Merle mentioned was that the court martial was to be held in the great cabin of *HMS Victory*. "That's not as unusual as it might sound. Dear old Victory has been used for a few courts- martial during the war as it is a requirement that they must be held on board a warship in commission and right now most of ours are too taken up with war work to be spared for a sideshow like this. *Victory* is usually reserved for officer courts-martial but I think your precious admiral want to make a show of your one so has demanded that it be held in this high-profile setting. It will be impressive enough."

Jane smiled wanly. "I have written out the whole story from my point of view. Would it be helpful for you to have it?"

"Oh yes Jane, that would be really helpful. Amongst other things we have to produce a Circumstantial Letter laying out the story. It normally comes from the commanding officer of the ship an accused is serving in so in this case it falls to Superintendent Welby to write it as your commanding officer at Plymouth. If it is anything like your canal report, I am sure your description will be very clear and to the point."

"How far away that canal trip seems now. I almost resigned to go off on the narrow boats, y'know, and right now that feels like an extremely attractive option."

"No chance of that now, Jane. You would not be allowed to resign until your case has concluded and even then, we hope you will stay in the Wrens."

"I suppose so but the Navy is hardly being encouraging just now, is it?"

"Bear up, Jane this will blow over soon enough."

CHAPTER EIGHT:
Preparations

"Jane, have you done anything else that you have not told me about? I ask because there is something very strange going on in the Admiralty about your court-martial."

Jane looked puzzled. "Not that I am aware of, father. Certainly nothing Naval."

"When I asked my contact there if he had any news, he said he had been severely warned off poking his nose into the matter and not to stir it up. So, there is something going on that we are not aware of. I spoke to Lady Ormond about it and she has got nowhere either."

"Oh dear, that sounds bad. Uncle George warned me before he went off to the eastern Med that some admiral, I think he said his name was Buffy, had taken against me for what I did at Dunkirk and was going to get me if he could. Might that be behind it?"

"Possibly but admirals usually have more to do than conduct petty vendettas against Wren ratings. I'll keep my antennae tuned but it doesn't look good."

"Oh well, thanks for trying."

"You seem remarkably calm about it all, Jane. A court-martial is a horrible thing to have to go through. I've sat on the other side of a few and they can terrify the strongest."

"Getting in a funk about it beforehand isn't going to help either. I need to keep a clear head to understand what is going on. And at least this stops me brooding about David. It's just all happened in such a rush, one damned thing after another, that I haven't had time to fall to pieces about it all. That can come when I have time to think."

The next day brought another letter from Merle:

Dear Jane

The full documentation is now to hand and therefore we need you at Headquarters as soon as possible. Please come fully equipped for attending your court martial. This is a 'Swords and Medals' occasion so please come with your best uniform and medals and please, a new hat. We are now based in Queen Anne's Buildings and a pass will be ready for you on arrival.

A round of telephone calls in the afternoon arranged for her to come to Lady Ormond's flat to stay and confirmed the day after tomorrow for arriving at Wren HQ.

All this was done quite calmly but as the train got ever closer to Paddington Station her nervous tension was rising unbidden. Lady Ormond was as welcoming

CHAPTER EIGHT: Preparations

as ever but confessed to being quite unable to find out anything more about David's demise or about the underlying drive in the Admiralty for Jane to be court-martialled. Jane's room was as immaculate as ever with her assorted clothes all beautifully pressed. Rufus the bear got an ironic pat from Jane then she changed into one of her white evening dresses for dinner. Despite the rationing restrictions this was as excellent as ever and the atmosphere agreeably relaxed. Lady O was sympathetic about the lost fingers with fellow feeling for lost limbs. She had adapted to only having one hand and although still a hindrance she was able to assure Jane that most of the previous use of her hand would come back, even demonstrating how to hold things with her forearm. Just for a little while Jane's potential troubles seemed a long way away.

The medals had been tucked away in Lady O's safe so first job next morning was to recover them, check that they were still clean and shiny, and ensure she had them all. With this detail in hand, she set off for Queen Anne's Buildings and inside an hour was sitting across the desk from Merle.

"Right Jane, the pile on my left is all the other cases I am working on just now. Yours is the rather larger one on my right. Temporarily I have come off other duties and am working full time on your case. As you can see there is a lot of it and I am amazed that sluggish old Admiralty has been able to produce so much so quickly. Somebody wants this to happen, very badly. One by one I want you to take every item here over to that desk in the corner and read it carefully. You have two days for that, then the director wants to see you to discuss a few matters. We have decided not to engage a barrister, feeling that an all-female presentation might make a particular impression on your court-martial. So, you have me as your advocate. The whole story of courts-martial is steeped in history going right back to an ordinance of 1190 for the third crusade which was nailed to the foremast of every ship taking part. The Statutes of Oleron in the Thirteenth century then codified sea law with themes going back to Roman times. Admiralty law is exceptional in the English system in being based on Roman law, not our own common law. There has never been a female presence on courts-martial. For historic reasons, the accused's advocate is known as the prisoner's friend and you will have to get used to me being referred to as such. In a case like this you do not enter any plea of guilty or not guilty. It is for the prosecution to make a case which shows you to be guilty. Any comments?"

"Gosh."

"You'll have to do better than that."

"Yes, I know Merle, but it is all a bit overwhelming."

"All right, the way to deal with that is to fully understand the brief so start reading."

For the allotted two days, Jane ploughed through the legalese trying to understand what each document was telling her. At a glance, the sum of the charges made her look like a major criminal and as she went along, she started to understand Merle's observation that they would take it bit by bit. She considered that two of the charges would be seen as baseless, one so vague as to be meaningless and only two that needed serious attention. But they really were serious and Jane's defence would have to be strong to persuade her inquisitors that they were very small items. In the civil courts a woman giving a single slap to the face of a man who had insulted her would not be considered a serious assault and barely register as worthy of the court's time. This point would be made in the defence. It was only the fact that Jane, a rating, had hit a naval officer in uniform on naval premises which made it a serious crime.

The next day Jane had an appointment with two very senior masters-at-arms. They had been despatched to take a statement from Jane covering the slap and what had led to it. Statement made, Jane read through it carefully before agreeing to its being a true record, as she knew it would be part of the prosecution evidence.

Then it was the Director's turn. Sitting in front of her, Jane felt the power of that calm but forceful gaze. "Well Beacon, you do seem to attract trouble. Second Officer Baker is assembling a strong defence and we will go on arguing about whether a Wren can be court-martialled at all, but at the moment we are losing that argument. The Navy's chauvinism is at full throttle just now. I need hardly tell you that there are enormous matters of principle for us which go far beyond your fate and these will never be far away when the court martial sits. So you may hear arguments which seem remote from your particular story but are important to the future of the Wrens. I gather you are taking this calmly so far. It is vital that you continue to stay calm and strong, especially when you first come into the great cabin and see your inquisitors arrayed in full Naval splendour. That is a daunting sight and any sign of weakness by you will play straight into the hands of those who would have us removed from the Navy. And believe me, there are still plenty of them. Your record will be considered and I don't have to tell you that it is exceptional for good and bad. We have laid plans for talking up the good while downplaying the bad and you will be led into saying the right things. We know about your capacity for arguing with anyone and everyone. This will have to be kept in tight control, used to speak clearly and strongly when you are defending yourself without annoying the President of the court by telling him he is wrong. The one good thing we have managed to do is to get two senior Wren officers onto the Board and while they must remain visibly impartial, they should be able to keep any extreme outbursts of chauvinism in check. All I can say otherwise is good luck and let us hope for the best." And with a nod of dismissal Jane found herself ushered out without actually saying a word.

Once again, she found herself in Merle's capable hands. "Tomorrow we will go through the five charges in detail and make sure you understand each one. Then the two Wrens who were on the buoy with you are being called in and briefed as witnesses. We are also calling the sister and nurse from your ward at Stonehouse Hospital as defence witnesses as they were there when you were insulted and saw the whole incident. We will go down to Pompey two days before the due date and meet with them to go through their testimony. Then I have to hand you over to the Provost-Marshal who has the legal responsibility of ensuring that you are presented to the court. Once he is in charge my role simply becomes your defence lawyer, your 'prisoner's friend'. I continue to have full access to you on board *Victory* where you will be held until the court concludes."

"Oh, I didn't know people lived aboard the ship."

"Apparently so. Facilities of a sort are available on board and you will be held in one of the senior officers' cabins close to the great cabin. There will be an armed marine on duty outside your cabin the whole time you are on board. Whether that is for your own security or to make sure you don't run away is unclear; probably a bit of both. I'll be staying in the barracks wardroom. We'll also have Third Officer Rubens with us. She is going along the same path as me, training to be a lawyer while working at Headquarters and will act as general assistant. She will be with us from tomorrow through to the end."

"That's an awful lot for one errant rating."

"Jane, I hate to say this but the matters of principle involved here are massive and, in a way, you have just become a cipher. That one slap of yours has been seized on to put the whole future of the Wrens in the balance."

"That's ridiculous. And from what you said before, the composition of the Board will be hostile even with two Wren officers on it?"

"It can't be too visibly hostile but you can bet it will not be trying to do us favours."

Jane was not good company for Lady Ormond that night, staying in uniform and deeply pre-occupied with the way matters were unfolding; but the port was as excellent as ever and wanly she tried to respond. The lady just had a wry smile and left Jane to it.

Third Officer Rubens proved to be a good addition to the team. A more mature woman but bright, brisk and cheerful, she seemed to have the documentation and arrangements firmly in hand and it was she who led Jane through the five charges in detail.

"Hello Jane and nice to meet our great heroine. Please call me Hilary when we are not on formal public business. Let's take the charges in their numerical order in the Articles of War. The first is number nine, '*Neglect of Duty*'. It states that 'Every person subject to this Act who shall desert his post or negligently perform the duty imposed on him, shall be dismissed from His Majesty's service, with disgrace'. The Act is the Naval Discipline Act and Wrens are not subject to it, the Admiralty themselves having decided they did not want their ladies to receive such rough treatment. So you can imagine what a rumpus their deciding to go ahead with this court-martial has caused. The neglect of duty charge relates to your leaving the buoy you were mooring *HMS Turkey* to, before she was fully moored up. One of the other charges relates to the same incident."

"But my fingers had just been crushed. Did they expect me to go on with the mooring like that?"

"That's what the charge says, but we are not rehearsing your answers here, just showing you what the charges are."

"Well, that one is grossly unfair for a start. And anyway, I checked that the mooring line could be heaved up and secured before I left. "

"Quite so and we think we can deal with both the charges relating to this, fairly easily. Let's move on."

"Next is the heart of the matter, Article sixteen. Believe it or not this comes under the *Mutiny* section and states amongst other things that 'Every person who shall strike or attempt to strike, or attempt to use any violence, against his superior officer, shall be punished with penal servitude.' Now I don't have to tell you this is the heart of the matter. As you said in your statement, you hit him with some force in the presence of witnesses and there is no getting away from that. Provocation is a strong mitigation and we will use it but at the least you will get a rap on the knuckles for this one."

"Bah. He asked for it."

"You might think so. I don't think the Navy will and we'll have to get your language a bit more suitable before you give evidence. Moving on, next is number seventeen, *Insubordination*. This states that 'Every person who shall use threatening or insulting language, or behave with contempt to his superior officer, shall be punished with dismissal."

"But it wasn't insulting, just very angry words."

"Yes, we know that and we do not expect serious trouble with it, but as part of a general picture it is bound to have some effect on the court's opinions. Let's not waste time on it just now as we consider it one of the weaker charges.

Next is number twenty-nine. This comes under *Miscellaneous Offences*: 'Every person who shall either designedly or negligently or by any default, lose, strand or hazard or suffer to be lost, stranded or hazarded, any ship of His Majesty, shall be dismissed from His Majesty's service with disgrace.' In effect they are saying that

CHAPTER EIGHT: Preparations

you hazarded the ship by leaving the buoy before she was fully moored up. This closely ties in with number nine and is two stabs at the same incident. I know your opinion of this so we'll not linger on it just now.

The last one is number forty-four and is a typical Captain's Cloak. It is a bit wordy so bear with me. This is also under the miscellaneous provisions and says, 'Any person committing any offence against this Act, such offence not being punishable with death or penal servitude, shall, save where this Act expressly otherwise provides, be proceeded against and punished according to the laws and customs in such cases used at sea.' Now, fortunately none of your five are punishable by death anyway but it does emphasise how major and important this case is. We suspect they have something up their sleeves here, the 'custom of the sea' is an ancient concept, a vague and in many ways outdated approach anyway. We are cautious about this one which in itself should be easy to defeat but we are wary of some sort of horned mine surfacing here. So that's what we are up against. It all makes you sound like a major criminal out of one little incident but that is why we are going to break it down into small pieces and demolish them one by one."

Jane took a deep breath. "Well, that all takes some absorbing. I understand that there isn't any plea at the start unless I plead guilty to the lot which we certainly don't want to do. Can I be found guilty of some charges but not others?"

"Oh yes, each stands on its own although there is obvious overlap."

"I suppose that is some comfort. Do we know why the Admiralty is going after me like this?"

"You will have to ask Second Officer Baker that one and I'm not sure she knows much more. I get the impression that your outstanding history has a lot to do with it."

Next morning Jane was late arriving at Wren HQ, having called at St Thomas's Hospital to have the stitches taken out of her hand. This had been arranged from Stonehouse with some discreet intervention by her father. Seeing the hand for the first time was disturbing, it looked unbalanced and the healed wounds had a bright pinkness to them which seemed to draw attention. But sitting on the tube no-one paid any attention to her and she wryly reflected that this was a bit like going into the mess for the first time after she had lost her virginity. Arriving at Merle's desk she showed off the hand, unbandaged for the first time and got a sympathetic but practical, "That's what this whole business is about."

The two brand new boat wrens who had been on the buoy with her were in the office and their testimonies were run through to ensure everyone was telling the same story. Both were deeply apprehensive about the whole business but were strengthened by seeing clearly that they would be well supported throughout. With three days to go until the opening of the court, tension was rising all round but it seemed to Jane that Merle was almost looking forward to the event. Merle had looked up the officer from the Admiralty legal department who would be acting as prosecutor and found that he was qualified as a barrister with his expertise in ship collisions; this meant that he might be vulnerable to lack of knowledge about insubordination. Merle gave the impression of a fighter who knows they had a good chance of winning the battle and looked forward to it.

Next morning they all gathered at Victoria station; Merle had reserved a whole first-class compartment and the run south was spent going through the story again. From Portsmouth Harbour station they walked along to the dockyard gate, spent five minutes convincing the gate police that they really were going to *HMS Victory* ship and one of their number would be staying on board, then presented themselves at the brow. The Instructions were to seek out the ship's Master- at-Arms, and this senior chief formally took possession of Jane on behalf of the Provost-Marshal. She was shown to her cabin which proved to be minute but gave her a strong sense of being at one with the great sweep of naval history. An evening meal of Cheesy Oosh was brought to her and at some point, a marine guard appeared outside her cabin door. Jane felt a strong sense of events powering forward, the process taking hold of her and sweeping her onwards to a crescendo of formality and authority that she was powerless to change or influence. She felt very small.

The next day was busy. Jane had had a poor night's sleep, her cot bunk being five feet six inches long which meant she slept with her knees sticking out the side. Even a pillow under them did not make it much more comfortable. Breakfast was a bowl of thin watery porridge which provided sustenance but no more. Merle and her assistant arrived early and set up on a table outside Jane's cabin. They had a minor disappointment to report: they had hoped to meet with the two nurses who would be witnesses, but they were now being called as prosecution witnesses so Jane's team was not allowed near them.

They were quietly going through their defences when a very senior master- at -arms arrived. "Good morning, ladies. My name is Gordon and I am the Provost-Marshal for your case. The accused is now in my charge and it is my duty to deliver her to the court." There was some general discussion about who was who and what the defence team's position was. Jane was cautioned not to leave her cabin without an escort and not to leave the ship at all unless granted his specific permission, "And that won't happen until after the trial."

When this gentleman departed, they completed their review then Merle gave Jane a long look. "Well Jane, this is it. Remember to get your medals securely pinned on and to be looking your absolute best. We will be with you from early in the morning and will enter the court shortly after you have been escorted in. I am expecting to

CHAPTER EIGHT: Preparations

open the defence for you but you must be ready to speak up calmly and clearly. This bruiser of a barrister from the other side will do his best to trip you up and you must stay calm; believe me, it will feel worse than being attacked by Stukas. And above all, stay calm when you first enter the court room. It is an awe-inspiring sight, the legal wigs and gowns and that row of senior officers in their very best uniforms, with cocked hats and gold lace everywhere. But we know your President, Captain Cathcart, is a decent and honest man who will do his best to keep the atmosphere cool and respectful. And at least we have our own two familiar faces to offer some balance to the Board. We have the right to challenge any member of the court that you don't like so don't hesitate to tell me if you want to. That's it I think so good luck and keep your end up." With that Merle stood up and gave Jane a brief hug, murmuring "Don't worry, you will be fine on the day." Third Officer Rubens settled for a more formal handshake, but with a warm smile.

CHAPTER NINE:
Into the Jaws

With Merle's instruction to look her best in mind, Jane decided to see if she could get a bath and hair wash. This proved to be a problem: the only abluting facilities for ratings were some open showers in a lower deck mess and hardly suitable for a stray female. Having been introduced to him, in the end the ship's captain offered his facility: a shower over a hip bath with no certainty about the water temperature but it was sufficient to get clean and shiny. Deeply grateful, Jane promised the captain a drink sometime which he seemed to regard with some irony.

Back in her cabin she pinned on her medals, having some difficulty in hanging them evenly. But that achieved, they made a fine display; would it impress the court or turn them against her? All along there had been a lingering hint of resentment in upper levels of the Navy about her collection and the danger of creating a bad impression was clear. But there was nothing she could do about that and where she was now, the Army was no help. Would it still want her if she was dismissed from the Wrens? This stray thought amused her and lightened her mood enough to be able to drop off but again sleep was poor.

She was up by six o'clock the next morning. Trying to shed the sense of foreboding hanging over her, she dressed with new black silk stockings and a fresh collar extra specially starched for the occasion. Merle and her assistant were on board by eight and quietly but firmly took charge of the situation. They had a final light run over the main defence points and waited patiently while Jane ate her thin porridge. At half past nine Chief Petty Officer Gordon arrived to ensure everything was ready and a few minutes later a lawyer arrived ready for court appearance. He introduced himself as the Deputy Judge Advocate who would be officiating at the court-martial for legal matters, his role to ensure correct procedure and fair play. Merle introduced herself as a qualified solicitor and the prisoner's friend; they would be having discussion of legal points during the trial. Then the bosun's pipes started to twitter as they piped the side for each of the very senior officers arriving at the brow for the court, each in his own good time. With quarter of an hour to go Jane put on her jacket, medals clinking as she did so. Third Officer Rubens looked in awe at the collection. "How can they possibly court martial someone decorated like that?" She asked, as much to herself as anything. At ten o'clock the three ladies solemnly shook hands, Chief Gordon produced a cutlass, held it upright and as required by

CHAPTER NINE: Into the Jaws

procedure took hold of Jane by the hand. At this moment there was a loud bang, a gun going off somewhere. Chief Gordon smiled. "Ah, they've fired the rogue's gun." He commented. The ladies looking mystified, he explained that a single gun is fired when a court martial starts, and at the same time a union flag was hoisted at the yardarm. "Now all of Pompey knows you are being tried."

Cutlass over her head Jane was led to the great cabin; despite the warnings the sight took her breath away. As instructed, she stepped forward, saluted and reported in usual form. The officers of the court were all in their best uniforms, frock coats with epaulettes, suitably belted and cocked hats worn. She was pleased to see Chief Officer Lady Cholmondley who by now must be well accustomed to attending at Jane's troubles with Naval authority. More surprising was to see Miss Currie, her OiC at Dover now showing a Superintendent's four stripes on her sleeve. They looked almost dowdy in their best but ordinary uniforms. Jane cast an eye along the officers sitting in judgement and to her horror, there was Captain Gribben. Their eyes met with instant recognition; he smiled briefly, a shark's smile with teeth showing. The prosecution team came in behind her then Superintendent Mrs Welby took a place in the middle. 'Good Lord' thought Jane 'half of the Wrens' top brass is here. They really are taking it seriously'.

The Deputy Judge Advocate, now in full wig and gown, asked Jane "Do you have a friend to assist you?"

Trying hard to control her fluttering nerves she answered as coolly as she could, "Yes sir, Second Officer Baker and Third Officer Rubens of the Women's Royal Naval Service."

"Let them be admitted."

Merle and her assistant came in and identified themselves.

The Deputy Judge Advocate now stepped forward and named each of the members of the court in turn. He turned to Jane and asked, "Do you have any objection to any of them?"

'It's now or never,' thought Jane. "Yes sir, I object to Captain Gribben."

Merle jumped visibly at this unexpected statement. The President rolled his eyes and Gribben himself snorted noisily. The Deputy Judge Advocate asked, "State your reasons."

"We have met before, sir, back in early 1940. I was a crew hand on a launch transferring from Plymouth to Dover and we had to put in to Haslar Creek to land an injured seaman after we had been shot up by an RAF hurricane. Captain Gribben appeared from somewhere and took it on himself to try to have me dismissed from the boat."

"Why was that?"

"Because I am female sir, and he does not believe that women should be involved with the Navy in any way. Knowing his views on this I do not believe I can get a fair hearing from him here."

The President intervened. "I see. Clear the court while this matter is discussed."

For ten minutes they all waited aimlessly outside then were recalled. The President looked Jane in the eye and said, "We have discussed your objection and do not uphold it by a vote of five to two. We are satisfied that Captain Gribben can be a fair member of this court as his personal views do not obstruct his sense of duty." He turned to the Deputy Judge Advocate, "Please proceed."

This gentleman asked Jane "Do you have any other objections?"

"No sir."

Each of the members of the court were then sworn in by him, in turn giving their oath to be fair, legal and impartial. The President then swore in the Deputy Judge Advocate in similar manner. That done, the Deputy Judge Advocate completed arraigning Jane by reading out the charges laid against her before inviting Superintendent Welby to read out the Circumstantial Letter. Her clear description of the two incidents left no doubt about the underlying facts of the case. After this the President looked at Jane and asked, "You suffered permanent damage, then?"

Jane simply held up her left hand. "Yes sir. Before this incident I had a full set of fingers."

The President nodded and addressed the court. "Ladies and gentlemen, this court-martial is the first time that a woman has been arraigned before us. Because of that we will not stick too rigidly to procedure, with some informality allowed to get at the truth while ensuring that correct legal process is accomplished. Our object is to achieve a fair hearing which deals correctly with the issues while giving a full airing of them."

He then turned to the prosecutor. "Commander Wolfe, kindly present your case." Commander Wolfe was an imposing figure, a large man with a heavy face and mane of grey hair. He rose slowly and dramatically to his feet and spoke in a deep booming baritone. "Ladies and gentlemen of the court, we have here today a simple case of someone suffering the consequences of her own inadequacies and then trying to deflect attention from them by attacking her superior officer. The Navy in its wisdom has specific rules to protect officers from this sort of behaviour and no less than five of the Articles of War have been traduced by her behaviour. Specifically, she hazarded His Majesty's Ship *Turkey* by leaving her post on its mooring buoy before the ship was secured and only by chance was the ship not left drifting helplessly around the Hamoaze. In the second incident Lieutenant-Commander Hobbins came to offer sympathy to the accused for her loss of fingers and was

CHAPTER NINE: Into the Jaws

assaulted for his pains. All five charges arise from these two incidents. I intend to call witnesses to both events. It should be pointed out that the accused has a long history of behaving badly including assaulting an able seaman on her first day in the Wrens. Subsequently she contravened one of the Navy's most powerful bans by entertaining a foreign officer in her cabin."

At this point Merle rose to her feet and caught the eye of the President. "Sir, may I speak?" On getting a nod from him she said "What we have here is not evidence, it is character assassination. The fact that she misbehaved when a green and naive new entry in the first month of the war has nothing to do with the matters under discussion here and what my learned colleague is saying is simply an effort to muddy the waters. I must request that he is kept to the point."

The President looked at him. "Commander Wolfe? Do you wish to respond?"

He shook his head. "No sir. With your permission I would like to call my first witness."

Leading Seaman Jones was sworn in. "Jones, you were the upper deck buffer in charge of the mooring party when *HMS Turkey* was moored to a trot buoy on the day in consideration?"

"Yes sir."

"Did you observe the mooring party on the buoy, and if so, did you see them having difficulties?"

"Yes sir. There were two women on the buoy with Petty Officer Beacon but they were having difficulty reeving the mooring wire through the ring on the buoy and Beacon here joined in. Between them they managed to get the wire through and attach the messenger rope. I had turned to supervise heaving up the messenger when there was a scream from the buoy and I saw Petty Officer Beacon's hand jammed between the wire and the ring. We slacked back and she was able to extract her hand. Then she jumped into her boat and they went roaring away."

"You were able to pull up the wire and secure your ship?"

"Yes sir."

"But if the messenger rope had parted you would have been unable to moor up?"

"I suppose so sir, but it was a good new rope."

"Quite so. Thank you, Mr Jones."

Merle now stood up. She asked the President "Sir, may I have permission to cross-examine the witness?"

"Yes please, Miss Baker."

She turned to the seaman. "Jones, as upper deck buffer, maintenance of mooring wires would be part of your duties?"

"Yes, that is right."

"What sort of condition would you say the mooring wire you used on this occasion was in?"

He shrugged. "Well, it was just a mooring wire like any other. They have a hard life, y'know."

"It is normal maintenance for any mooring wire that it should be oiled regularly and kept supple?"

"Well yes but we had been at sea for ten days in bad weather so that sort of thing had not been possible."

"And is it not the case that if wire ropes are allowed to get rusty, they become stiff and harder to work with, as well as having strands break and become snags sticking up?"

"Yes, I suppose so but I told you we'd been at sea for ten days with no maintenance possible."

"But the state this wire was in must have taken longer than ten days to get as rusty as it was? Can you recall when last it had been oiled?"

Leading Seaman Jones looked nonplussed. "No, I can't really."

"Which means you were using a dry rusty wire to moor with. Did that really seem like a good idea?"

"Well, it was the best one we had."

"Ah, so the rest of your mooring equipment was in even worse condition?"

Leading Seaman Jones was looking distinctly unhappy with this turn of questioning. He just nodded.

Merle turned to the President. "That is all my questions for now sir, but I shall refer to this evidence during the defence case, with your permission."

The President waved a hand. "Please do. This is most interesting." He turned to Commander Wolfe. "I believe you have further witnesses to call?"

"Yes sir. I would like to call the nursing sister and nurse who were on duty on the ward that Beacon was in, when the assault on Lieutenant-Commander Hobbins took place."

With the two nurses sworn in, Mr Wolfe turned first to the senior. "Miss Ogilvie, you are an experienced nursing sister?"

"Yes indeed, I have been a sister with Queen Alexandra's Royal Naval Nursing Service for nine years, and before that in a general hospital for six years."

"So you are familiar with the Royal Navy and its ways?"

"Oh yes I have dealt with all levels of the Navy along the way, from admirals to naughty boys."

"Right. You were on duty on the afternoon of Thursday eleventh December when the incident occurred? If so, please tell us what you observed."

CHAPTER NINE: Into the Jaws

"Lieutenant-Commander Hobbins came in demanding to know which bed Miss Beacon was in. Having found her he marched up to the foot of her bed and said some fairly strong things. These seemed to incense Miss Beacon who was in a low state anyway. She got out of bed and went up to him; they exchanged a few more words and were glaring at each other then, quite abruptly, she slapped his face with her good hand. This was not a normal female slap; there was a lot of power in it and she knocked him over. I was surprised by the ferocity of it. After that he charged out of the ward saying threatening things and she got back into bed."

"That was it?"

"As far as the incident is concerned that was it. I heard no more about it for a few days then a Wren officer spoke to me on the phone. I had been led to believe I would be called by the Wrens as a defence witness but then I received a summons to this court martial as a prosecution witness and gave Commander Wolfe the evidence he asked for."

"Is this your first court martial?"

She smiled. "No sir, this is my fourth one. The others I attended as a medical witness."

"Right, thank you for testimony."

He turned to the young nurse who was looking much less self-confident.

"Miss Keller, what is your experience.?"

She spoke in a whisper. "I have been a FANY for nine months now. This is my first time at anything like this."

"What did you observe on the relevant afternoon?"

"Well really just what Miss Ogilvie has described. I went to Miss Beacon's bed when the officer came in and I could see she was getting very angry. I don't think she liked what he was saying. From there she behaved as Miss Ogilvie has described."

"Did you think Miss Beacon was behaving badly?"

"Well very forcefully but I didn't think it was my place to judge it. She is a famous heroine and not someone for the likes of me to doubt."

"Quite so. Thank you, Miss Keller."

Merle stood up. "May I have permission to cross-examine Miss Ogilvie?"

"Yes please Miss Baker."

Merle looked at the coolly confident nursing sister. "Miss Ogilvie, nine years in the QARNNS means you know how to keep your yardarm clear?"

She smiled. "You could say so."

"And did you do anything following this incident?"

"Oh yes. I was so startled by what was said that I made a point of writing it down as soon as the officer had left the ward, as close to word-for-word as my memory could bring it back."

Merle turned to the President "Can we have permission for Miss Ogilvie to read out what she wrote down?"

"I don't see why not." He turned to the Deputy Judge Advocate, now sitting quietly at the end of the row. "Any legal problem with this?"

"No, I don't think so provided it is relevant."

Commander Wolfe had been getting increasingly red-faced and annoyed through this exchange. "Sir, I must protest. Miss Ogilvie is my witness and if she has anything important to disclose, she should have done so to me."

"Well maybe. Miss Ogilvie, is there any reason why this note of yours was not shown to Commander Wolfe?"

"He never asked for it. All he was interested in was what happened and I have described that. I have learned the hard way to answer the question, no more and no less."

A gentle titter of laughter went round the court.

The President, smiling broadly, said "All right Miss Ogilvie, you may read out your note."

Sister Ogilvie smiled in return and said "This is what I wrote sir, Lieutenant-Commander Hobbins' words as best as I could recall them immediately after he had left the ward. "You really are a silly goose to be getting involved in stuff like that. Women's place is in the kitchen, tending their babies, not trying to pretend that they can do a man's job. I was told I should be sympathetic but I don't feel in the least that way, just annoyed that a stupid woman like you got yourself where you shouldn't be and paid the price. You deserve whatever you got, and now perhaps you will just quietly go back to your kitchen and stop pretending you are good for anything else. I shall lodge a complaint every time I see one of you stupid ninnies in a boat. It really shouldn't be allowed." That was it, sir. They exchanged a few more angry words then Miss Beacon slapped his face so hard it knocked him over."

There was a silence for a minute then the President asked "You are quite sure you got this right? It could be important."

"Well, I wrote it down no more than five minutes after the actual happening as I suspected it could be important. I may have an odd word different but certainly not the main part."

Merle looked at the President. "May I continue, sir?"

"Yes please Miss Baker, this is really very interesting."

"Miss Ogilvie, I only have one more question. Did Lieutenant-Commander Hobbins appear at all physically threatening?"

"No. Miss Beacon is substantially taller than him and did rather tower over him

CHAPTER NINE: Into the Jaws

while they were arguing."

"Thank you. No further questions but I would like permission to refer back to this evidence during the defence."

"Granted." The President then turned to the Deputy Judge Advocate. "Can we have this note as an exhibit?"

"It really should have been notified beforehand to be admissible as evidence but as a supporting document we can accept it."

"Right. Miss Ogilvie, may we have it please?"

So it was handed over and both nurses left the court.

The President looked at the prosecutor. "Do you have any more witnesses to call, Commander Wolfe?"

"Yes sir, I now wish to call my witness in chief, Lieutenant-Commander Hobbins. It was he who raised the complaint against Miss Beacon in the first place."

The lieutenant-commander stood up. Even in his best uniform he looked rumpled and scruffy. After swearing in, Commander Wolfe eyed him keenly. "Lieutenant-Commander Hobbins, you have been in the Navy for how long?"

"Twenty-five years sir."

"Which makes you a very experienced officer, skilled at your job?"

"Yes indeed."

"That would mean that you were upset when the mooring party left you on the day in question, before mooring was complete?"

"I was horrified. We were in narrow waters with other ships around us and severely limited room to manoeuvre. I was relying on the wire at the bow to hold the ship."

"And you felt that your ship had been put at hazard by this desertion?"

"Yes indeed sir."

Commander Wolfe turned to the court. With a dramatic sweep of his arm he said, "Surely the word of a captain left unsupported on his bridge is sufficient to establish that the mooring party had put the ship at hazard by running away?"

He turned back to Lieutenant-Commander Hobbins. "Now sir, moving on to your visit to Miss Beacon in hospital, what was your intention?"

"To offer some sympathy to her."

"But according to what we have heard that was not what you said?"

"Those are lies. I do not know why the nursing sister should perjure herself like that, but what she said had nothing to do with what I said."

Merle and Jane had jumped to their feet. "Sir, we must protest." But the President held up a peremptory arm "Miss Baker, the Lieutenant-Commander is Commander Wolfe's witness just now. Kindly sit down and be quiet. Your turn will come."

Commander Wolfe smiled and turned to his witness again. "Now sir, you said a few kind words to Miss Beacon and for that she jumped out of bed and hit you so hard you fell over?"

"That's right. I was utterly taken aback by it."

"Did you warn her that she was committing an offence under the Articles of War?"

"Well, I didn't phrase it like that but I did warn her it was an offence."

"She knew full well it was wrong?"

"Oh, she must have done."

"But that did not stop her?"

"She seemed to me to be completely out of control."

"Indeed. That is all I have to ask you just now."

Merle then stood up. "Lieutenant-Commander Hobbins, when you were mooring up you still had full use of your screws and rudder?"

"Yes."

"So you were not all that hazarded by the departure of the mooring boat because you could have manoeuvred?"

"Well yes but I did say that we were in a tight space with other ships around us."

"But you got to the buoy without any difficulty?"

"Yes of course. I am a competent ship handler with many years' experience."

"Which means that you would not really have been at hazard if you had had to try again?"

"Well I felt abandoned by those silly girls."

"But that is not the same as being hazarded. Are you saying you would not have been able to handle your ship to get out of trouble?"

Lieutenant-Commander Hobbins was getting redder of face. "Yes of course I could have handled her. You are trying to suggest I am incompetent when that is not true."

"No, I am suggesting that you were not really at hazard at all and if you are as good as you say you are, you would simply have tried again. But in fact, you were moored up perfectly well by the efforts of the buoy party and were never in hazard in the first place."

"That is arguable."

"Perhaps. I would also like to ask about what was said by you in the hospital. You have stated firmly that Sister Ogilvie lied in reading out her recollection of what was said. Why on earth would an experienced QARNNS sister of many years' experience lie on oath when there was no interest for her in telling anything but the truth? And why on earth would Beacon hit you if you had said nice things to her?

CHAPTER NINE: Into the Jaws

I hope you are aware of the dangers of committing perjury in this setting."

"Dear lady, I have no idea why she would and I think Beacon is a dangerous out of control person who needs dealing with."

"I understand you are unimpressed by Wrens doing work other than domestic chores?"

"Yes ma'am. This unfortunate business has made it clear to me that women are not safe to be let out of their God-appointed roles."

"And those are?"

"Oh, domestic work and looking after their babies."

"You would not have a Women's Royal Naval Service at all?"

"No of course not. I think it is quite wrong for women to be doing things like this. They should not be allowed to get above themselves and think that they have a right to be doing men's work."

Captain Gribben muttered "Here here."

Merle gave him a withering look and asked, "You expected trouble when you saw Wrens on your mooring buoy?"

"I knew it was bound to end in tears, and my doubts have been amply justified. You women should not be doing things like this and this court martial gives a chance to stop it now."

"You surely don't think the whole WRNS is on trial here?"

"Well yes I do rather because none of this would have happened if men had been on duty."

Merle turned to the President and quietly asked "is that the view of the whole court?"

The President smiled and said "No, young lady. We are here to try specific charges and not the whole of the Wrens. Lieutenant-Commander Hobbins' views are his own."

"In that case why is he being allowed to air them?"

"I was waiting to see if there was anything relevant to this case. Perhaps at the edges we see some explanation as to why he and Miss Beacon did not see eye-to-eye."

"But hopefully nothing that will influence our decisions here?"

"That is a matter for the court. Now it is time to adjourn for lunch so kindly conclude this discussion for now. Clear the court."

CHAPTER TEN:
The Defence

"Good afternoon ladies and gentlemen. I hope you are well fed. I am advised by the defence that Miss Ogilvie wishes to make a statement in support of her evidence to the court. As Miss Ogilvie is a prosecution witness it is necessary for them to recall her and to invite her to make it. Commander Wolfe, are you happy to do so?"

"Well sir, this is most irregular but if you insist, we will comply. So yes please, ask Miss Ogilvie to return."

With the Sister duly returned the President eyed her sharply. "Miss Ogilvie, I understand that you wish to supplement your evidence. I trust that what you have to say is relevant."

Commander Wolfe took over. "Miss Ogilvie, this morning we heard your evidence of the conversation in the hospital but that has been directly rebutted by Lieutenant-Commander Hobbins. Are you sure what you said is accurate or could you have been mistaken?"

"Sir, I am completely certain that my evidence this morning was correct.

I have been advised that this morning I was accused, under oath, of lying. I wish to register the strongest possible protest over this accusation. My whole life has been based on honesty and within my profession my word is accepted as the truth without question. To be accused now of perjury at a court martial, which is what this amounts to, is a devastating blow to me and could destroy my career. I know that what I said this morning was the truth, having witnessed it, and I refute in the strongest possible terms any suggestion that I did or said anything but the truth. I have no idea why Lieutenant-Commander Hobbins should suggest otherwise but I demand that it is recorded here that I am stating, on oath, that I did tell the truth."

Commander Wolfe looked startled by this statement but the President cut in.

"Thank you, Miss Ogilvie, your protest has been noted. You are aware that in making this protest you are in effect accusing Lieutenant-Commander Hobbins of perjury? That is a profoundly serious allegation to make against a serving naval officer."

"Yes sir, I have no wish to do so but am left with no choice to clear my own name."

The President turned to the Deputy Judge Advocate. "Tell me, can we record both versions without imputing a lie to either?"

The Deputy Judge Advocate looked pained by the thought. "I am afraid not, sir. We are required to adjudicate and decide which version we believe is the truth."

CHAPTER TEN: The Defence

"But that is impossible. Are you saying that we have to label either a respected senior sister of the QARNNS or a serving naval officer, a liar?"

"As we have been presented with a direct conflict of evidence it is our duty to decide which we think is the true one."

"But surely neither of these people would lie to a court-martial?"

The Deputy Judge Advocate allowed himself a weary smile. "I am afraid you are being rather generous with your view of human nature, sir. When a conflict like this arises, it is usually because one party has an interest in steering the view of the court in a particular direction to his benefit. When a party has no personal interest in the outcome, they tend to be more honest because they have no reason not to be."

"But presumably the shorthand writer has recorded the verbatim record?"

"Yes indeed sir but that does not take away from the requirement to decide which version you think is the truth."

"But we will have to hear the defence case before we can make any judgement?"

"That is so but then you have to decide."

"I see. Can I sound the views of the Board on this?"

"Yes sir, you are required to do so and to take a vote on which evidence you prefer."

"I suppose we will have to bear it in mind, then. Thank you, Miss Ogilvie and I hope your career is not affected."

At this point Commander Wolfe intervened. "There is one other witness to this altercation, sir. That is Nurse Keller. Can you recall her to repeat her testimony?"

"Yes, I suppose so. Please recall Miss Keller."

Nurse Keller looked very young and terrified as she returned to the court. Commander Wolfe took charge. "Now, Miss Keller. You said that you were by Miss Beacon's bedside when the disagreement with Lieutenant-Commander Hobbins took place?"

"Yes sir."

"Would you please repeat what you heard him say?"

"He said something to the effect that Miss Beacon wasn't capable of doing the job and deserved everything she got, or words to that effect."

"That's all?"

"Well there was more, something about silly ninnies in boats, but I don't recall it more exactly."

Commander Wolfe stood very close to Nurse Keller and towered over her, fiercely looking down at her. "Now, Keller, is it possible that your recollection is not correct? Might Lieutenant-Commander Hobbins have actually said something else?"

The nurse looked puzzled and even more scared. "I don't think so sir."

He boomed at her, his face inches from hers. "I put it to you Miss Keller that perhaps you heard much kinder words being said but got them muddled up in your mind."

She shook her head, trembling and on the verge of tears. She whispered, "Well I suppose that is possible but I don't think so."

"Ah, you think it is possible? There is doubt in your mind and perhaps what you thought you heard was not what was actually said?"

Now she did burst into tears, shaking her head and cowering back from Commander Wolfe. "I just don't know sir. I told you what I thought I heard and so did Sister Ogilvie. Please, I am totally confused now."

Commander Wolfe turned to the court. "So, we have established that what was alleged to have been said was perhaps not actually what was said and we have Lieutenant-Commander Hobbins' testimony to that effect."

"Thank you, Mis Keller. That will be all." The shaking weeping girl was escorted out of the court and was heard crying noisily outside.

After a short silence in the court, the President took charge again. "Right, Commander Wolfe, have you anything else to present to the court?"

"No sir, although I will be wanting to cross-examine the defence witnesses."

"Yes of course. We will proceed to the defence case. Miss Baker, is the defence case ready for presentation?"

"Yes sir."

"Kindly proceed."

Merle turned to the court. "Ladies and gentlemen of the court, the prosecution was correct in saying that, at heart, this is a simple case. The actual happenings, as described in the Circumstantial Letter, of the two broadly related incidents, which in turn lead to the five charges laid against my friend, were not in dispute to begin with. That was until we heard alternative versions of the hospital incident which have left confusion which I will try to deal with. Unlike the prosecution's broad-brush approach, throwing mud about wherever it may stick, I intend to look at each individual charge in isolation, taking the charges relating to each incident in groups. I will be working with my witness in chief, the accused, Petty Officer Wren Jane Beacon and with your permission, sir, I would like to be involving her while addressing the court in general." Commander Wolfe interjected. "I must also have a chance to cross-examine Miss Beacon."

"Oh yes Commander Wolfe, you will get your turn. Miss Baker, this is a slightly unusual approach but I see no reason why you should not follow it."

"Thank you, sir. I will call Miss Beacon now."

After Jane was sworn in, Merle turned to the court again. "Let us consider the

CHAPTER TEN: The Defence

incident which gave rise to everything else, the difficulty Miss Beacon and her Wrens had in reeving the stiff and rusty mooring wire through the buoy's mooring ring. This was part of a wider picture: *HMS Turkey* was a slack and slovenly ship, dirty, unkempt and poorly run. We have heard from Leading Seaman Jones that the poor condition rusty mooring wire being used was nevertheless the best one they had. The crew were lounging about on the forecastle dressed in any old bits of clothing and their general attitude was slack and careless."

Lieutenant-Commander Hobbins had gone purple of face during this description and prodded Commander Wolfe in the ribs. The prosecutor rose to his feet and bellowed "Objection! This is not relevant to the case." He towered over Merle, slim, blonde, five feet five inches tall, and roared "Withdraw this. It is utterly irrelevant." Unlike the wretched Nurse Keller, Merle was not about to crumble under his fierce gaze and dominating presence. She stood very straight and spoke quietly but clearly. "Oh, but I think it is, Commander Wolfe. Matters like this are of great importance to seamen and always tell a lot about a ship's commanding officer."

At this point the Deputy Judge Advocate intervened. "Miss Baker, you are getting too far away from the point you set out to make. Kindly restrict your presentation to matters within the legal bounds of what you are saying. And Commander Wolfe, please sit down and allow Miss Baker to present her case."

Merle smiled "Thank you, sir, and the correction is noted. Let me return to the position on the buoy. We have clearly established that the two Wrens on the buoy, newly confirmed as boat crew Wrens, were unable to bend the mooring wire through the mooring ring. Miss Beacon, their trainer during the boat crew Wrens' course which had just completed, saw that they were in difficulties and joined them in pulling on the wire. She is well practised at 'buoy jumping' as the Navy calls it and came to help. They were all wearing heavy leather work gloves as is normal for this sort of work. When Miss Beacon's glove got caught in one of the many snags sticking out of the wire, the run of events which has led to this court martial was set in train. When her hand was crushed between wire and ring and it was obvious that she was seriously injured, her instinct was to seek medical help. By then they had managed to reeve the wire through and attach the messenger rope which would be used to hoist the wire up and back onto the ship's foc'sle, thereby allowing the ship to be fully moored up. Which means they were not leaving the ship in a helpless position. Miss Beacon, can you confirm what the position was then?"

"I was in intense pain from the accident and leapt back onto my launch. I did check and saw that the ship would be able to heave up the wire to complete the mooring so we could clear off without leaving it in difficulties. I recalled my two Wrens from the buoy and we set off to seek medical help for me."

"Thank you Beacon. The two charges relating to this incident both say, in effect, that Miss Beacon deserted her position thereby putting the ship at hazard. Article Nine says that every person who deserts their post or negligently performs their duty shall be dismissed the service. No mention of hazarding the ship, which is covered by Article Twenty-nine. This says in its circumlocutory way that any person who hazards any of His Majesty's ships whether designedly or by default shall be dismissed the service. Although the charges following from the two Articles are presented as separate cases, it is necessary to conflate the provisions of both of these Articles to make a case at all and while this is possible it is stretching the intentions of the Articles considerably to do so. We have heard that in fact the ship could and did moor up perfectly safely so it was never really at hazard and Miss Beacon did make sure of this before she departed. With blood running from her glove and in intense pain, seeking help was a perfectly natural thing to do. Summing this up, we contend that there is no case to answer under these Articles as the ship was never at hazard in the first place and Miss Beacon's actions were neither negligent nor intentional. If I may I would like to conclude this part of our defence by calling together our two witnesses. These are the two Wrens who were on the buoy with Miss Beacon and may be able to further our understanding of the difficulties they met in handling the wire."

The Deputy Judge Advocate responded. "Beacon will have to sit down, then. We cannot have different witnesses testifying at the same time."

Jane sat down and the two Wrens were sworn in.

Merle sipped a drink of water then began again. "Pocock, you were one of the Wrens trying to secure *HMS Turkey* to the mooring buoy?"

"Yes Ma'am."

"Why was it proving so difficult?"

"The wire rope we were handling was as stiff as a metal rod and wouldn't bend. It was full of snags so we had to be very careful where we took hold of it which also made the job more difficult."

"Even two of you were not able to do anything with it?"

"No Ma'am we were pulling together and not getting anywhere."

Merle turned. "Now, Walters, have you anything to add to what Pocock has just said?"

"Not really ma'am. With the lack of anything secure to stand on, it was difficult to get a decent purchase to pull on the wire."

"But Miss Beacon joining in helped?"

"Oh yes indeed. She is amazingly strong and was able to bend the wire around the ring. From there we were getting on well until her hand got trapped and squashed."

CHAPTER TEN: The Defence

"Did it occur to you that you should have stayed until the mooring operation was complete before leaving to get help for Miss Beacon?"

"Oh no ma'am. Petty Officer Beacon said let's go and she is not someone you argue with."

Merle had a little smile at that. "Is there anything else either of you wish to say?"

"Not really, just that we are desperately sad to see what has happened to Miss Beacon who we all look up to awfully much."

"Thank you both." Merle turned to the President. "That concludes my interrogation of these witnesses."

The President looked at Commander Wolfe. "Do you wish to ask any questions?"

"I certainly do, sir. Do you two silly girls really think you can do jobs like mooring ships up?"

They both looked mystified. "Well yes sir, apart from the unfortunate accident we did this one successfully."

"But put the ship at hazard in the process. That is hardly a recommendation, is it?"

"But we didn't, sir. She was perfectly well made fast and if the wire hadn't been such a mess, we would have managed on our own without any bother."

Commander Wolfe was looking irritated. He adopted his leaning over them pose, glared hard and said "I put it to you that it was only good luck that you did not put the ship at risk and really the job was beyond you. Girls should not be doing jobs like this and the sooner you stop pretending you can do them, the better."

Wren Pocock, a big strapping girl with a well weathered face, glared at him. In her soft Devon accent she said "I have been in boats all me life sir and done much more difficult things than that. All the girls on our course are perfectly well able to do boat jobs. I won't have it that we are not up to the job."

"But you could never moor a battleship, could you?"

"It takes fifty sailors to moor a battleship sir, and I am sure fifty Wrens could too."

A small rumble of laughter went round the court at this vision and Commander Wolfe shrugged. "No further questions."

The President and court had been silent while these exchanges had gone on, but now he spoke to Merle. "Does that complete your defence on the first incident?"

"Yes sir, and we are ready to go on to the second element."

"It is now 1640 and I think rather than have to break off in mid-presentation, we will stop the proceedings here. Let us adjourn for the day now."

The Deputy Judge Advocate and the court officer took charge and cleared the court. Soon there was the shrill twitter of the bosun's pipes as the august members of the Board took their leave.

Jane's defence team squashed into her tiny cabin to debate the day. Merle was hoarse from so much talking but felt that overall things had not gone too badly. "This unspoken agenda to get rid of the Wrens is rumbling away in the background but I don't really feel they have made much of a case, have they? Pocock was excellent."

Jane looked unimpressed. "That's all very well but what about me?"

"Well Jane, tomorrow is the difficult bit. We know we can't deny that you hit a superior officer and have to concentrate on the provocation angle. Hobbins telling flat lies may make that more difficult and no doubt that is part of why he did it. There may be a balance of benefits to be struck."

"Let's hope they are feeling kind, then. Even now I don't want to be chucked out."

"All things being equal that is unlikely." The conference was broken up by a steward arriving with Jane's supper. Tonight it was that old naval favourite, a cheesy hammy eggy which she tucked into with relish. She changed out of her best uniform and medals and lay back on her cramped little bunk, thinking over the day's proceedings. She woke up again late in the evening, crawled under the covers and slept soundly between stirrings to ease her bent knees.

The defence team had reassembled by 0830 the next morning but by now they had everything as well prepared as it could be, so when the Provost Marshal arrived and raised his cutlass to lead Jane in, they were ready.

The President eyed Merle "Are you ready with your defence?"

"Yes sir. Like yesterday I would like to have Miss Beacon with me as I go through our case."

"We agreed yesterday so that stands."

"Thank you, sir. Today we are considering the second incident which occurred at Stonehouse Hospital when Lieutenant-Commander Hobbins visited Miss Beacon when she was recovering from the operation to repair her damaged hand. This has given rise to two charges, one under Article Sixteen that she struck her superior officer, and one under Article Seventeen that she used threatening or insulting language, or behaved with contempt, to her superior officer. This second charge I think we can dismiss directly. Tell me, Beacon, did you use insulting language or behave with contempt?"

"No ma'am I did not. I was fizzing with rage at what he had said but there was nothing insulting or premeditated about it. I had only met him for the first time when he appeared at the bottom of my bed a couple of minutes earlier."

"Thank you. Although it is part of an overall picture, I am sure we can dismiss that charge as a separate entity. Now we move on to what is the central heart of this court martial, the charge under Article Sixteen that Miss Beacon struck her superior officer. It is a well-established fact that she did so and we have not sought to deny it. Therefore, she stands guilty of the charge under Article Sixteen. But provocation is

CHAPTER TEN: The Defence

allowable in mitigation under the Naval Disciple Act and it is our contention that Miss Beacon had been subject to extreme provocation from Lieutenant-Commander Hobbins by what he had just said to her. Despite the injuries she had received caused by his poorly run ship she had no malice and no interest in having any dispute with him and most certainly would not have struck him had he not provoked her into doing so. Miss Beacon, what were you doing before you were provoked?"

"Oh, I was just lying in bed feeling fairly low. I was totally surprised when Lieutenant-Commander Hobbins charged into the ward and started abusing me."

"Ah yes, his abuse of you." Merle turned to face the court. "Members of the Board, you are aware that there are two versions of what he said, shouting at Miss Beacon from the bottom of her bed. There is Sister Ogilvie's written record, and Lieutenant-Commander Hobbins' alternative version which denies Miss Ogilvie's account. Really, we must approach this from common sense. The question has already been asked, why on earth would a senior sister, a lady with a respected career and high standing, give anything other than the truth of what transpired and she was witness to? She has no interest in the outcome and no vested interest in Miss Beacon's future; she was simply doing her duty by recording what transpired. There can be no reason to doubt her testimony, recorded virtually verbatim and carefully presented. Then there is the deeply doubtful alternative version of what he said, offered by Lieutenant-Commander Hobbins. Miss Beacon, if he had said what he claims to have said, would you have climbed out of bed, confronted him and slapped his face?"

"No of course not. I would have been pleased to see him. I am not an out-of-control person looking for the next officer to assault, as the prosecutor has implied. I have not risen to petty officer in the Wrens without knowing how to behave correctly in naval terms."

Merle resumed. "One other small aspect of my learned colleague's presentation merits mention. In his demolition of Nurse Keller, he used her phrase "yes I suppose so" to support his contention that she had mis-heard Lieutenant-Commander Hobbins' rant. It will not have escaped your notice that he avoided using the second half of Miss Keller's sentence, "But I don't think so." This selective use of her comment completely changed the sense of what she said and I contend that his use of it should be deleted from the record."

"Very interesting Miss Baker and duly noted but we will not be removing it from the record. Your corrective will go alongside it."

"Thank you, sir. Ladies and gentlemen of the Board, there is another aspect of this matter to consider, and that is whether a single slap by a woman, in response to an insulting verbal onslaught, is such a terrible matter? If you brought a claim like this to a civilian court, I am sure it would be laughed at. It is only the fact that it was an altercation between a rating and an officer which gives the matter any significance. I know that is important to the Navy but as we adjust to the new reality under wartime conditions, the Navy and the Wrens must work out a sensible balance between naval good order and discipline, and some degree of chivalry and acknowledgement that we are women. This was acknowledged when the Admiralty refused to bring the Wrens under the Naval Discipline Act so this court-martial is exceptional but demonstrates that weCed never beyond the reach of the Act's provisions. This means that a degree of common sense is going to be needed in keeping relationships healthy. Women are perfectly capable of doing a lot of things which are new to them and to the Navy, and the rubbing of this fact up against older more prejudiced views of women's place in the world is bound to produce moments like we have here. We have heard strongly expressed traditional views on this already and that is at the heart of this case. Miss Beacon is one of the most successful and dynamic Wrens we have and is bound to stick out a bit in consequence. Therefore, in reaching any conclusions about how culpable she is for slapping Lieutenant-Commander Hobbins, this wider dimension should also be in your minds."

At this point Captain Gribben interposed. "This rather implies that you think the Wrens should continue to expand and to work in all sorts of naval occupations. Do you not think this rather detracts from their being female?"

"No sir, not for one minute. It is Wrens' policy that we should remain feminine, even when doing jobs traditionally seen as male. We are perfectly capable of combining the two and being effective in both."

Captain Gribben allowed himself a snorting laugh. "So you think that being a girl allows you to hit your superior officers?"

"That is not what I said sir and no, of course not, Wrens should not be allowed to get away with things. But is a female slap the equivalent of a male punch? When it threatens good order and discipline the answer is yes. When it is contained and simply a defensive act perhaps a gentler level of punishment may be appropriate. Within or outside the Naval Discipline Act, we need to be clear about these things and perhaps today is a first step along that road. I certainly hope so."

The President had sat silently through this speech. "Miss Baker, your eloquence is admirable but perhaps we should get back to the matter in hand. Have you anything else to say in Miss Beacon's defence?"

"There is only the matter of the final charge, brought under Article forty-four of the Articles of War. This is so vague as to be meaningless. We had expected something to emerge in the charges but nothing has and we say that it should be struck out forthwith."

CHAPTER TEN: The Defence

"Thank you, Miss Baker. I will have it looked at."

"In which case Miss Beacon's testimony is finished."

The President turned to the prosecutor. "Commander Wolfe, do you want to cross-examine Miss Beacon?"

"Yes sir I do but it has to be said that Miss Baker's speech has dealt with no few of my points. Now Miss Beacon, we have heard very little from you about what Lieutenant-Commander Hobbins said to you as you lay in your hospital bed. We know what his version of that was. Why do you think that something else was said?"

"Because I heard something else. Miss Ogilvie's note was an accurate record of what I heard too and was why I got so angry about it."

"Ah yes, you got angry. I put it to you that you really are an intemperate character, easily going out of control and becoming a danger to those around you. Just the sort of person who would end up on a charge of assault. Yet your friend makes great play of the Wrens being feminine. The two do not really reconcile with each other and if the Wrens are more typically like you than the fragrant females Miss Baker suggests, we have to ask if the Navy wants any of you at all."

"That is a neat way of trying to get rid of us but you would have to look at our record and ask how many times something like this has occurred. The answer is not at all until now. We are a well-behaved and reliable support to the Navy and trying to generalise out of my case would be deeply mistaken."

"I see. No further questions."

The President took charge. He turned to the prosecutor, "It is common for you to sum up your case at this stage. Do you feel a need to?"

"I'm not sure that I do, actually. The case has been amply recorded by our shorthand note taker and is really quite simple."

The president turned to Merle. "Miss Baker, have you completed your presentation?"

"Not quite sir. We wish to call a witness to character before we complete."

"Very well, let us hear him."

"It is Superintendent Mrs Welby, sir, Wren officer in charge at Plymouth and Beacon's early commander. Informally she is about the third most senior lady in the Wrens."

Mrs Welby was sworn in and stood to speak. "I could go on at some length about Petty Officer Wren Beacon but will try to be brief. She joined the Wrens at Plymouth, under my command, on 3rd October 1939. From the start she was exceptional, being a brilliant success as a first experimental boat crew Wren and despite various disciplinary issues along the way has been an outstanding success ever since. Like a lot of exceptional people she has an enormously strong character

101

which means that sometimes she does things her way which the Navy does not like, the most outstanding being her expedition to Dunkirk in a naval cutter to rescue many thousands of soldiers, showing incredible bravery in the process. It is from that which her medal collection originates, but also the tribunal set up to try her for disobeying orders not to go. It did not take any action against her. Since then she has progressed in naval boats and in the first half of last year was in command of a launch on the Thames with the very first all-Wren crew. Vice-Admiral Boyd VC, in command on the Thames, wrote a glowing testimonial to her abilities after her boat was used as his Admiral's barge. Recently, she was on the training staff for the first Wrens' boat crew training course and contributed significantly to its success. It was directly after that, that the unfortunate incident on the buoy took place which has led to today. It is our strong wish within the WRNS that we retain her services, believing that her value greatly outweighs her more wayward characteristics which we have under control. We commend her to the court as someone well worth keeping. Thank you, sir."

The President gave her a long look. "And thank you, Mrs Welby, for that glowing testimonial. Have you anything else to say?"

"No sir."

"In which case, thank you again." Mrs Welby smiled sweetly at her two colleagues sitting on the Board and left.

The President turned to Merle. "Miss Baker, have you anything else to contribute?"

"No sir, that concludes the defence."

"That being so, it is lunch time and time to adjourn. After lunch, the court will meet as jury on its own and we will recall all the other members when we reach our verdicts."

Jane found she had little appetite for the naval dinner she was offered, the tension tying knots in her stomach. Not for the first time, she found this waiting was worse than being dive-bombed by Stukas.

CHAPTER ELEVEN:
The Processing Continues

The waiting group were finally called back into the court at 1500 after it had deliberated for two hours. The Deputy Judge Advocate rose to speak. "Wren Beacon, you have been tried on five separate charges. The court has considered each of them and found as follows: On the first charge under Article nine of the Articles of War, leaving your place of duty, it finds you guilty. On the second charge, under Article 16, striking your superior officer, you have admitted your guilt. On the third charge under Article 17, insulting or showing contempt for your superior officer, it finds you not guilty. On the fourth charge under Article 29, hazarding *HMS Turkey*, it finds you not guilty. The fifth charge under Article 44 has been dismissed as having no substance. Your service record will now be tabled and added to the minutes of this court. Do you wish to say anything in mitigation before sentence is pronounced?"

Jane pulled herself up to her full five feet ten inches, clinking her medals in the process, and said, "Yes sir, I do. On the first charge, did the court really expect me to stay to watch a wire being hauled up and secured when I could see that I had been seriously injured? This was the result." And she held up her fingerless left hand. "Evidently you felt that I should have stayed or you would not have reached the decision you did, but it is a singularly harsh view of duty. On the second charge, which I have admitted to, I must plead extreme provocation to explain my behaviour. We Wrens are accustomed to sexist attitudes and having to put up with abuse about our presence. But by any standards what Lieutenant-Commander Hobbins said was primitive chauvinism. I know he has offered a different view of what was said but it has no validity and the implication that I am an out-of-control rating looking for the next officer to assault is nonsense. I was provoked into my actions, not helped by one circumstance which had nothing to do with the actual event but certainly influenced how I was feeling. Just a few hours earlier on the day Lieutenant-Commander Hobbins called, I had received a telegram telling me that my husband was missing in action, presumed killed. As a result, I was at an extremely low and sensitive ebb anyway."

Captain Gribben cut in at this point, saying sneeringly, "Who was this unfortunate husband? Some nice artificer no doubt."

"No sir, my husband was Lieutenant-Commander Lord David Daubeny-Fowkes, in command of *HMS Bowman*."

The President had jumped and gone white at this, staring hard at Jane. "You are David's wife?" He whispered, as much to himself as to Jane.

"Well I was sir. I am his widow now."

"Oh dear. So you are in fact Lady Daubeny-Fowkes?"

"Yes sir."

"That being so, where does the Jane Beacon come from?"

"That is my maiden name sir, and I made a conscious decision to keep it after I married. I am fairly well known in the Wrens as Jane Beacon and it has to be said that Petty Officer Wren Lady David Daubeny-Fowkes is a bit of a mouthful for everyday use."

The President looked close to tears himself. "Why was I not invited to your wedding? He was my protégé for a time."

"That list was not mine, sir, so I'm afraid I cannot help you there."

Commander Wolfe had risen to his feet. "Sir, if I may, I have to protest at this which has nothing to do with this court's deliberations."

The Deputy Judge Advocate said "He is right, sir. Even as mitigation her marital status is only relevant to this court inasmuch as it explains her sensitive state when Lieutenant-Commander Hobbins came to see her."

The President sighed. "Yes, I suppose so." He looked hard at Jane. "Have you anything else to say?"

"Just one other thing, sir. I have been tried on five counts under the Articles of War which are intended to keep good order in time of war. Yet the events leading to the charges laid against me were not in the least warlike and have the consequence of taking what was a relatively minor accident and turning it into a series of potentially criminal and life-changing charges. I do feel that the Navy and the Wrens must come to some accommodation which takes the serious criminality out of humdrum little incidents. The Articles of War are a mighty instrument to be used like this and I want to put on record a suggestion that something less draconian is used for unfortunate incidents like the one which is being tried here."

"Thank you, Lady Daubeny-Fowkes. Have you anything else to say?"

"No sir."

"In which case clear the court while we consider sentence."

Outside, Merle gently grinned at Jane. "Well done, Jane. That shook them up a bit."

"You were pretty eloquent yourself."

"Yes well, we had worked out something like that beforehand, knowing that they were going to be coming after the Wrens in general. I think we have dealt with that one pretty finally, don't you?"

CHAPTER ELEVEN: The Processing Continues

"Well yes, but what about me? It didn't help me so much."

"Sorry Jane, we had to do it to secure the Wrens in the Navy."

"You mean I came second to some wider concern?"

"I am afraid so."

"Well thanks. Let's hope the court thinks more about me."

Merle sighed. "I really am sorry Jane, but I did warn you that greater forces were in play. There are still those in the Admiralty who would like to be shot of the lot of us and some of those saw this minor incident as an opportunity to make a much greater case that we were no use to the Navy. Well I think we've nailed that one down."

They waited about at a loose end for another hour before finally being called back in. Once again, the Deputy Judge Advocate took the lead, addressing Jane directly. "Wren Beacon, the court had to consider and make public which version of Lieutenant-Commander Hobbins' talk to you it preferred. After a great deal of deliberation it has decided on balance to favour Sister Ogilvie's account as being more probable and decided – just - to accept that with a dissenting minority opinion recorded. This means that your plea in mitigation is fully accepted and has born strongly on our sentencing. Striking a superior officer is a serious matter which goes to the heart of naval discipline. This cannot be justified under any circumstances and if we had preferred Lieutenant-Commander Hobbins' version of events your punishment would have been much more severe and included dismissal from His Majesty's service. However, we have concluded after much discussion and debate that you were severely provoked and therefore, we have decided to award more lenient punishment. Accordingly the court sentences you as follows: First, that you be reduced to the rate of ordinary Wren. And second, that you serve thirty days' detention and receive no pay during that period. The court has decided not to exercise its right to deal with your decorations which remain. Do you understand?"

Jane was too dumbstruck to do anything more than whisper "Yes sir." So that was it: The Wrens had been preserved at the price of her being cast into the wilderness. She now had a criminal record to add to the other injustices. Somehow at this moment her urge to stay in the Wrens was wavering seriously.

The President spoke. "This Court-Martial is now dissolved. Provost Marshal, ensure that the prisoner is kept securely. Ladies and gentlemen of the Board, thank you for your efforts. Clear the Court and haul down the Union Flag." Soon the shrill twitter of the bosun's pipes pierced through the ship once more as the Board members took their leave.

Half an hour later Merle negotiated her way past the sentry at her cabin door and joined Jane. "Don't worry, we will look after you. Thirty days' detention in your case will mean being cooped up in a Wrennery somewhere and we'll organise something to keep you occupied. As for your rating, we'll fix that again soon enough. Your career in the Wrens will not be blighted by this and already we are thinking of some interesting projects for you."

"I don't suppose I will be on the boat crew training team though, will I?"

"Eh no, probably not. Or not for a while, anyway. We'll leave that one open. I must get back up to London this evening to deal with the fallout from this business but you will stay here for a day or two more while they sort out the paperwork then your nice friendly Provost Marshal will organise your move to a Wrennery and some sort of security arrangement while you are there. I'll pop down to see you again when your time is up. And Jane, don't take it too hard. You have no idea how much your taking this on the chin for the greater good is appreciated at the top level in the Wrens."

"Well thanks Merle. I'll have another medal."

Even another cheesy hammy eggy did little to brighten her mood.

Another poor night's sleep, brooding over the unfairness of how she had been treated, left her less than enthusiastic about another bowl of watery burgoo in the morning. No-one came near her and by mid-morning restlessness got the better of her. She looked out of her little cabin and found the marine guard still standing patiently outside her door. "Do you suppose I could be let out for some exercise? It's pretty small in here."

"I can't leave here but a regulator comes by once an hour and I'll ask him."

She was slowly eating a plate of indeterminate meat stew when the regulator looked in. "I gather you want some exercise. I've told your sentry you can go on the upper deck to walk but he must keep an eye on you the whole time. Do not try to run away."

Jane gave that a lopsided smile. "Don't worry, I shan't run away. I've too much at stake to blow it like that."

The jossman nodded. "All right then, you can walk on the upper deck for two hours, morning and evening."

"Well thank goodness for that. Being cooped up here is not much fun."

Stew and duff eaten, she collected her sentry and while he sheltered in the fore end of the quarterdeck, Jane resolutely marched up and down for her allotted two hours. Despite trying to be detached and cynical about the whole business there was a sense of being somewhere special about the upper deck. The great mass of masts and rigging above her made her feel very small but uplifted at the same time by the powerful reminder of the naval tradition she was in the midst of. She paused by Nelson's plate marking where he had fallen and couldn't help looking up, seeing in her mind's eye the rigging of other great ships towering alongside full of sharpshooters trying to catch her. A cold shudder went through her at the thought, a reminder of tougher times and how slender survival was amid war. Diving Stukas seemed the closest modern sort of thing, raining death from above on the toiling crew below. Somehow this put her travails in a perspective; knuckles rapped and being cooped up in a Wrennery for thirty days seeming trifling by comparison. Then it was back to pacing up and down, bowsprit to quarterdeck. The Navy might not want her, yet at the same time it was wrapping itself round her ever more deeply. This sense lingered with her through the evening, leaving her wondering about which great Nelsonian officers had occupied her cabin and what it must have been like at Trafalgar. In its present peaceful state, it was difficult to imagine the thunder and crash of battle as this little cabin must have experienced it.

Next day was the same, walking on the upper deck when not confined to her cabin, with no-one coming near her. By day three she was beginning to wonder if they were just going to leave her where she was for thirty days when her Provost Marshal arrived. "Right, Beacon, be ready to move tomorrow morning. My people will come to escort you to your new abode. Do you have your work gear with you?"

"I am afraid not. I only have my tiddly uniform with me as I was expecting to be moved on more quickly than this."

"Right, I'll get it sent to you. You really are being a pioneer." And with that enigmatic comment he left her to her solitude again. That night the unfairness of her position crowded in on her ever more strongly with a deep resentment at how that slack inadequate ship's captain had led to her being the victim. Fingers gone, a criminal record acquired, her usefulness to the war effort casually dumped, it was all just too much. She spent the evening picking the crossed anchors off the sleeve of her uniform jackets.

It was late the next morning when three armed masters-at-arms arrived and threw her cabin door open. "Are you Wren Beacon?"

Getting a nod from her the senior one said "Right, get your gear and come with us." She was marched off the ship with one jossman behind her and the other two closely alongside, guns at the ready. "This is a bit much isn't it? I'm not violent, y'know."

"All prisoners are moved this way. Just be thankful we didn't handcuff you as well." Jane gave them a very doubting look. They marched her to a large grim-looking three-story building and left wheeled into its entrance block. "Right, here we are." The senior regulator shook hands with an older marine sergeant at a reception desk. "Right Killer, here's your new miscreant. Bit different this one."

Jane was looking around in alarm. "I am supposed to be going to a wrennery now. Where on earth is this?"

"This, dearie, is the Detention Quarters and we have the dubious privilege of holding you for the next thirty days."

"But that can't be right. The DQs are for men only and in any case, I was told quite clearly I would serve my thirty days in a wrennery. I am not staying here."

"Oh yes you are. Your papers were delivered here yesterday by a four-ring captain in person and we don't argue with orders like that."

"This is ridiculous. Can I have a phone, please? There's been a huge mistake here and I need to speak to my office right away."

"I am afraid not. Once you come in through that door and your paperwork is correct you are cut off from contact with the outside world. From this moment you do not speak to anyone except your warders. You have no idea how much trouble has been caused by having you landed on us. We have brought in two Wren petty officers to look after you and adapted one of our holding cells here in the reception area for you. But it's too late for you to be contacting the outside world."

Jane was looking around her, utterly stunned by this development. "I just don't believe this. There must be a mistake somewhere."

"No, no mistake. The captain who came in yesterday was quite explicit that this was where you were to come, and the committal papers say so quite clearly. So here you are for the next thirty days."

The Jossmen who had brought her nodded to the sergeant, now joined by two other mature chief petty officers, and left, a solid front door swinging closed behind them. Jane felt utterly trapped. "I just don't believe this" she muttered for the umpteenth time. "It has to be a mistake."

"No mistake dearie. Everything done correctly. Now come and see your cell."

Bewildered, she trailed round a corner into a short corridor with three solid doors off it. With a flourish the sergeant flung open the end one. "Here you are. We've tried to make it a little comfier for you by slinging a hammock and putting in two blankets. You're lucky – a sailor would have had to sleep on the wooden bench there under just one blanket."

She was then led back to the reception area where two mature Wren petty officers were now waiting. Jane looked at them and wailed "Oh no." One of them was Chief Petty Officer Jenkins who had administered her caning back on pro course. This lady smiled, a shark-like grimace with no friendliness in it. "Hello Beacon, we've got you again."

A sudden wave of desperation swept over Jane. Like a cornered animal she wildly looked round for any way out but there was none. This was madness, some weird parallel world with no connection to reality. Only this was reality, as Chief Jenkins took her firmly by the arm and led her back to her cell. "We are under orders to treat you like one of the men as far as possible, so your routine will be like this. That shiny bucket is your heads. You slop it out each morning and must keep it clean and shiny. Use grit shaved off that brick mixed with the pusser's hard cake soap next to it. It will be inspected daily so don't neglect it. You get into the ablutions block once a week to wash yourself and your clothes. You will go on Saturday to avoid the men who use it on Sunday. The DQs is keen on fitness so you will get the same regime as the men. You will be given the gym from 0630 each morning and a PTI will give you a good workout. Then you will have the obstacle course to yourself for an hour at lunchtime when the men are in their cells. You go round that at the double. If you give us any trouble at all we will simply extend the length of your stay here. You must not speak to anyone except Chief Frone or me unless they speak to you first. Is all that clear?"

Utterly bemused, Jane could only nod.

"Right, come and get your kit." She picked up her suitcase and kitbag from reception and changed. Somehow an elegant doeskin best uniform seemed totally out of place here; there was nowhere to hang it up so she folded it carefully into the top of her suitcase and pulled on a pair of trousers. Chief Jenkins appeared in the doorway again. "Chief Frone or me will be around and with you all the time and you will do exactly as we tell you. Punishment is quick and severe here so don't step out of line."

Jane looked at her in horror. "You're not going to cane me again, are you?"

"No, Beacon, we are not allowed to do that now, more's the pity. A good thrashing would do criminals like you a whole lot of good to my mind. But we have other ways of punishing you if need be." And with that Chief Wren Jenkins marched off. Not long after one of the chiefs appeared with a hunk of bread and some cheese along with a billycan of tea. "Here's your supper. Next meal is burgoo at 0800. Sleep tight."

The door thudded shut with a terrible finality, the rasp of key in the lock the final touch in her humiliation. In despair, she sank down on the wooden bench and cried wailing tears of frustration and anger at her helplessness.

CHAPTER TWELVE:
Correction

Her first night sleeping in a hammock was a new experience for Jane. Having adjusted to the shape of it and made sure she was not going to fall out, she found it relaxing and despite a seething rage running through her she slept well. Chief Jones arriving again was less welcome. The cell door was flung open and a bellow of "Rise and shine, come on there, look lively," jerked Jane into consciousness. "All you'll need are trousers and a white top; get dressed smartish." Jane was led to the gym which proved to be large and airy. A typical naval PTI – physical training instructor – crossed clubs prominent on his sleeve, took charge. "All right, warm up by doubling round twenty times then you'll meet the equipment." For an hour Jane was driven round mats, weights, the vaulting horse and climbing ropes. It gave her whole body a thorough workout which left her feeling better. The last few weeks had been all about stress with little physical release and letting it all out was doing her good. The PTI was quite impressed "You are in good shape, aren't you?"

Jane curled a lip at him. "You could say so."

He looked at her again. "Been in the wars too. Was that all action?"

"I bet I've seen more action than you have, sunshine. Shrapnel does a lot of damage although I've been lucky and avoided the bullets so far. Do you know what a bullet sounds like when it passes so close to your head that you can hear it?"

"Can't say I do; I've never been that close to one."

"Well I have and for the briefest of moments you get a sucking sound. Not nice but better than stopping it with your head."

"I was warned you were a bit different; now I see what they mean."

The return of Chief Jones stopped this chat and Jane was led back to her cell. "Now slop out your bucket. I'll show you the heads first time then you'll do it yourself right after your gym session each day." Jane dutifully did as she was told, feeling that this had a familiar ring to it. What was that? She puzzled for a moment or two then it came back. Of course, this was a bit like life on a narrow boat and she could put the lessons from that to good use to survive here. Back in her cell, a bowl of porridge was passed in to her with another pannikin of tea. "Do we get sugar or milk with this?"

"No, porridge is porridge here and you eat it as it comes."

Jane shrugged and ate it. At least it was more solid than the watery gruel on board *Victory*. Her bowl collected, the cell door was swung shut again but not, she noticed, locked. Left on her own she stretched out on the hammock and tried to sort out what on earth she was going to do. Thirty days here seemed too much to contemplate but perhaps she might have to? That was a grim thought. She was left alone until midday when Chief Jones arrived again accompanied by a small hard-faced Chief Wren. "Beacon, this is Chief Frone. You will obey her as you do me if you want to get out of this place in one piece and on time. Now come with us, it's your turn on the obstacle course."

Led out into a large yard, Jane saw a circular course of ramps and walls and hurdles. "You will go round this at the double for the next hour. Now get cracking." There seemed little to do about it except obey orders, so she set off, going at a steady jog. "Faster, faster," bellowed Chief Frone. An hour of this left Jane panting and sweaty but otherwise feeling good. As she set off back to her cell the first of the afternoon matelots were emerging from the cell block. Seeing her, they pointed and smiled but stayed oddly silent. Jane was puzzled by this; cheering, wolf whistling and suggestive comments were so much a part of everyday life in her male Navy that their lack seemed unnatural. She queried it. "I told you, Beacon, that you speak to no-one except us and then only when spoken to. The sailors are subject to an absolute silence rule same as you and woe betide you if you make any noise. It will add at least a week to your sentence."

'Why do they have to be constantly threatening me' she mused. 'It is not as though I am being difficult.'

This brief reverie was interrupted by the marine sergeant barging in. "All right, lunch time." He handed her a pannikin with some nondescript green soup and a baked potato. This consumed, she waited for the main course to arrive. When she queried its arrival, she got a sour laugh in response. "That's your lot dearie. You needn't expect to get fat in here."

"Good heavens, that wouldn't feed a fly. I can't possibly do all that physical exercise on as little as this."

"Yes you can and yes you will. Now don't argue." And with that he stamped out of the cell banging the door behind him. It was beginning to dawn on Jane that her thirty days here might be difficult in some ways. Fit yes, but much more so, hungry and lonely. How on earth was she going to occupy herself?

Around four o'clock Chief Frone appeared with a hunk of bread, some cheese and a pannikin of tea. "Enjoy your supper. That's your lot until tomorrow morning." The cell door slammed shut and the rasp of key in lock told its own story. She lay in her hammock and thought about the last few weeks. The injustice that she should have an accident and end up locked away, a marked criminal, seemed so utterly gross and unfair that it dominated her mind. But behind that lay other, deeper, thoughts.

David was dead. Her mother was dead. Her home was a ruin. The boat she had brought on to have the first successful Wren crew was going brilliantly in someone else's hands. And she had been reduced to an ordinary Wren again. Everything that was important to her had been stripped away and she felt very empty. It would be so easy to turn her face to the wall and dwindle away because there was no point in doing anything else. These crowded thoughts grew larger and larger as she lay there, physically tired but emotionally strung out and resentful. She tried her old mantra "Dammit, I will not be defeated" but it had a hollow ring to it when so much of her present life was not hers to control. She suspected that the way to survive in this place was to be as co-operative and agreeable as seemed necessary to keep the staff sweet and to take advantage of the physical opportunities they seemed to think were essential. Well, she would show them that she was fitter than their little exercises required. But the long solitary hours, locked away in her cell, that was not an appealing prospect.

Next morning saw the same routine, except that on returning from the gym and slopping out, Chief Frone snarled at her, "You must clean your bucket every day. You didn't yesterday and it shows. As soon as you have had your porridge, get cracking on it."

The whole procedure of scraping dust off the brick, mixing it with pusser's hard soap and using the abrasive mix to polish up her bucket, took half an hour working under close supervision from Chief Frone. "From now on do it yourself without having to be told."

'At least it whiles away some time,' thought Jane, looking at the gleaming result. From then on day succeeded day following exactly the same routine. The next interruption to it came when Chief Jones barged in after porridge. "Right, Beacon, today is washday for you. Bring your toiletries, towel and any clothes you want to wash and follow me." The washhouse was a substantial space obviously equipped to deal with multiple matelots so there was plenty of room for one girl. Chief Jones came in with her. "You get six buckets of hot water for yourself and your clothes so make best use of them. Better to do yourself first then dhobi your clothes. Now strip off and get washing."

Startled, Jane said "What, just take everything off here? Aren't there baths or anything?"

"No, Beacon, there are not. You take your clothes off and dowse yourself with as much of you water allowance as you like, remembering that you need it for your clothes as well."

"Well, all right but I am not doing it in front of you. Kindly take yourself outside while I'm washing."

CHAPTER TWELVE: Correction

"No I do not. I stay here to make sure you do it properly."

"Oh do me a favour, you think I don't know how to wash myself?"

"That's not the point. You are under supervision here and it is my job to make sure you do as you are told. Now strip off."

"I object to this. Who do I complain to?"

"You don't, young lady. Those are direct orders from the set-down routine here and if you don't comply you will get a week or two added to your sentence. Come on, we haven't got all day."

Taking a deep breath, Jane stripped to bra and knickers. "Come on, those too."

"This really is the final humiliation. I suppose you want to see your handiwork?"

"I'm not with you?"

Defiantly Jane pulled off her knickers and presented her bare backside. "Look at those stripes. You did that and you have not been forgiven."

Chief Jones curled a lip. "Save your breath, girlie." But there was a gleam in her eye that Jane had never seen before and Chief Wren Jones was breathing heavily, almost panting. The six buckets had been lined up and were cooling off rapidly because of the delays arguing. Still seething, Jane washed herself all over with one, washed her hair with a second and set about her dirty clothes with the rest. It was a strange sensation washing her clothes while stark naked and dripping wet. Jane poured the last half bucket over herself as a final gesture of defiance and stood there waiting for the next instruction. "Wrap yourself in your towel and go back to your cell. Your clothes will follow."

Shrugging her shoulders Jane walked the length of the corridor with just a skimpy towel round her, passing various male warders as she went with each obviously eyeing her. Her cell was rapidly becoming somewhat of a retreat, a bolthole away from the endlessly prying eyes. Chief Jones slammed the door and Jane was once more alone, virtually naked and rapidly getting cold. But at least she was in her own little bit of privacy. By the time she was called for her run round the obstacle course she had pulled some clean clothes out of her kitbag and was dressed, calmed down and ready to take them on again. Even the thin soup and baked potato arriving for lunch seemed a welcome confirmation that the other routines of the place were uninterrupted by the washday humiliation.

Into the second week of her incarceration and always hungry she was working out how to get along with her jailers so that their opportunity to heap further abuse and humiliation on her was limited and there was no doubt that, fit as she had been, she was rapidly getting a lot fitter. But the long evenings locked in her cell were dragging. For the first time in weeks she had time to think, and her thoughts were not happy. Why did David seem so unreal? She had loved him with a passion yet his departure seemed remote, the memories more like a film than the bare stuff of actuality. Her mother's loss was a much more immediate pain, raw and deep and all through her being. But above all her mind seemed filled with a burning sense of injustice that she was locked up in a cell because of other people's incompetence and the machinations of a vengeful Admiralty. That really hurt and brooding over it just stoked the fires all the more. Alone in her cell her world seemed wrapped in a grey cloud pierced by flashes of fury about her situation. By the end of her second week she found herself crying in the evenings; through the day she was kept active enough for her mind to focus on the immediate, but when that cell door thudded shut in late afternoon with sixteen hours on her own to come, she found she was getting less fierce and what had been her rage-fuelled determination was sliding into a deep dark pit of despair.

Stripped naked for her second wash day, she was startled to be given a gentle slap on her left buttock by Chief Frone with a "Come on, hurry up". Jane whirled and very nearly let fly with the slap that had got her into this trouble but pulled up short. "Keep your hands off me," she snarled.

"Silly girl, don't you know how to keep your warders sweet? One word from me and you will have your sentence doubled. Just relax."

Jane eyed her with a venomous fury. "The first time blackmail was tried on me I gave in to it. I know a bit more now and I know what your game is so keep your hands to yourself. It's bad enough having you ogling me but I can live with that. The rest is out of bounds."

Chief Frone shrugged and turned away. "We'll see about that."

This little incident added to Jane's sense of being very alone and helpless in her incarceration. She knew that keeping the staff friendly was making a difference to her life but how far was she expected to go to keep them sweet?

The third week seemed to enlarge her sense of isolation, of being trapped in a world of misery and despair which she was finding progressively more difficult to resist. In the long night watches locked in her cell she brooded more and more on the unfairness of her situation, alone and deprived of her loved ones. Their loss, her sense of injustice, and her sense of helplessness somehow all seemed to be mixed together in one black vortex.

By the following Saturday, and wash day again, Jane's resistance was low and she had decided to mentally shrug if Chief Frone wanted to pat her buttocks. It seemed a small price to pay for keeping on good terms with her. So she was a bit surprised when both Chiefs came into the wash house with her. Knowing what to expect she stripped off without being told and set about washing herself. Wet and soapy, she was totally unprepared for Chief Jones grabbing her arms from behind

CHAPTER TWELVE: Correction

and nodding to Chief Frone who stepped close and ran her hands all over Jane's body while Chief Jones kept her clamped close. Jane wriggled and squealed but was held firm. She was released after a couple of minutes and told to get on with washing her clothes. Chief Frone left. Shaking with a mixture of fury, disgust and despair Jane tried to do as instructed but struggled to keep her hands still enough to do anything. With the session finished Jane returned to her cell in just a towel as before. Chief Jones eyed her from the doorway. "You are due for release next Friday. Just keep your nose clean for a little longer and you should get out on time." Jane scowled at her but said nothing.

Alone that night Jane howled with misery, the still vivid memory of hands roaming over her body adding to her sense of helpless isolation and the unfair way she had ended up in this situation. Her world seemed to be ever blacker and her capacity to resist it ever weaker. During her last week's incarceration she found herself bursting into tears during the day as well; she still performed in the gym and ran effortlessly round the obstacle course barely out of breath at the end of her hour on it, but this was on autopilot, her mind in turmoil and despair. At night her will to resist had gone completely and she cried all night, sleeping badly with fresh nightmares to add to the faces from long ago.

Second Officer Merle Baker was reading up the law on a particularly difficult case of a Wren who had stolen a captain's bicycle to go adrift to see her boyfriend, when her phone rang. "Hello, Portsmouth Detention Quarters here. We've got this Wren of yours ready for discharge but there are no instructions for her and she is not in a fit state to be left on her own. What do you want us to do?"

"Good question but I'll sort something out. Hang on, did you say Pompey DQs?"

"That's right. We've had her here for the last month and now she's due to be let out."

"But that can't be right. She was supposed to be in a Wrennery for her detention. What on earth is she doing with you?"

"We were given instructions by a four-ring captain and the paperwork came straight from the Admiralty, all correct, so we've had her. Bit of a first for us, having her here. Now she's sitting on a bench in our reception area crying her eyes out and all we can get her to say is that it's not fair. Can you people make some arrangement to take her off our hands, please?"

"Well this is all very strange but yes I'll do something about it."

An hour later a small tilly turned up to collect the miscreant Wren and took her to the hospital at Haslar where, still weeping, she was put in a private room and installed in bed with instructions to stay there.

PART THREE:
SAPHO'S SONG

CHAPTER THIRTEEN:
The Slow Road Back

It was early afternoon the next day before Second Officer Baker got to Haslar Hospital to see Jane. She was unprepared for the weeping crumpled inert body she found lying there. "Jane, jane, what on earth has happened?" She was equally unprepared for the snarl she got back. "This is all your fault. It's so bloody unfair locking me up so your precious Wrens could be saved. I hate you all." And she wept more loudly.

Since getting the phone call from Portsmouth Detention Quarters, Merle had been busy finding out what had happened. She had found that Wrens Headquarters – which basically meant her – had been deceived by someone in the Admiralty into believing that Wren Beacon was being sent to a Wrennery for her detention when in fact they had arranged for her to be sent to the DQs and had not told Wren HQ. Copies of the relevant forms were now produced to Merle and the critical signature made clear who had enforced the arrangements – one Captain Gribben. So for a month, while intensely busy with other work which stopped her enquiring about how Jane was getting on but presuming she was active in a wrennery, Merle was unaware that in fact Jane had been suffering much harsher treatment. Now she saw the consequences.

"Oh Jane, this is terrible. Have they been mistreating you?"

"Oh, a bit but it was the solitary that really got to me. Do you have the slightest idea what it's like in DQs?"

"I am afraid not, Jane. We thought you were in a wrennery working on a project, not languishing in solitary in the DQs."

"Sixteen hours a day locked up on your own. It's enough to drive you crazy. And it's all so bloody unfair. One minute you tell me I'm the best Wren around, the next you take me away from doing anything useful and leave me to rot in a prison cell. That's just not fair."

"Didn't they let you out at all? Y'know, for some exercise or something?"

"Oh yes, I got plenty of exercise and I've never been fitter. 'As fit as a butcher's dog' seems to be the way they say it. I actually liked that bit but it was the solitary that got me."

"Well I'm afraid it is done now and all we can do is try to help you get better. If it is any comfort to you, your position in the Wrens is secure but you'll have to be a lot better before we can deploy you again."

"Deploy me? Deploy me? Is that all you can think of, you utterly uncaring bitch! I am a criminal now, to add to all the other injustices on my record and all you can think of is how to get more work out of me. I'm done with the lot of you. I think I'll just go and live on my boat."

"Oh dear, oh dear. Would it help if we tried to get some assistance for you? I presume you can't stay here indefinitely. I think I will look into what we can do for you. Some psychiatric help perhaps."

"I don't need some trick cyclist meddling with my brain. Just an end to the unfairness you have heaped on me."

"Even so, there might be some help there. Listen, I am staying at the barracks here tonight and I'll come and see you again in the morning. Have a good rest and we'll see what can be done for you. I am so sorry Jane, please believe that sending you to the DQs wasn't our idea."

"What difference does that make? The result is the same. If you had been in the least caring you would have seen what had happened and got me out of there, admiral's orders or no admiral's orders. I hate the lot of you."

Merle shrugged and stood up to go. "I'll see you tomorrow and perhaps we will be able to do something for you. Are they giving you anything here for your state?"

"Just a sleeping pill."

"Does that help?"

"To sleep, yes. But that's all."

"All right, I'll see you in the morning."

It was late morning before Merle returned and by then she had news from a busy morning making enquiries and arrangements. "We are going to move you to a different hospital where they will be better able to help you. I've got a car arranged for 1400."

"Why do I have to be in hospital at all? There's nothing wrong with me. Just stop all this unfairness and I'll be fine."

"Well physically, maybe. But you are not mentally settled at all, are you?"

Jane shouted, "I told you there's nothing wrong with me."

"Nothing that a bit of help won't sort out and don't worry, this will only be for a few days."

"Then can I go back in a boat?"

"We'll see. I will come with you when we move to the other place. Meantime I will leave you to dress and pack ready."

"Oh, all right."

Merle returned with the car which proved to be a large American saloon and once out of Fareham its Wren driver headed west. Jane just sat curled up in a ball

CHAPTER THIRTEEN: The Slow Road Back

in the corner of the back seat.

'Royal Victoria Hospital' said the sign as they swept in through the entrance and pushed on through extensive grounds. The hospital itself proved to be a collection of one and two storey buildings. A nurse met and showed them to a single room which looked out over the Solent. "O God, how I long to be out there" whispered Jane. "First decent sight I've seen for a month." Merle smiled "Don't worry, you will be back there soon enough. Just let the staff here help you find your feet again."

"I told you there's nothing wrong with me, "shouted Jane, "Just resentment at the unfairness of it all." And to her chagrin she burst into tears again.

"Yes Jane, I know but perhaps the people here can help you get things a bit better ordered. Do try to let them help you."

"Is that an order?"

"Jane, you know I don't give you orders but it is what we want for you. Believe me, we all want to see you recovered and doing good things again."

With that Merle left. Jane turned to the nurse who had been quietly witnessing this and asked, "where is this place?"

"It's called Netley and it is an army hospital which helps personnel from all the services. I think you will find it a pleasant place to be."

'Lieutenant R P Woods' said the name on the door. Ushered in the next morning, Jane found Lieutenant R P Woods to be a youngish woman sitting in an armchair by the window. At one side her polished but bare desk gave nothing away. She stood up and smiled at Jane. "Good morning, Miss Beacon. I hope we can help you while you are here."

Jane shouted "I keep telling people there is nothing wrong with me that sorting out the unfairness wouldn't solve in five minutes. Why do you all behave as though I've got a screw loose?"

Lieutenant Woods smiled again. "Yes, we understand that and perhaps you might like to tell me why you feel you have been treated so unfairly?"

"I don't feel it, I know it. You try thirty days in the DQs and see how you like it."

"Tell me about it, then."

This proved to be a trigger and for several hours Jane stormed on about her court martial and the DQs and how one fat incompetent little Lieutenant-Commander was the cause of her losing her fingers and all the misfortunes she had had heaped on her since. She marched up and down Lieutenant Woods' office waving her arms about while that lady sat quietly interposing a question here and there to keep Jane going. Strangely, at the end of this explosive session Jane felt better and was able to eat her lunch, the first meal she had managed for several days. There was another session in the afternoon but not so noisy as Lieutenant Woods probed Jane's background and service record.

Three days later Lieutenant Woods had left her seat by the window and was sitting behind her desk when Jane came in. Jane's service records were spread out and it was clear that Lieutenant Woods had been studying them carefully. "Well, Miss Beacon, you have quite a record and I see now where the medal ribbons came from. Tell me about your Dunkirk adventure." This set off Jane's twenty-minute routine about that expedition. Her audience sat smiling quietly during this performance. At its end she said, "Well Beacon, you may feel deeply angered by the way you have been treated lately but there's nothing much fundamentally wrong with you that a period of less pressurised activity would not resolve."

Jane butted in. "I keep telling you all there's nothing wrong with me and it's quite normal to be upset by the way I have been treated."

"Quite so, but the combination of factors has left you in a disturbed condition. I am sending a report to your headquarters today saying that all you need is some peace and quiet to recover full effectiveness and that you can stay here for a day or two longer until your people arrange something for you. I don't think I need to see you again but if you want to talk to me, I can be available."

"Well thank you for that but I think I'll be all right."

The nadir Jane was going through co-incided with one of the lowest points in Britain's fortunes in the war. The entry of America into the war following Pearl Harbour held out a long-term promise of immense power and productivity coming in on the Allies' side but in the short term it simply gave Britain another enemy to contend with as Japan swept through East Asia. The fall of Singapore shortly after the sinking of the battleships 'Prince of Wales' and 'Repulse' was about the most bitter blow Britain was given throughout the war. At the same time it was struggling in the war in North Africa and simply hanging on to prevent the Germans sweeping through to the Middle Eastern oilfields.

Close to home, the Navy was given a very red face when the German battle cruisers 'Scharnhorst', 'Gneisenau' and 'Prinz Eugen' escaped from Brest, steamed up the English Channel and safely reached Germany with very little interference from chaotic disorganised British Forces. Although it put the German ships further from serious conflict and in the longer term it proved a blessing in disguise, at the time it was a serious publicity coup for the Nazi war machine. In the North Atlantic the U-boats were sinking large numbers of merchant ships trying to bring badly needed supplies to Britain and the Navy's attempts at getting a grip of this menace were peripheral to their effectiveness.

All this meant very little to Jane, focussed on her own woes. Two days after Lieutenant Woods had signed off Jane, a formal letter from Second Officer Baker arrived, drafting her to Dartmouth Wrennery without specific duties, and enclosing a travel warrant. Things moved rapidly after that; a bus was laid on for 1000 which

CHAPTER THIRTEEN: The Slow Road Back

took a variety of people to Southampton station. Calm and in control of herself Jane sat at the back then found her train to the west. Inevitably it was late and packed but did run and by 1830 she was catching the Kingswear Ferry to Dartmouth. She located the Wrennery and presented herself to the quarters officer. "Ah yes, Wren Beacon. We've been notified about you, coming without specific duties. Petty Officer Smith will be looking after you. You will find her in the regulating office next door."

Going into their office, Jane found just Petty Officer Smith who was immaculately turned out in typical regulator fashion. Jane looked at this young lady, finding something naggingly familiar about her. "Hello Jane, how nice to see you again. I gather you've been having a hard time of it lately."

"You could say so. Do I know you from somewhere?"

"Yes Jane you do. Remember pro course two? A particularly struggling little Wren you knew as Dora?"

"That's really you? No, I don't believe it. My goodness. I see the resemblance now but you're utterly changed."

"Yes well, there was room for improvement. And you were right: there was a future for me in the Wrens. You've no idea how much that little suggestion of yours carried me through to finding my feet in this outfit."

"Do you mind if I sit down? This really is a complete surprise."

Jane looked across the desk at this apparition; blonde hair immaculately coifed, face perfectly made up and pin-sharp uniform exactly fitting a filled out and sleek female body. The transformation from the scared, scrawny little waif on pro course two was utter.

"Right Jane, now you are over the initial shock let's discuss practicalities. I know the story of why you have been sent here without specific duties to recover your equilibrium. Just chucking you into the main wren quarters, sharing with twenty-odd other girls seemed a bit much under the circumstances so I've arranged for you to have the other bunk in my cabin which will give you a bit more privacy and peace to settle down. It's in the next-door building. You will have to mess with the other Wrens but they are a friendly lot so I don't think that will be a problem. They will be curious about you so I have put out a buzz that you are going to train as a regulator with me once you are fully recovered. That should keep them from being too nosey. There's an enormous heap of mail for you in my cabin. Some of it is addressed to Lady Daubeney-Fowkes. Is that really you?"

"Yes Dora, that's my married name for what it's worth. You know my husband was killed just before Christmas?"

"Yes Jane, I've heard the story and it's no wonder you were down. Hopefully, Dartmouth will help you recover. It's a nice peaceful corner despite the efforts of the Naval College. Come on, let's get you settled in."

Dora's cabin proved to be a comfortable if small space, with the bunk made up ready for her. Once inside, Jane was a little startled to be given a big hug by Dora and a smacking kiss, full on the lips. Disentangling, Jane remarked "I haven't had a full embrace like that for months; I'd forgotten how nice it can be."

Dora smiled. "You're welcome any time. One little thing we must do is get you a new hat. I don't suppose you noticed with all the other stuff going on in your life but the basic Wrens' hat has been changed. The old pudding basin like you still have has been replaced by a nice beret version of the sailor's round hat and that thing you are still wearing is no longer official uniform."

"Is that right? Well fancy that, a new hat. Where do I get it?"

"They are on issue from the clothing store. I'll take you there in the morning."

After a good night's sleep and a decent bowl of burgoo Jane felt fit to face the world again. First off was a trip to the clothing store where she was fitted for the new hat. Jane rather liked the hat; its arrival had been a major event in the Wren universe, greeted with enthusiasm in all quarters. Having been issued with one, she bought another one.

From there she returned to Dora's cabin and without specific duties she tackled the pile of mail that was waiting; some of it had been following her for several months, mail of any sort being banned at the Detention Quarters.

Sorting through it, she divided it into personal letters, official stuff and a handful of letters addressed to Lady Daubeney-Fowkes from a firm of London solicitors. These had to be opened first. The first dealt with her status as David's widow and the title she had acquired. It made it plain that she was entitled to use the Daubeny-Fowkes name but was not to expect to be involved with that family in any way. The second laid out her husband's provisions for her in the event of his dying. He had made a fresh will just a week before he took his ship to sea again, and effectively left all his wealth to his wife. This included substantial sums in the bank, shareholdings and other investments, and for her to become the beneficiary of his trust fund which would pay her one hundred pounds a month in perpetuity. It would be necessary for her to attend at their offices for probate to be settled and legal documents to be signed and witnessed.

The third letter advised that she would have some responsibilities now that she had a title and again these needed to be discussed and some legal documentation required signing. Their last two letters were brief nagging ones asking where she was and please would she respond to their previous missives? 'Right', thought Jane 'that needs immediate attention'. It was no wonder that her husband had been dismissive of her concerns about spending too much.

CHAPTER THIRTEEN: The Slow Road Back

Lady Ormond's letters showed that she knew about Jane's court martial and its consequences but not that Jane had been locked away in the Detention Quarters. She wondered if Jane might like to have a more formal arrangement as the Lady's adopted next-of-kin with some rights assigned to her. What those rights were, remained unclear. There was a brief note from the Wrens Director herself, wishing Jane a speedy recovery and expressing the hope that she might find active involvement with the Wrens of interest once ready for service again. Jane suspected that her off-the-cuff threat to leave the Wrens to go and live on her boat, had reached the Director's ear. More disturbing was a shortish letter from Arthur. Jane had rather hoped that the Marchioness cutting her off would mean that Arthur would also fade out of her life, but no such luck. He seemed as keen as ever to get together with her. 'I know what you want, sunshine,' she thought to herself, 'and you're not having it.' Two letters from her father were full of family news and it was clear from their tone that he did not know about her abrupt disappearance into the enfolding grasp of the DQs. The rest were from friends and Wren acquaintances, all of which needed answers of some sort. This left Jane in a quandary. Should she tell the whole world that the Navy had seen fit to lock her up for thirty days and that she now had a criminal record, or simply to say that she had been out of circulation for a bit? In a wartime world where people did not ask about others' activities, she could probably pass off her missing time as 'Don't ask questions' and have that accepted. Whether she could refrain from talking about the court martial and the DQs was another matter, and she decided to say nothing in the letters she was writing but not to hold back with anyone she met. She was still industriously writing when Dora came in. She came behind Jane, wrapped her arms round her and gently kissed the back of her neck. "So you are communicating with the world again. I suppose that means you are feeling a bit better too?"

"Well maybe. I still get spurts of pure rage when I think about what the Navy has done to me."

"In these circumstances rage is positive. It's when you feel defeated that it all goes negative."

Jane stood up and turned to face Dora. Again, she was hugged and kissed and the gentle warmth of the embrace was soothing. Something about that set Jane quietly weeping again. "Oh please Dora, don't make me cry."

"But you must get it out, Jane. Don't worry, I don't mind if you have a weep from time to time. Let out the bursts of anger as well. In the privacy of this cabin I shan't be upset by it."

"It's very good of you to be so accommodating. I really don't think I deserve that sort of kindness."

"Jane, it's not an exaggeration to say that you saved my life on the pro course. I have an enormous debt of gratitude to you and if being a bit helpful and kind helps you, it is the least I can do. Believe me, I really feel very sad to see you in the state you are and we are determined to try to get you well again."

"Not another one trying to get more work out of me, are you?" The sudden vehemence of this startled Dora and she took a step backwards. "No no, Jane. That wasn't what I meant at all. With this war on we all have to do our bit but I think you've done yours ten times over already. If you want to go and hide on your boat that's your choice but you do have a lot more to give the Wrens if you want."

Jane shook her head in bewilderment. "Right now I really don't know what I want."

"And right now you don't have to want anything particular." Dora stepped in and took the gently weeping Jane in her arms again. "Just let it all flow out. Try to let go of your anger and sense of unfairness. We all know you have been treated very badly indeed but it's history, Jane. Just a little, try to look forward and see the light on the horizon."

Jane shook her head in confusion but couldn't resist a little smile through the tears. "All right, Dora, maybe you are right. It's just getting there that is so hard just now."

Dora very gently pushed Jane onto her bunk, stroked her hair for a minute then straightened up. "I've got rounds in five minutes so I'll have to go. Hang on to the slack, Jane and don't give up. Between us we will make you better."

The morning brought a bright and fresh early spring day so Jane took a walk round the area and found Dartmouth a pretty little town with the waterfront never far from view. Getting back to the quarters in time for lunch it occurred to her that she needed more exercise than a gentle stroll. Enquiries would have to be made but for today a walk was enough.

CHAPTER FOURTEEN:

Closer

After a couple of days Jane had life a bit better organised. She found that she could borrow a rowing boat and take it for a trip each morning, so the heavy exercise was arranged. Returning hot and sweaty from that, the flood of mail that was coming in kept her occupied till lunchtime and the afternoons were spent exploring. She was still getting spurts of rage from time to time and always hovering in the background was a dark cloud of sadness at her recent losses which tended to bring on a fresh burst of weeping. Dora's hugs and kisses helped, their sympathetic gentleness in stark contrast to the harshness of her recent treatment. She was in no hurry for a social life but asked Dora if she had a boyfriend or any sort of a social life. "Me? Boyfriend? Bah, who needs men. I had enough of them and I'm happy to live without now."

Remembering what Dora had come from before the Wrens, Jane wasn't altogether surprised by this attitude. Her beginnings had been so different to Jane's that she had some difficulty imagining what it must have been like. But there was no doubt about Dora's presence now, busy and apparently fulfilled.

Turning in to sleep was Jane's most difficult time, when the memories of her mother and even more so of her husband came flooding into her mind. There were some nights when she could not hold back the tears and she silently lay there dampening the pillow. The raw memory of David could hit hard at times as it came to the forefront and then it was difficult to stifle the sobs. After some nights of this Dora, changed for turning in, came over to Jane. "Is it worse than usual, Jane?"

Jane nodded. "I'm missing David and the life we had, so much."

Dora stroked Jane's cheek then abruptly climbed into Jane's bunk, cuddling up close. Through the thinness of their pyjamas this was a much more intimate cuddle but Jane found it warm and soothing and clung onto Dora, weeping into her neck. "All right Jane, take it easy, just relax and let it out." And she gently murmured soothing noises while stroking Jane's back and neck.

Waking in the morning Jane was stiff from the cramped sleeping position, the bunks being narrow for one person let alone two, but some of the tension inside her had eased away. A good full power rowing trip up the river helped and she found herself feeling much better; this set her wondering if there were any light and simple jobs that she could do. Dora was dubious but agreed to investigate, getting a warning that it had to be outdoors. The result of that was a suggestion that she might work in the bosun's store, splicing ropes, making rope fenders and the likes, which while not outdoors was close enough to keep her happy. Early in her time in the boats Jane had been horrified at the possibility of being sent to the bosun's store at Dover but somehow it seemed a much pleasanter option now. A bosun's store has one of the most pungent and evocative smells to it that any seaman could wish for – a mixture of shiny new rope and ropes soaked in Stockholm tar, and cans of linseed oil and colza oil. Just going into it floods the senses with the aroma of the sea and ships. The Dartmouth store was typical and Jane's spirits lifted. Inside she found a very old chief petty officer, two wrens and a large shaggy dog. "Hello, I'm Lucy and this is Joanna. We're both recovering from injuries so not fit to go back to the boats yet but this is a nice little place to stay tucked out of the way."

Jane looked at them. "Were you both on boat crew training course one?"

"Oh yes, you had us for our week on the boat. Luckily, we both managed the boat boom without much trouble. But things must have changed drastically for you to be back to plain Wren and in a quiet corner like this."

"Yes, things did rather come apart after that course. I now have the dubious distinction of being the only Wren to have been subject to a full court martial. But I'm surviving. What's the dog called?"

"We call him Rover because he keeps wandering off. He's chiefy's constant companion."

The Chief butted in. "What are you good for? Can you splice and make rope fenders?"

"I can certainly splice but how good I'll be without fingers, I don't know." And she held up her left hand.

"Working here will certainly harden that hand off. I'll work with you and show you how to make rope fenders. C'mon girls let's get busy."

For some days, the damaged left hand hurt a good deal as it was subject to rough work, but Chiefy was right – it did harden off soon enough.

Jane had drawn a good deal of comfort from Dora cuddling up with her in bed, so when it was suggested again Jane was willing. This was a more intimate encounter: after kissing and cuddling for a while Dora unbuttoned Jane's pyjama top. She started and wriggled a bit at this but the hand caressing her breast sent sensations of warmth and pleasure through her body and she relaxed into its message. They fell asleep like this, Jane feeling more content than she had for some time.

Working in the bosun's store was proving therapeutic as well. Each morning Jane went rowing for an hour until thoroughly warmed through, then headed into the store. Old Chiefy proved to be a good teacher and it did not take Jane long to master the art of fender making. From that she was moved on to various other bits

CHAPTER FOURTEEN: Closer

of scrimshaw and the sense of creativity pleased her. She was feeling better in other ways too. Dora was joining her in bed each night and her gentle caresses helped Jane move away from the nightly memories which caused her so much grief. This gentle caring was a balm and each day Jane felt more comfortable in herself, and in having Dora in bed with her. After a week of this Dora said, "Let's not bother with pyjamas."

"What, you mean go to bed naked?"

"That's right; get as close to each other as we can."

Alarm bells suddenly rang in Jane's mind. "I'm not sure that is a good idea, is it? You are being awfully nice to me but isn't that a bit too close?"

"No, Jane. I think you'll find you like it. Come on, let's try."

Jane shrugged and gave in, still with misgivings. But the warm closeness of Dora's body against her own was soothing in its way and she relaxed into it. By now she was accustomed to Dora caressing her breasts, sometimes kissing them and stirring warm feelings through her. So, when they got into bed naked the next night Jane was accepting of the closeness and accustomed to Dora's hands wandering about her body. But this time they slipped between her legs and found her clitoris. Again Jane jerked and tried to wriggle away, "No Dora, that's too far, we really shouldn't do this."

"Why not? It's a perfectly natural thing to do. Just relax and let me do it to you. I think you'll like it."

Briefly Jane resisted but the skill in Dora's hand was proving highly effective. Within minutes Jane climaxed, an explosive release of pent-up urges that seemed to go on and on. Coming down from this and returning to the world around her Jane wept gently. "Oh God I needed that. Thank you, Dora, but really we shouldn't have done it. This is going in ways that I don't know about and I think we should stop this now."

"But Jane, we've only just begun. Believe me, what we're doing is natural, expressing our feelings for each other through our bodies as well."

"Well yes, I'm used to that but only with men. Doing it with a woman just doesn't seem right somehow."

"That's because you've never thought about this before. I'll bet your upbringing was entirely about relations with men, now wasn't it?"

Jane nodded dreamily, her body still glowing. "Yes, I suppose it was, now you mention it. It has never occurred to me to get intimate with another woman; it simply hasn't been in my world and I still suspect that I really belong to going with men."

"You can be both, y'know. But I am here and this is now so relax and let this bit be natural to you." Dora's hand slipped between Jane's legs again and before long there was a second explosive result. It took Jane longer to come to her senses again second time round and when she did, she simply hugged Dora close, gently drifting off to sleep in this close embrace. There was a third session in the morning before Dora had to rush off for her duty all of which meant that Jane was in a dazed dreamworld when she took her rowing boat out. But she felt cleansed, brighter and fulfilled for the first time in a long time.

From there Jane's world seemed to come together again. Work in the bosun's store was curiously satisfying as she learnt more rope working skills. Both Lucy and Joanna recovered from their injuries and left to work on the boats again, leaving Jane to the quietly skilled instruction of old Chiefy and the affections of the dog. In bed, a daily diet of fulfilling sex allowed Dora to introduce Jane to other skills to satisfy them both, some of which Jane found quite startling. She knew about oral sex on men but on another woman was a new idea which she took to after some initial resistance. Jane became steadily more committed to activities with Dora and a strong bond of mutual affection was building up from the direct bodily contacts.

It was late April before this idyll was interrupted. First, a letter from the Daubeny-Fowkes solicitors demanded to know when Jane might manage to come and see them to deal with paperwork which was being delayed by her absence. Then, within a few days a friendly but direct letter from Merle asked how Jane was getting on and when she might be well enough to come and see them at headquarters. Jane was now feeling very well, thank you, so it looked as though she would have to join the outside world again. She wrote to both enquirers and also to Lady Ormond begging a bed for a few days. In the meantime her twenty-second birthday passed by. Dora and she went out for dinner to celebrate and although the meal was constrained by rationing, they had a cheerful evening. Another exchange of letters and a phone call to Merle set up a London visit for the end of the first week in May; Jane sent her tiddly uniform to the cleaners, its sleeves now bereft of badges, which Jane had carefully put away. She then packed a suitcase with spare uniform and other essentials. Jane had taken the precaution of buying a first-class upgrade to her travel warrant so although the train was packed, she found a seat with a group of senior RAF officers. Arriving at Lady Ormond's had a feeling of coming home again. She said hello to Rufus who had waited patiently in his seat by the window and looked out an evening dress from storage. It was the first time Jane had been in the flat since she left for Portsmouth and her court martial. That felt like ancient history given how much had gone by since but the Lady's welcome was as warm as ever and Jane entertained her at dinner with a slightly expurgated version of all that had happened since. There was news for her, too. Lady O explained that through her contacts she had learned a fuller story. The Wrens Director had created a major fuss when she heard what had happened to Jane. She was determined that there would not be another chance for one of her Wrens to be sent to the DQs and in the shifting sands of politics at the Admiralty the senior admiral who had engineered Jane's trial and locking up, found himself seriously unpopular with his fellow Admirals. He had been quietly moved to a safer position and had been admonished for allowing his obsession with 'getting' Jane to cloud his judgement. He was now placed where he could not reach her despite still being very angry that she had not been dismissed entirely from the Wrens. Even better news was that Captain Gribben had been "allowed" to retire gracefully to a quiet backwater and now had no executive authority in the rest of the Navy.

When Jane arrived at Merle's desk at 1030 prompt the next day it was to a warm welcome. "Hello Jane, how nice to see you so much better. When do you think you might be ready for boat duty again?"

"Oh, now really. I think I've forgiven you all for my treatment and going off to rusticate on my boat isn't as appealing now as it felt early in the year. What are the plans?"

"Well, I've got a few of pro course two together for dinner tomorrow night which I thought you might enjoy. We are all going to the Savoy where your name seems to work magic. *Kittiwake* is still going strong under Punch's capable hand. I've arranged for you to join them for a day later in the week so you can have a nostalgic trip down the Thames. And there are several special projects lined up which might suit your particular talents. They are not finalised yet so I'll say no more at this stage but assuming you are up to it I think you will not be bored. The Director is expecting you in twenty minutes' time so be ready for that."

"That will be enough to be going on with. It's funny, in the past I would have thought of Dartmouth as a dead little backwater but this year its peace and quiet have really suited me very well. Why did you send me there?"

"It was Dora Smith's idea. She's been based there for a while now and when she heard what had happened to you, she suggested that Dartmouth and her tender care might just be the thing to let you get back on your feet again. It is remarkable the way she has blossomed given the chance."

"Yes, she really has come a long way and it is lovely to see her so well now. I gather she can be a bit of a terror among the Wrens if they get out of line. She has been enormously helpful in letting me recover and come to life again."

"Yes, her affections seem to work wonders."

Alarm bells rang in Jane's mind at this. Her relationship with Dora had seemed like a private matter but was Merle hinting at knowing about it?

"Although she is pretty strict with them, the Wrens there think highly of her for being caring and considerate at the same time."

Jane relaxed. Merle's comment was more general but it was a quick warning about being discreet. She had never thought about it but presumably a relationship with another woman would be frowned on just as much, if not more so, than her other activities had been.

"The Director is ready to see you now." And once again Jane found herself escorted into the presence by Merle. She saluted and reported in proper order and was waved to a seat. "Hello Beacon, I am relieved to see you recovering well. That single slap of yours has caused more grief and upheaval than any other minor incident I can recall. I don't suppose you thought much about it when you did it."

"Ma'am, the truth of it is that I didn't think at all. I just lost my temper with that nauseous little man and reacted. Well, I've paid a heavy price for it. I can't say I like DQs."

"That's hardly surprising but your court martial and involuntary stay in them has allowed us to clear up a good few uncertain arrangements and relationships between Wrens and the Navy. There won't be any other Wrens go to the DQs and although it remains a theoretical possibility, we have been able to establish much more clearly the rules for sending any other Wren for court martial. So to that extent we appreciate the way you stood up to the treatment you got and we are happy to keep you in the Wrens which I gather you have now come round to being willing to stay in. Is that right?"

"Yes ma'am, so long as I'm doing something useful that helps the war effort I will stick with it. One of the things that really annoys me about the last few months is what a waste it has been. I could have been doing something useful instead of mooning around feeling sorry for myself. Hopefully, that is now finished."

"You will have to tell us, Beacon, but I see the familiar fire has come back so I presume that means you are ready to engage with the war effort again."

"Yes indeed ma'am. Have you any idea yet what I might be doing? Hopefully in boats?"

"Oh, certainly in boats Beacon, but there are several possibilities and we are waiting for the Navy to make its mind up about them. But it won't be long now."

"That is good ma'am. I was a little afraid that my outbursts earlier might have turned you against me so to find that is not so, is good news for me."

"Beacon, we are a little more understanding than that. I know there's a war on and discipline must be maintained but we are more considerate than to turn against you after all that you have done for us. When I interviewed you at the end of your probationer course, I marked you down as exceptional but troublesome. I don't think I have changed my opinion since but your service has been outstanding and the good has always outweighed the bad. If you can just keep that up, we will make

CHAPTER FOURTEEN: Closer

sure you are properly looked after."

Jane smiled, a rueful lopsided twitch of her face. "All right ma'am I will try."

And with that she got the nod of dismissal.

The next day was quite different. She presented herself at the solicitors' office at ten o'clock as instructed, dressed again in her best tiddly uniform. "Lady Daubeny Fowkes," she told the enquiring receptionist and found herself escorted straight into the inner sanctum of the senior partner's office. Two others were summoned to join the meeting. "Good morning, Lady Daubeny Fowkes. I gather that your naval duties have prevented you coming to see us sooner but it is not too late to deal with your late husband's will and what he has left to you. Were you aware of what he had arranged for you?"

"No, not at all. He never mentioned writing a new will or making any arrangements for my benefit. To be quite honest, nothing like that occurred to me as I was well provided for by my own family and had no particular need for more. Your letter rather hinted at him leaving his trust fund to me but I have no idea what that means."

"Yes well, rather more than just his trust fund. You are now a wealthy woman, which means that you will have to give thought to the management of your wealth which, of course, we will be happy to assist you with. His assets are mainly in three parts: One, cash in the bank. Two, stocks, shares and other investments. And three, the income from the trust fund. He has bequeathed some minor goods and chattels to you as well but they are of little consequence. Firstly, the cash in the bank: This stood at sixty-two thousand pounds eleven shillings and sixpence as of last Friday. It is, of course, on deposit and earning interest. Do you have a bank account?"

"Yes indeed" and Jane handed over her Coutts & Co cheque book. The senior partner's eyebrows went up at this. "You already had a Coutts & Co account?"

"Oh yes, my father banks with them. He's a successful doctor which means that we are a comfortable upper middleclass family and when he offered to let me have an allowance each month, he arranged an account for me. Does this cash get transferred to my account?"

"We would recommend that you leave it where it is and we will arrange for title to the account to be transferred to you. It can be linked to your current account so that you have access to the funds whenever you need some. We have the forms for this to hand here which just need your signature to complete the transfer."

"Oh, fine, whatever is best. I've never had much to do with money and my needs at present are very simple so I am happy to leave it where it is. Might we perhaps transfer five hundred pounds to my account for working demands?"

"That can be arranged. Are you sure it is enough?"

Jane thought of her own account with ninety pounds in it. She had felt quite rich with that so dropping five hundred pounds into it seemed astronomical. "I think that will do me for now. I've never been a spendthrift so I don't suppose I will spend much of this, certainly not right away."

"Right, Lady Daubeny Fowkes. Moving on to the complex part, the investments, Lord David preferred to keep his investment holdings on a long-term basis only making changes when he felt it necessary and we recommend that you do the same. The biggest part is in Government bonds and blue-chip companies. Lord David liked to keep a small part for more speculative investments which may or may not prove to be worthwhile. It is up to you whether to sell these or keep them for the chance that they might come good."

"I am afraid I know nothing about investing, blue chip or speculative. But if they are only a small part let's leave them where they are for now and at some stage I'll try to educate myself about this sort of investing."

"All these will have to be re-registered in your name. There is nearly three hundred thousand pounds' worth of investment in total, all in negotiable securities which shows just how wealthy you have become. We will ask for our stockbroker to make the arrangements if you would sign this authority for him to deal on your behalf. And lastly, the trust fund. All of the Daubeny Fowkes children have identical funds and Lord David's is now transferred to you. You cannot touch the principal but the income comes to you at one hundred pounds a month. We are the nominated trustees of the fund but you also become a trustee because you are the beneficiary and it will be necessary for you to meet with us on a quarterly basis to discuss the affairs of the trust."

"Gosh. That's an enormous amount. What do I do with all this money?"

"Invest it, spend some, support charities but look after it so that it does not dwindle away."

"I was bequeathed a yacht. Presumably I can spend a little on its maintenance?"

"Yes of course, that is just the sort of expenditure which your current account is there to support. Now, you have to sign the legal documentation appointing you a trustee. We have it drawn up ready here."

For some time Jane signed form after form. She tried to look at them and absorb what each one was for, but found herself losing track of them. With all this completed the senior partner leaned back, smiled and said "Your brief marriage has been remarkably beneficial to you. Did you know this when you married Lord David?"

"Good heavens no. Money was never mentioned. With this blasted war going on our focus was on being together. We loved each other very much, y'know and I would like to think that I made him a happy man for the short period we were together. We were just two young people coming together because we wanted to be.

CHAPTER FOURTEEN: Closer

I suppose with all this money and trustee responsibility I will have to learn to look a bit further than driving naval boats round the place but it will take a little while for the consequences of all this, to sink in."

"Well, there is no need to be in a rush. Everything is tightly tied up and safe, which is more than can be said for our personal safety. Now, might we invite you to join us for lunch?"

"Well, that would be very nice of you, Mr Hepplewhite. Thank you."

Over lunch in Simpsons she gave them the twenty-minute story of Dunkirk, extended by rather more detail about her rescue of the men trapped on a burning, sunken destroyer and how one of them proved to be her future husband. Then, throwing caution to the winds, she went on with a description of her court martial and the dubious pleasures of thirty days in the DQs. "So here I am, being well fed where only a few months ago I was surviving on very thin gruel. The last six months have been a crazy roller coaster ride and the Wrens are quite keen for me to be doing something for them in boats again, very soon. It looks as though I will be busy again and whether you get hold of me at any time is going to be a bit of a lottery but that's life in a blue suit in wartime. Give me plenty of notice if you need my presence any time."

CHAPTER FIFTEEN:
Moving On

Dinner at the Savoy with five of her colleagues from probationer course two was a lot of fun. Punch, now a petty officer, was relaxed and positively giggly although the air of authority which she carried with her was more noticeable. Evadne, still with her strong Rhodesian accent, kept them all entertained with reminiscences about the wildlife back home. They were all in uniform and Jane was pleased to see that both boat Wrens had their white lanyards prominently across their chests. Alicia had come up from Liverpool specially to join them and was loving being a despatch rider. Camilla, dainty as ever, was now a second officer working somewhere in the Home Counties. "Cyphering, y'know. Can't say more." And Merle was in good form, talking about legal issues and how important it was for the Wrens to have legal capability of their own. For a while Jane just let all this flow over her, enjoying hearing about other people for a change. Inevitably she had to take her turn and her description of the DQ's caused a few moments of silent thoughtfulness before she moved on to telling everyone of how well Dora was doing now. It was agreed that they would meet again in September.

For Jane, the next day was a pleasure as well. She was at Lambeth pier by 0730, back in her bell bottoms and boating rig and was delighted to be handed a cup of tea by Sparrer on arrival. It was clear that the *Kittiwake* crew were a deeply settled and smooth-running outfit as the boat moved off for its daily routine. There were stores and mail to drop off at half a dozen points down to Gravesend and back and Jane was invited to take the helm again. She felt distinctly nervous about this, realising with a start that she had not actually been on a boat like this since the day she lost her fingers almost six months before. It was a sunny blustery day with a couple of berthing challenges where Punch had to quietly guide Jane but no-one said anything about her rustiness and she just had to accept the help. After so much teaching other people, Jane found it rather odd to have to be told what to do but accepted it with good grace and made a mental note to try to get some practice in again before she left Dartmouth. There was an odd conversation with Punch. "Going in a ship will be a bit strange after the stuff you have been used to."

"What's this about a ship? No-one has said anything to me about one. Tell me more."

Punch grimaced. "Oh, sorry. Oi should not have spoken out of turn because it's just second-hand comments I picked up. Enough said." And would not say any

CHAPTER FIFTEEN: Moving On

more. But clearly there were moves going on in the background that had not been mentioned yet to Jane.

That night at dinner she gave Lady O a brief sketch of the change in her fortunes and asked if she could look to the lady for advice if she needed it. "Yes of course, my dear, if I can but I am no expert. But having raised this topic there were some things I wanted to discuss with you as well. You know that both my brothers and my fiancé were killed in the first war and my parents are long dead. This means that my family's wealth has all devolved onto me, not that I ever sought it. My legal next-of-kin is an elderly and distant cousin living in Scotland. In addition, I am not getting any younger myself and must be looking to the future. I have discussed what to do with my solicitors and I would like to name you as an alternate next-of-kin if you are willing. Also, most of my wealth is tied up in a trust; the solicitors are trustees as am I but we badly need some younger blood on it. Would you be willing to become a trustee? We can arrange for it to let you have about one hundred pounds a quarter in expenses for your efforts."

"This is all very considerate of you, Lady O. Yes of course I am happy to help you in any way I can, although with David's bequests available to me I hardly need the money. Does this involve regular meetings?"

"Only two a year, usually held at my solicitors. There is one other matter to discuss. This flat is owned by a limited company which in turn I am the sole shareholder of, and the staff here are all employed by the company. Like the trust I need new blood on the company board. This would involve you in the affairs of the flat and people. Although most of it is done as we go along, we still have to have formal meetings from time to time as well as a proper Annual General Meeting and you would have to have some understanding of what goes on here. The staff all know you by now and trust you to be sensible about the place. I would like to gift you twenty-five percent of the shares in the flat's owning company to make it worth-while for you. If this is acceptable to you, we'll do a tour of the place in the morning."

"What can I say, Lady O? This is enormously generous of you and yes of course I am happy to help in any way I can. I just hope I can live up to your expectations. You know I have no experience in business matters like this and when David's lawyers dumped all this onto me yesterday, I felt totally overwhelmed and out of my depth. Really, I can only offer common sense to you. Will that be enough?"

"Yes of course Jane. I've seen enough of you by now to feel confident that your common sense will be adequate to deal with the fairly simple matters you would be expected to participate in."

"This is all so remote from my Wren life – it's only three months since I was locked up in a DQs cell and living on very thin gruel. The contrast is so utter that I find myself wondering if one or other of these experiences is real. I am due to resume boating work for the Wrens very soon now and who knows where that might take me? On the one hand I'm really looking forward to being on a boat again and in the fresh air, but on the other all the money and responsibilities I have had landed on me these last few days make me feel that maybe I should be a bit more careful with myself. I suppose the next thing I must do is make a will. It hasn't seemed necessary up to now."

"Yes Jane, you should certainly make a will. I'm surprised David's lawyers didn't insist on that when you were with them. For the rest, if I were you I'd get back in the fresh air, enjoy being a boat girl again and let it all sink in. There's no need to be rushing into anything right away and your finances will gently look after themselves for a bit. Once you've got some perspective on it all perhaps I can help you a bit with decisions. I will be instructing my lawyers to make the arrangements to put tonight's discussions into action. Apart from that, let's leave it lying quietly for now."

Sleep did not come easily to Jane. Turning over the momentous changes of the last two days she felt both an enormous weight and an opportunity beyond her wildest imaginings. But for sure life would never be the same again. On the long train journey back to Dartmouth next day Jane was left in a daze. Trying to think about the events of the last few days she found impossible, her mind going off at tangents whenever she tried to concentrate. Arriving at the Wrennery she waved to Dora in passing but it was a much more passionate embrace and kiss as soon as they were alone in the cabin. Jane had come to one clear decision on the run down: she would not tell anyone outside a select few, about David's bequest to her and her changed fortunes. So although it was lovely to see Dora again, Jane only told her the social news and that she was likely to be drafted away sometime soon. The disappointment on Dora's face on hearing that, told its own story. "I suppose it is inevitable that you will have to move on now you are recovered but Jane I love you and don't want to lose you. At least I have the comfort of knowing that I repaid my debt to you by helping you recover from the shattered state you were in when you arrived here." And to Jane's dismay, Dora collapsed into floods of tears, perched on Jane's bunk sobbing heavily. "Dora, there wasn't really any kind of debt; I just did what seemed right at the time and I am happy that it worked out so well for you. If anything, I owe you now. Our close relationship has opened up a new world and given me so much strength to face outwards and be useful again."

"Do you love me, Jane?"

"That's a difficult question to answer. Yes, I love you and our relationship which has shown me many new aspects of life. But do I love you like I did David? No, I haven't loved anyone else like that and I wonder if I ever will again. I really don't

CHAPTER FIFTEEN: Moving On

know, Dora. Do you only love women now?"

"Yes Jane, I am what they call a lesbian with no interest in men. I wasn't looking to do anything more than help you get better but one thing kind of lead to another and now I love you utterly. Please don't turn away from me now."

"Dora, I wouldn't do that. But what happens if I meet another man and fall for him? I've been very happy in my relationships with men and I can see me going back to that. This whole business of loving you physically is so new and different for me. It has all been delightful and has given me a deep emotional bond with you but it isn't going to stop me wanting to have a man again. I'm sorry if that disappoints you but I can't pretend to be what I am not. You did say that I could love both and maybe that's how I will be. I just don't know."

"But you won't go with another woman?"

"Dora, I wasn't looking for it when you and I got together and I certainly don't intend to go looking for it again. But who knows what might happen? I am back to having a life and want to live it to the full. Until our getting together I had always assumed an emotional life would be with a man. But now? I am confused and just don't know. Come here." And Jane wrapped her arms round the weeping bundle and hugged her very close.

By next morning, the immediate emotional storm had blown over and they both went to their routines. Jane rowed up the river, looked in on the bosun's store which had acquired another Wren in the meantime, then came back to the cabin to deal with a pile of mail. Among several letters from the solicitors was one confirming that David's main accounts had now been transferred into Jane's name, and that five hundred pounds had been transferred to her Coutts & Co account and was available to spend as she chose. Given that she had no plans for spending any of it, this did not mean a lot but it was comforting to know that cushion was there. It did not stop her from attending pay parade and having her Wren pittance deposited in her hand but its sheer insignificance gave her an inward wry smile.

A day later she arranged to call on the boats officer. She came smartly to attention, saluted, and reported in correct form. "Yes, what do you want?"

"Sir, I have fully recovered and expect to be drafted to a boats job somewhere, very soon. In the meantime, I wondered if I could be useful here and get back in practice handling boats."

"Now let me get this right, Beacon. You were found guilty at a court martial of assaulting an officer, were disrated and served time for your crimes. I have seen you in the bosun's store cheerfully making scrimshaw items which seems to be about your level. I have no intention of letting a menace like you lose in my boats so the answer is no, you may not get some practice here. If anyone else is daft enough to take a chance on you that's their business but I will not be one of them. You may go."

Absolutely seething Jane saluted and stamped out of the office. Just how much damage had been done by her recent disasters had been really rubbed in and made clear in that brutal five minutes. From now on she would have to carry the weight of a criminal record with her no matter how much Wren HQ might say they wanted to keep her.

On the Saturday there was a letter from HQ. Inside were forms and a rail warrant plus a semi-personal letter from Merle.

Dear Jane

The Navy has now made up its mind about several projects and we are appointing you to one of them. On receipt of this letter you should proceed to Plymouth directly to take over VIC 5. Report to Plymouth boats officer for further orders on arrival and be prepared to operate remotely for some time. I hope to come to see you once you have arrived at your operating station.

Yours truly

"Dora, I'm afraid the draft order you dreaded has come. I am being sent away immediately and I'll travel tomorrow. Sorry but it was inevitable."

By now Dora had recovered her equilibrium and took the news calmly but that night was a tear-stained affair without much sleep as they clung to each other. Jane felt guilt as much as love in this departure. Dora had done so much to help her get back on her feet, giving her heart to Jane in the process, and at the end of it was being left behind, discarded like an old jersey. What could she do to make it better for Dora? With her new-found wealth there was the option of offering money but might that make it worse, an insult and suggestion that the whole affair had just been a transaction in passing? She would explore that cautiously. Getting dressed in the morning she casually said "Y'know, Dora, if you ever need financial help do let me know. I would see it as a privilege to help you if the need arose."

"Well thanks Jane and it has to be said that Wren's pay is not terribly generous. I'll let you know if the need does arise." And the topic was left at that.

By late morning Jane was on her way to Plymouth and for once the trains ran to time. Coming into Boats Officer's office at Flagstaff Steps felt very familiar.

Formalities over he gestured to Jane to sit. "Nice to see you again Beacon and I'm glad you have recovered. How much do you know about your next appointment?"

"Almost nothing. I am to take over a thing called VIC 5 but what that is and where, I'm afraid is a mystery."

"Well, I don't know much more but I do know a Wren crew will be arriving tomorrow. You are getting a tiffy and two stokers to run the machinery. VIC 5 is in the basin round the corner and you are to take her to Weston-Super-Mare to take

CHAPTER FIFTEEN: Moving On

part in some secret trials. It will be a good test of your seamanship to get her round Land's End and up the North Devon coast. If you look on the chart you will see that Weston-super-Mare has a small harbour at Knightstone Island for the boat to lie in. On arrival you are to report to *HMS Birnbeck* where these trials are being carried out. That's about all I can tell you except that you are to be ready to go by next Monday, weather permitting."

"Right, sir. Do I draw on you for stores, and is this VIC 5 a coal burner or an oil-fired thing?"

"Oh, coal fired, I'm afraid. She is one of a class of stores boats the Navy is building and they are all coal-fired. She is almost brand-new but modelled on the old Clyde puffers, I gather."

"Bah, that's a bad start. I've done my share of coal shovelling and it is a complete pain."

"Ah, so you've been in a steamer before?"

"Oh yes, at Dover and Portsmouth. They were old picket boats but I gather this VIC 5 is something else entirely."

"Yes indeed. I will see you again tomorrow morning to arrange storing and victualling."

An evening with her father restored some sense of balance in her life to Jane. She had decided to ask his help with her unexpected new wealth and his calm sense of proportion gave her some understanding of how to live with it. They agreed that the five pounds a month he had quietly been subsidising her with, could be transferred to younger sister Sarah although he declined Jane's offer of repaying what he had given her already. Jane noted with interest that in this new house, Eunice had a bedroom next to her father's and although she still performed her cooking and housekeeping duties there was a proprietorial air to her which was new. 'I'll bet they are married before this blasted war is over' she thought with a wry inward smile.

Next morning her father dropped Jane at the dockyard gate and she found VIC 5 in the basin. Her jaw dropped; this was a little cargo ship, quite unlike anything she had been involved with before. Cautiously she made her way on board and looked around. There was a little cabin aft with two bunks but the main crew accommodation was in the bow of the ship, in the foc'sle head. Jane was having a look round the engine room with its vertical boiler and two-cylinder steam engine when a tiffy and two stokers turned up. The Chief Engine Room Artificer, a seasoned old operator with Navy written all over his faded uniform and face, gave Jane a sour look. "I heard we'd got some of you Wrens for a crew. Do you know the first thing about taking a ship to sea?"

"It won't be the first time, that is for sure. This thing is a bit different but we'll manage. How long are you going to be with us? I can't think that the Navy will waste your experience on this little lady for long."

"Naw. My orders are to see you to your destination then leave you to it. By then these two herberts" – and he pointed at the two silent stokers – "will have learnt enough to be able to run the thing for the day running I gather you'll be doing." They set about getting life into the boiler and Jane was with them learning a bit about the machinery when she heard female voices on the quayside. "Oi reckon this is the one." Jane froze. That voice sounded very familiar; recovering rapidly she shot up on deck to see the entire *Kittiwake* crew standing on the quay. "Good heavens, what are you lot doing here?"

"We've come to be your crew, Jane. Oi heard that you were going to be doing this new job which might be a bit different so we figured you could do with a reliable crew and here we are. Can we come on board?"

"Well I never. Yes of course. You can put the kettle on."

Settled in the mess room Jane asked, "But Punch, you've been your own skipper for a long time now. Surely you don't want to go back to being Jimmy the one?"

"For you, Jane, yes oi do. Wouldn't do it for anyone else, but for you no problem. It sounds like you're going to need a good crew with you."

"It sounds to me like you know more about this project than I do. Do you know we have to take this thing round Land's End and up the Bristol Channel? That'll be a challenge in itself never mind what the job is going to be when we get there."

Suki spoke, "Yes well, we're support for some sort of research project but we don't know what that is." With cups of tea all round they spent an hour catching up before their tiffy looked in to report steam on the boiler, the engine apparently in good order and that they needed coal. Knowing they had only four days before they were due to sail there was a rapid handing out of jobs to get ready, Jane watching the casually assured way Punch organised both her Wrens and the stokers. There was going to be some hammock sleeping with the engine room crew aft and the girls in the foc's'le head.

PART FOUR:
BEYOND THE STYX

CHAPTER SIXTEEN:
A Little Excursion

"Will you show us round the engines, please Chief?"

"Yes certainly but I'm having difficulty sorting you out. Who is skipper among you lot?"

Jane smiled and held up a hand. "That's me, Chief"

"But that makes no sense. You are a plain Wren in charge of a petty officer and two leading hands? Pusser does some strange things but that is a right upside-down arrangement."

"It might seem so but amongst us it makes sense."

"So I'm expected to take orders from a woman? And a basic one at that? I don't like that at all."

"Don't worry chief. It's only for a few days and we'll try to keep the orders down. It won't be so bad really."

"Well maybe. Do any of you know anything about engines?"

Suki held up a hand. "I know petrol and diesel engines but these steamers are new to me. I believe it's the boiler that is the tricky part?"

"It can be but these little up-right jobs are pretty easy. Main thing with them is to keep up steam."

For the next hour, the rather bemused crew were introduced to simple and compound engines, condensers, various pumps, thrust bearings and the oiling routine to keep it all running smoothly. They were introduced to the boiler and how to stoke it, shovelling coal from the bunker at the ship's side into the blazing fire that was the heart of the plant. Its safety features and the need to keep water in it were emphasised. With the down-below tour finished the chief led them up onto the bridge. "These little ladies are unusual in having control of the engine worked from the bridge. That valve wheel by the compass operates the valve that lets steam into the engine. The handle next to it with rodding onto the engine is for ahead or astern. If you are working the engine, remember that it must be stopped before you can change direction. I think I'll make a point of being on the bridge going in and out of port to make sure that you treat it properly."

Jane took charge. "Thanks chief. I gather we need bunker coal. How much, and what else do you need?"

"Oh lubricating oils and grease. We don't seem to have any. And we could do with topping up the feed water."

"Won't tap water do?"

"Only in emergency. All steam boilers like their feed water pure and free of impurities. But they'll be used to supplying that here. You should see how fussy they are on the destroyers."

A long list of needs was compiled then the chief and Jane went to see boats officer. He did a double-take at the length of it all but accepted the need. Later in the day a passing dockyard train dropped off a wagon full of coal. Jane looked at it. "Is that enough for us, chief?"

"Probably yes but we'll see how full the bunker gets. Can we get started on it right away?"

"We'll have to I suppose 'though I hate the job. If we shovel it to the bunker access can your boys stow it?"

"Yes, I suppose so. Are you sure you girls are up to it?"

"Just you watch chief. C'mon girls, into boiler suits or your scruffiest uniform. This is a filthy job."

Suitably dressed they emerged to work out how to open the wagon door, get coal cascading from it onto the quay, and from there to shovel it direct to the bunker opening. Sparrer and Evadne worked in the wagon while Jane, Punch and Suki shovelled from the quay. Three hours' hard work had them all black of face and gritty of hair, but their fuel was all in with the ship's bunker virtually full.

Chief looked impressed. "Well, you girls certainly know how to work. I hope the rest is as good."

"Just you watch, chief."

The ablution facilities on VIC 5 consisted of a board with a bucket-sized hole in it, down in the foc'sle space, so Jane led a raid on the nearest Wrennery. Suitably clean and shiny they bought fish and chips on the way back and settled into their new quarters. Two more busy days of taking stores, figuring out where to put them, and getting everything to work had them at it from early to late, but when they rose on Monday morning their little ship was ready for sea. "All set to go, chief?"

"Oh, engines are ready and the boiler is steaming well. I can't think of anything else we need to do. When are we off?"

"If we sail at noon, we'll get the tide with us round the Lizard which is always a help. The forecast isn't too good for doubling Land's End so we'll just have to see what it's like when we get there. Because we have no idea what this little lady will be like in a seaway it will all be 'try it and see'."

Chief nodded gloomily and disappeared down below without a word. True to his word he re-appeared on the bridge at noon, looking around as though expecting some disaster. Boats officer came to see them off with a couple of matelots who let

CHAPTER SIXTEEN: A Little Excursion

go the mooring lines till they were singled up fore and aft. Jane looked at her Chief. "All right to go? Got plenty of steam?"

"Yep, we're nicely nudging the red line."

"Fine then, we're off." Jane put the wheel hard-a-port, signalled to the after party to let go, and called "Dead slow ahead". The chief pushed the arm over, opened the steam valve a little, and watched. As the ship pulled on the fore spring, the stern slowly came off until the ship was at forty-five degrees to the quay. "Stop engine." The basin was cluttered with other ships and boats but there was a way through. "Let go forward." With the fore spring cast off Jane called "Slow astern," and watched while chief put the rods over and opened the steam valve again. Remembering to midships the rudder, Jane watched closely as the ship slowly gathered sternway. It proved responsive to its rudder so with small movements of the helm Jane was able to steer astern out of the basin and into the river. There she straightened out; chief gave Jane a satisfied nod, and they were outward bound. An aircraft carrier easing its way gingerly into the Hamoaze rather got in their way but it proved possible to go round it. Jane had a great surge of joy as her little ship rose gently to a slight swell coming in. With the engine running full ahead the chief disappeared below to check that all was well. But his two stokers, silent types who got on with their jobs, actually knew their work well and one of them was already going round the engine with the oil can. On the bridge Jane threw off her hat and luxuriated in the wind in her hair. With a fresh breeze from the west the ship ambled along at a steady seven knots, her south-westerly course keeping her close to the sheltering land. Punch joined Jane on the bridge, smiling broadly. "It's always good to get away, isn't it? How are we going to arrange the watches?"

"Well, I thought you and Sparrer could be one watch while Suki and I make the other. I've heard that Evadne is an ace cook so maybe she could be out of watches and keep us fed. Does that suit you?"

"Yes, that would be fine. Do you want to take the watch to 1600? I'll send Suki up to join you."

"All right Punch, see you later."

As the ship got down to Lizard Point the effect of the freshening Westerly started to make itself felt with growing sea and swell to set VIC 5 pitching her head into it. By the time Lizard was astern the motion had become thoroughly unpleasant, with the ship butting its head into a short steep sea and the wind a snarling force. With her bow high despite the forepeak ballast, VIC 5 was pounding her forefoot at intervals to double the unpleasantness as Jane found when she tried to go into their foc's'le accommodation. Speed was down to five knots, less at times, but the sturdy little vessel kept pushing on which was fine for the ship but thoroughly unpleasant for her crew. Jane re-joined Punch on the bridge. "Y'know, I wonder if we'll get round Land's End in this. I can't help thinking we'd be better off anchoring in Penzance Bay for the night; the forecast suggested it should ease off tomorrow and back southerly which would make getting round a lot easier."

Punch smiled "Y'know, Jane, oi was thinking something like that meself. Let's do it."

"Have you looked at our anchors? Stowed on deck with a cat davit to handle them. Are you all right with that?"

"Oh yes. That's what the barges have so I'm used to it."

It was falling dark by the time VIC 5 arrived in Penzance Bay. Punch was true to her word and dropped the anchor without difficulty, they gave a good scope of chain and breathed more easily. In the Bay's shelter the ship lay quietly and the seasick members of the crew appeared on deck again. After an initial grumble about the delay the chief accepted their position philosophically.

"I think we ought to keep the watches going overnight, just keep an eye on her in case she drags. Chief, can we keep the engines at immediate readiness?"

"Yes, I've arranged that already. My lads will keep a good head of steam up."

Through the evening the wind rose. Gusting to a full gale at times but the ship lay quietly. By daybreak it had backed four points and was quietening down. Evadne cooked up a substantial breakfast for everyone and once that had been cleared up the weather had eased sufficiently for them to get going again.

There was a brief holdup while the chief and Punch worked out how to get steam on the windlass, and another pause while the foc'sle party catted the anchor, swung it inboard and lashed down. It was a bumpy trip until they were able to turn north but that put the swell on the beam and VIC 5 showed a strong tendency to roll so much that they all had to hang on to keep their feet. With the Longships Lighthouse close abeam they were able to turn more north-easterly, putting the weather behind them and with the wind backing steadily it came off the land once more. VIC 5 surprised them by working up to eight and a half knots as they sailed up the North Cornish coast. That night it fell deepest black and with no lights to guide them there were a few anxious hours as they steamed ahead into complete darkness. In the early hours of the next morning, blindly pushing ahead, they found themselves in a really rough patch with stiff upright waves breaking over them; a thoroughly unpleasant half hour followed. Punch had joined Jane on the bridge, woken by the ship's motion. "The notes I was given suggest this must be Hartland Race, which at least tells us we're not going to go aground. Nasty place this for grounding."

Punch nodded. "That's some sort of good news, I s'ppose. Should we alter a little more to the east? Wouldn't want to bang into Lundy."

CHAPTER SIXTEEN: A Little Excursion

"That's debatable. I think we're getting between them as we are. I'll be glad of daylight."

By daylight Lundy and Hartland point were astern; their guardian angel had seen the ship pass safely between them in the dark and they pushed on to the east.

By mid-afternoon they were off Weston-Super-Mare and looking at their close-in navigation. "Apparently this Knightstone Island isn't an island any more. It's connected to the land with buildings on it, and the quay we're looking for is on its west side. Because of the huge tides here it dries out at half tide and next high water is half past eight tonight so we'll not get in before about six o'clock or so. Or at least that's what my notes say. Might as well slow down meantime. Can you see where this quay is?"

Punch was using their only pair of binoculars to scan the shore. "There's what looks like a clump of houses further out than the rest just on our starboard bow. Can you see them?"

Slowly they pushed their little ship towards the shore until the island that wasn't, was plainly visible. Suki now had the binoculars and suddenly shouted "Hang on, there's a boat like us in there. Look!"

"So there is. That's useful; my notes said there would be two of these little ladies doing the job. That must be the other one and our orders are to tie up alongside it."

Cautiously they nosed in; a toot on the whistle brought a couple of matelots out onto the other ship's deck and by the time they pulled in alongside the whole crew had turned out to greet them. An AB seemed to be in charge, ordering them about to get fenders out and be ready to receive VIC 5's mooring ropes. To Jane there was something naggingly familiar about him; another of the half-remembered faces that she struggled with.

Tying up completed, this half-remembered face came aboard and shook Jane by the hand. "Hello Jane, great to see you again."

'Oh Lordy' thought Jane, 'another one I should know'. She smiled at him and asked tentatively "Dunkirk?"

"That's right, Hooky Jane." That brought it all flooding back: on the beach sorting out an upturned whaler, towing it to and fro for a morning, and a killick in charge. "Of course! Hooky Tommy isn't it? Did you get back to *Venomous* all right? And what brings you here?"

"Like you I've been up and down the rates, got my chief's buttons but a complete arsehole of a lieutenant gave me such grief that I lost it and whacked him. Got a court-martial and six months in DQs as a result. They would have chucked me out of the Andrew completely if they weren't so short of men and I otherwise had a spotless record. Did you know this is a suicide job?"

"My story's the same but at least I only got thirty days' DQs. That was bad enough. And what's this about a suicide mission?"

"We're the guinea pigs for some clever new way of dealing with mines. Round the corner is Birnbeck Pier and a bunch of boffins have taken it over. They try out all sorts of clever new gadgets there. Now it's mines and too bad if they blow us up."

"So we are expendable? Oh dear, I don't think my crew know that. I was told we were day running; are we expected to live on board this primitive little thing?"

"Naw. You will see there is quite a community at *HMS Birnbeck* including a bunch of Wrens doing the catering. You'll be able to mess with them."

"That's something. It's probably too late to make our number today so we'll sleep on board for tonight then I'll have to find them in the morning. But I take it this is a snug enough lie for the boat?"

"Yes, safe enough. We leave one person on board overnight as a watchman just in case but nothing has happened so far. I'll be around in the morning and can show you where to go."

"Thanks Tommy, we'll do the same then. See you in the morning."

Jane was looking around when her Chief ERA appeared on deck, kitbag on shoulder. "Right, I've done my job and I'm off. Your two lads know the job now so you'll be all right. It's been easier working for you lot than I expected but enough is enough. Good sailing." And with that he swung down the pier to where a taxi was waiting. 'Ships that pass in the night,' thought Jane. 'I never even had a chance to thank him. Oh well, that's life in a blue suit I suppose.' And she turned to seeing everything settled for the night.

HMS Birnbeck proved to be a spindly walkway from the shore to a little island with a collection of buildings. Beyond that was a short pier of the sort that excursion paddle vessels tied up to before the war, disgorging their day trippers to sample the delights of Weston-Super-Mare. Disused since the start of the war, the Navy's Department of Miscellaneous Weapon Development (DMWD) had found it. This group of brilliant if eccentric boffins worked on many forms of equipment, no few of which were for use on or in water. Birnbeck proved ideal for their particular needs. The enormous tidal ranges of the Bristol Channel allowed them to work on items dried out on the seabed at low water, but underwater at high tide. Official permission to use the establishment having been given, it was taken in as another dry land frigate and the DMWD put it to good use throughout the war. Universally known as the "Wheezers and Dodgers", the department had an impressive collection of scientific and technical brains, but these civilians in uniform tended to have scant respect for naval protocol or ways of doing things. The glue that held them together was a fierce determination to contribute in any way they could to winning the war,

CHAPTER SIXTEEN: A Little Excursion

both developing new weapons and working out ways of countering enemy ones.

When Jane walked out the pier to report, she had no idea of the informal but driven atmosphere she was walking into. Enquiring around, she was told to report to a Lieutenant-Commander Richardson. Coming into his office she snapped off her best naval salute, smiled dazzlingly if lopsidedly, and reported in usual fashion. "Ah, so you're the Wrens we are getting for the anti-mine work. Do you know anything about mines?"

"No sir, we know a lot about boats and little ships and doing things with them, but the nearest we came to mines were a few that blew up in the Thames. Those were quite spectacular."

"Right. What I want to do is get both the VIC crews together and give them a short talk on what we're doing. It is to counter German magnetic mines. Can you assemble here this afternoon?"

"Yes sir, we'll be there."

From there Jane sought out the Wren third officer in charge of the domestic side of life at Birnbeck. She proved to be a rather harassed middle-aged lady far more interested in looking for some missing tins of rice pudding than in dealing with Jane. "Yes, what do you want?"

"We're the crew from VIC 5, the little ship which is going to be doing experimental work here for a few months. We'd like to victual in and mess here, please."

"Why? What's wrong with staying on your ship? I don't have time for any more Wrens here."

"The ship is a very basic little thing and we wouldn't make any more work for you, ma'am. We look after ourselves and just need accommodation and meals."

The third officer glared at Jane. "Sort it out with the chief. It's her people who will have to feed you."

"Thank you ma'am and I will do just that."

The chief proved to be much more amenable, seeing no problem with adding seven mouths to her catering, and she was able to point out an unused little room which they could treat as their own. There was a stock of bunk bed iron frames which Jane's crew would have to set up for themselves. The stokers could find quarters with the other matelots on the site.

With this fixed Jane headed back to VIC 5 and briefed everyone on what the arrangements would be. "I'd keep away from the third officer who seems unimpressed by having five of us landed on her."

As instructed the crews of both ships assembled in the mess hall at 1400. Lieutenant-Commander Richardson led the instructions. "Your work is going to be steaming your ships up and down over magnetic mines. As you doubtless know, degaussing ships to remove their magnetic signatures has successfully dealt with the magnetic mine menace. But we are trying to get one step further by projecting a magnetic field far enough ahead of a minesweeper to detonate a mine before it is close enough to damage an approaching ship. Your ships will be equipped with generators and special equipment to do this, and we will have scientific staff on board to work it. They may need some assistance from the ships' crews as the experimental rigs we will have on board are quite large and cumbersome. The whole ship is magnetised and our equipment then concentrates the magnetic field into projecting in a particular direction, in this case ahead of the ship.

"Now, magnetic mines work by detecting the change in the earth's magnetism as a metal object passes by, and actuating a trigger mechanism which in turn sets off the explosives. Our calculations indicate that we should be able to project the magnetic field about three hundred yards ahead of the ship which is close enough but is an adequate distance not to blow the ship up. We have a dozen unexploded German mines to use for testing purposes. Their explosives are still in them but we have disconnected them from the triggers so you should be safe unless Gerry has secreted some other means of setting them off. What we want you to do is steam your vessels along a prescribed line towards the mines which we have laid out on the intertidal strip here. By doing that we can get at them at low water when they are dried out and see if the de-activating has worked. This means in turn that you will only be able to work for a period over high water each day and we will have to see how much useful testing we can get done. Our experts will be experimenting with different settings and field strengths each day until we hope to get it right. We have provided for up to two months' work but expect to come to conclusions sooner than that.

We will start tomorrow morning putting our gear aboard your ships and hope to have it ready in two or three days. Thereafter we will plan to be working each daytime tide until we know something. I hope all that is clear. Any questions?"

It was Punch who spoke up. "If we sail right over the top of these mines, we could be triggering them closer than your three hundred yards. Doesn't that remove any way of telling whether your system has worked at the distance you want?"

"Good question. We may have to arrange something so that you peel off at three hundred yards rather than sailing in a straight line. At the moment the mines are laid out in a straight line. We'll have to see if that is the best way of arranging them. This is experimental work and we have to be prepared to change our approach at any time."

Questions over, both crews shifted their gear and got settled into shoreside accommodation. There were minor grumbles about the fairly basic provision but

CHAPTER SIXTEEN: A Little Excursion

it was better than trying to live on board the ship. Next morning a lorry drew up on the quayside, and the sailors on VIC 6 topped their derrick to swing aboard a sizeable generator followed by half a dozen units with dials and control wheels on them. The Wrens pulled VIC 5 along the quay and the process was repeated. The boffins then wired up the various units and once set up, started their generators. By the end of the day they had electricity running through the different units and warned that it would take several days to get everything calibrated and functioning properly. This seemed to Jane like a good chance to top up the bunkers but found no-one at Birnbeck in the least interested in coal. The Wrens in the galley ordered a dozen sackfulls at a time from a local coal merchant but that would not last for long as bunkers for the ship's boiler. It soon became clear that bunker coal was an item which had not been thought of, with the boffins uninterested and the harassed third officer much too busy with her domestic concerns to be interested. "It's your own problem and nothing to do with the Birnbeck setup." Suitably dismissed, Jane cabled a message to her favourite boats officer at Plymouth and he at least was able to take action, referring her to South-West Command which in turn referred her to the admiral commanding the North Devon coastal area. His technical chief dealt with the problem and a day later a lorry load of best Admiralty bunker coal drew up on the quayside. The contrast between this basic physical need and the fine tunings of the boffins setting up their equipment was stark. It meant another day of hard physical labour for the girls who alarmed the third officer by arriving back at their quarters covered in coal dust and in need of more hot water than the system was likely to deliver.

CHAPTER SEVENTEEN:
On Taking a Deep Breath

Several days of waiting with increasing impatience saw the VIC crews with immaculate ships but little else to do. In late afternoon Lieutenant-Commander Richardson came aboard, disappeared down the cargo hold to confer with the technicians then called Jane and Tommy together. "It looks like the equipment will be ready to go tomorrow, they just need a few final adjustments to have it all working properly. High tide tomorrow is 1427 in the afternoon, which means you should be afloat by midday or so. Can you be ready to come round to Birnbeck as soon as you are afloat and we'll finalise your activities? We need to put out buoys to mark the beginning and end of each range, then we'd like to try a first run or two to test everything."

The two captains nodded agreement "We'll be there."

The VICs, like their puffer forebears, had hulls designed for working off beaches and being able to slip away from berths as soon as they came afloat. So, on a bright and blustery day with just a few inches of water under them VIC 5 closely followed by VIC 6 eased away into deeper water, went round the corner and hove to just off the Birnbeck steamer pier where a group of boffins and matelots were waiting. There was some shouting and waving of arms, the message seeming to be that the ships should come alongside. There they loaded little yellow buoys with their ground gear and took on a mix of boffins and technicians including Lieutenant-Commander Richardson. "The mines are laid out in two lines bearing nor'-nor' east from either end of the pier here. What we want to do once we have laid the buoys, is for one ship then the other to run up its line of mines without the magnetic field equipment being switched on. We have wired the mines to send a signal to the shore when their fuses are activated so we will know right away if we have had any effect on them."

With buoys placed, VIC 6 took the first run with nothing happening, then VIC 5 followed up along the inshore line of mines. They had to go close to the pier to hear the results shouted across which caused Jane to casually remark "Y'know, if we had a walkie-talkie for contact with the shore, this would be a lot easier."

"Hmm" said Lieutenant-Commander Richardson, "You're right. We'll fix that." And four days later the ships had a day off while radios were installed on board. A similar set was placed in a small booth on the pierhead. With the radios in place and working, the operating of each run over the mines was greatly improved. Quickly they settled to trying various frequencies and strengths, but for the first couple of

CHAPTER SEVENTEEN: On Taking a Deep Breath

weeks results were disappointing with no obvious effect on the mines. It was decided to put small buoys on each mine so that the ship's distance from each one could be more accurately judged. Frustratingly, the mines were only priming when the ships passed over them; the attempts at projecting the magnetic field ahead were not succeeding. Lieutenant-Commander Richardson was joined by Commander Norway, an engineering expert with an aeronautical background and intense debate produced a lot of calculations but no results. Another boffin had been summoned to join the brains struggling to make sense of it. This proved to be a Wren second officer who Jane took one look at and exclaimed "Esther! What a co-incidence. Are you a boffin these days?"

Second Officer Goldstein smiled. "Yes, I suppose you could say so. My speciality is the physics of electricity and magnetism which is a very similar subject so I've been summoned to add my tuppence worth to the deliberations here."

"Well I never. We must catch up some time."

"Yes of course. I'm not sure how long I will be here but we can manage something."

After another day of experimenting with frustratingly negative results, the two crews debated the lack of success from a seamanship angle. Punch said "Oi wonder how wide their beam is. Half the time, to keep going along the line of buoys we're having to allow a bit of leeway. Oi'll bet the beam is missing the mines."

Jane picked up on this "You're right, y'know. Their beam points straight ahead so if we're not going directly at the mines, we must be missing them. What do you think, Tommy?"

"Sounds reasonable to me. They either need a wider beam or some way of pointing it."

Jane stood up, dropped her empty tea mug into the bucket and said "Right, I think we'll go and suggest this to them. C'mon, Punch, let's go and see the boffins now."

The two Wrens found the boffins working at a blackboard covered in chalky calculations. Giving Esther a friendly nod, Jane said, "Might we be allowed to suggest something? We've been debating the lack of success and wondered about something." She went on to explain about leeway and how they often had to allow some to keep to the mine line which meant that their bow was not pointing straight ahead. Might that mean that the magnetic beam was not pointing at the mines?

There was silence for a minute while the boffins looked at each other. "Well, it is a field rather than a beam but it is a directional one so you just might be on to something there. What do you suggest?"

"Can the field be widened without losing its strength? If you can cover a wider area, the leeway allowance would have to be very large to point the field away from the mines. Alternatively if you could direct the field so it always pointed along the line, you would get the same results."

"How very interesting. Thank you Beacon, you are onto something here."

"It was Johnson's idea, sir. By looking directly at the problem she often comes up with answers."

They all turned to look at Punch. "You are a remarkable young lady, Johnson. What education do you have?"

"Oh, a bit, sir. Oi did my leaving certificate and me dad always made me think first rather than just go rushing in. He is well known for thinking things through."

"Doesn't it just go to show that the best answer is often the simplest and all our brain power counts for very little by comparison. Thank you both for suggesting this. I think we need to do some more calculating to work out how we can widen the field, then figure out how we adapt the equipment but it certainly looks as though you may have cracked it. Thank you so much."

Jane waved a hand in a mock bow. "You're welcome."

While this experimental work was going on, Sparrer and Suki had been making enquiries of their own. It turned out that there was a lively social scene in Weston-Super-Mare because of the large RAF bases round about. "You know the Crabfats; they do like their little entertainments and the dances are pretty lively. The girls in the galley here go regularly and have a great time. The Winter Gardens on a Saturday night is supposed to be the best. Shall we try?"

Jane felt less than enthused by this but everyone else was for it so she allowed herself to be carried along on the wave of energy. It was the first time she had been dancing in a long time and by finding a few airmen who were good dancers she managed to enjoy it despite herself. Working this funny little ship was turning into one of her better postings; the boffins seemed happy as long as she produced the ship on the end of the mine line when it was expected. She had also made a point of getting to know her two stokers, without whom she would not have gone far. Willie and Joe had been rather left on their own to begin with, but when Jane suggested they might join the girls going dancing they did not need to be invited twice, and bit by bit they were drawn into the group.

B y now the high tides were morning and evening so the work was a couple of hours in the morning and a slightly longer session in late afternoon. The routine was the same: come round and heave-to close to the steamer pier to establish radio contact. Decide which ship would go first, and as it reached the end of its line the second ship set off. Circuits like this were kept up throughout the working period with the technicians varying their settings. With three different forces to drive and

CHAPTER SEVENTEEN: On Taking a Deep Breath

control the field to deal with this was a constant process, checking with the shore after each run to see if any effect had been observed, before they had to return to Knightstone Island's berths, squeezing in on the last of the falling tide. With no officer directly over them the two ships' crews enjoyed a good deal of freedom and the unmilitary but driven atmosphere at *HMS Birnbeck* was appreciated.

Continuing with their daily routine, VIC 5 took the first morning run and was coming to the end of its line when an enormous explosion shook the little ship. jane jumped and wheeled round to see a huge column of water and smoke towering up with VIC 6's bow peeping out of it. This bow slowly pointed into the air then slid backwards into the cloud.

"Punch, get the jolly boat swung out. Suki, get some ropes ready. Sparrer and Evadne, get ready to receive survivors." Even as she was giving the orders, a horrified Jane swung VIC 5 round and headed to the cloud, now settling down. Of Vic 6 there was no sign, just debris floating on the water. Two heads were swimming away from the debris field and a body could be seen floating in it. There was no sign of anyone else. The two live matelots were quickly recovered, shaken but more or less unharmed. One was a deckhand, the other a stoker who had popped up on deck for a quick smoke. The floating body could not be reached from the deck, so they topped the derrick, swung the jolly boat out and within minutes Punch had sculled over to the body in the water, pulling it in over the boat's stern. "Take him straight ashore," shouted Jane. She brought VIC 5 alongside the steamer pier where a large crowd had gathered. Sick in her stomach she called out "What on earth happened? Did one of the mines explode?" Lieutenant-Commander Richardson, with overall responsibility for the trials, was pale and shaking, near to tears. "Well, it must have but goodness knows how. What a disaster. We'll have to call off the trials while we investigate. Are you girls all right?"

Still trembling with the horror of it, Jane nodded mutely then stepped ashore. The body Punch had picked up was laid out on the pier where Jane could see it. This disaster just got worse. "Oh Tommy." She wailed. Another sad memory to add to the ever-lengthening list. He looked undamaged, his face smooth and body intact. 'I suppose the blast must have got him' she thought in a vague way. 'Gerry might not have done it directly but there's no escaping them, is there?'

With the onlookers dispersing Lieutenant-Commander Richardson made an effort to pull himself together and take control. "Beacon, I suppose you had better take your boat round to its berth and wait. It doesn't look as though we will be doing any more trials for a while."

By now Suki had joined them. "Do you know, I was with your technicians just as we turned away to go to the rescue and everything was working just as it should.

I'll bet we had got the mines to trigger as planned so what on earth caused one of them to explode right under the ship is a real mystery. Just as your plans were working in practice this happens. What a shame."

"That may be so but it looks like the whole way of working is too dangerous for everyday use. Quite apart from the uncertainty of it, if the system is going to set mines off right under the sweeper it's not something that is going to commend itself to the Admiralty."

"Well, shall we come back tomorrow and make the system work? At least you would have that to show for your efforts."

"Oh come on, we can't expect you to put your ship at risk like that."

"But we've been at risk like that since the start, haven't we?"

"We didn't think so. What is really disturbing is that we thought the explosives in the mines were completely disconnected and incapable of going off. What we missed is another puzzle to deal with. If one can explode like that presumably any of the others could too."

"Oh all right, we will go and park the ship for now, but it seems a shame to give up because of a setback, even a major one like this."

"The Admiralty will terminate our license to play with dangerous stuff very rapidly if we go blowing up their ships and sailors. They tend not to like that. We know it's wartime and risks have to be taken when we're looking for more clever ways of doing things, but there are limits."

With VIC 5 tied up on its own back on the Knightstone wharf, it was a subdued crew who brewed up and sat silently round the table. Eventually Punch spoke. "I s'ppose that's an end to it? Seems a shame really. What do you think, Jane? Could we go on?"

"Well maybe I could but I can't ask you lot to take a risk like that. I don't much care if it is dangerous after all the other things I've been through and lost, but you four have boyfriends and lives to live for. Surely you wouldn't want to put your lives on the line needlessly? And what about Willie and Joe?"

The two stokers had been as silent and reserved as ever. Willie shook his head slowly. "We just do what we're told. I don't think this is any different. If we're tasked with keeping the ship going up and down the mines, that's our orders and we'll do what we're told. Can't say I am awfully keen on the idea but if we have to do it, we will."

There was a thoughtful silence round the table, each person deep in their own reflections.

Back in the mess at Birnbeck the whole place had a subdued air to it. There

CHAPTER SEVENTEEN: On Taking a Deep Breath

had been a plan to go dancing in the town but somehow that didn't seem like the right thing to do any more. By now all of them had seen their share of death and destruction but this one was closer, more immediate and personal, with the thought that it could just as easily have been them who got blown up always at the back of their minds. As the tide ebbed the twisted remains of VIC 6 emerged. It was a scary sight. The little ship had been broken into two parts, with the forward part bent and mangled and the mast hanging over the side in abject apology. The after part was demolished: the boiler was poking out of the remains of the superstructure which had collapsed in on itself. The funnel had disappeared. At low water, a detail of matelots was sent to find and extract the dead bodies then there was a general survey. "The only good thing in this is that the ground is firm so we'll be able to get machinery out to it to remove the remains. What a mess."

Nothing more was said by VIC 5's crew but a silent determination grew up. Next morning there was a maximum effort to make VIC 5 as clean and shiny as possible, even the funnel was given a lick of paint over the rusty patches and a new blue ensign was hoisted. With the ship coming afloat Jane went round to the boffins' lair to report ready for duty, but found no-one there. Eventually she found the boffins in conclave and gave them her very best salute, "VIC 5 all ready to come round and carry on, gentlemen."

Lieutenant-Commander Richardson looked startled by this. "Oh, we weren't thinking of doing anything else until we worked out what had gone wrong. You can't be put at risk like that."

"Well sir, we have managed three weeks without any problems and yesterday we actually made the system work as you expected. It does seem a pity to give up just as we are succeeding."

"Success in one way perhaps but total failure in another."

"That is true but not a reason to give up. Let us at least try again today."

"Beacon I am staggered by your bravery but really the answer should be no."

"Leading Wren Brownlow has all the settings recorded and we know we can repeat what we did yesterday. You don't need to put your technicians aboard; we'll do it all. Just have someone manning the shore station."

Just then a tooting on a steam whistle had them looking out to see VIC 5 hove to just off the pier, her generator running and ready to go. "There you are, sir, let's go to it."

Until an hour after high water the little ship ran up its range of mines, Suki and Evadne in the hold working the instruments and Punch doing the ship handling while Jane kept up the communications and general oversight. Repeatedly they made the system work. With the mines in their own range all triggered at a safe distance they turned to VIC 6's row and made them work as well, taking care to avoid the battered wreck lying just below the surface. With the tide well into the ebb they finally gave up and squeezed onto their Knightstone berth with the last few inches of water to float them. They were all sitting in the foc'sle mess having a cup of tea when there was a hail from the shore. "VIC 5 ahoy! Can we come on board?"

The crew climbed up onto the deck to find Lieutenant-Commander Richardson with a couple of his assistants and an unknown Commander. "Yes of course, sir."

The Commander introduced himself in a Canadian twang as Commander Goodeve, in charge of all the Directorate of Miscellaneous Weapons Development. He had been appalled at the explosion the day before and had come rushing down from London to see what was going on. Jane briefed him on what they had done that day, Suki showed him her notes with the settings which had worked as they should and Punch explained their ship handling to achieve it. "Well I must say, it is remarkable of you young ladies to have gone out there today and proved the system. I was watching you from the shore and fully expected you to be blown up at any moment."

Jane smiled. "We didn't think that was likely, sir. We had been over those mines hundreds of times by today without any mishap and we think yesterday's disaster was a rogue happening. So our calculation was that we should be pretty safe and that has been proved."

"You had better come round to Birnbeck and we'll go through this more fully."

A couple of hours careful debrief followed, showing all their workings and results. At the end of it Commander Goodeve said decisively, "Right, these trials are now concluded. You can return to your own base with our deepest thanks plus admiration for your bravery today. That was a quite exceptional thing to do, especially as it allowed us to see the system can actually work. We will consider these results but my immediate instinct is that it is a risky way of sweeping magnetic mines when we have degaussing to fall back on as an effective way of neutralising the things. But well done and again my thanks."

A calmly self-confident Leading Wren had been with the Commander, saying nothing but monitoring closely what was going on. As the meeting broke up, she came across to VIC 5's crew and introduced herself. "I'm Frances Randall. I've been working with this outfit for a little while now, specialising in unmanned target aircraft models but I lend Commander Goodeve a hand from time to time with other matters when Wrens are involved. He wasn't at all sure what he would find down here so brought me along to have a look but I must say you seem to be thoroughly organised anyway. You've obviously done a lot of work on boats already and what you did today was outstanding. I'll just tell him to let you get on with the job."

This was addressed to Punch as the senior crew member. Then Randall looked at Jane's medal ribbons quizzically. "Are you the Dunkirk Wren by any chance?"

Jane smiled. "Yes, you could say so."

"No wonder you were willing to take a chance today, then. For sheer naked courage, to go out today knowing that you could be blown up at any time was quite exceptional. But I suppose you are used to that."

"I don't think you ever get used to it, but it's no worse than a soldier going over the top knowing that a machine gun may be waiting to chop him into bits. This war has got us women much closer to dangerous action, y'know."

"I suppose that's so but it was still an awfully brave thing to do. I think Commander Goodeve is still a bit shaken up by seeing you out there today sailing up and down."

PART FIVE:
BEYOND SURVIVAL

CHAPTER EIGHTEEN:
Eastward Ho!

There was a flat feeling in VIC 5's crew as they came aboard the next morning. Suddenly there was no high demand on them, no tests to run or danger to defy. The ship was immaculately clean anyway so polishing the brass offered little in the way of occupation. "I had better call Plymouth and see what they want done with the ship," said Jane but no-one paid much attention. She took herself off to Birnbeck and the upshot of various phone calls was that they were to take the ship back to Plymouth then be ready for fresh deployments. Jane arranged for the technicians to come and remove their equipment from the hold, ordered two lorry loads of coal and arranged victualling for two weeks. With all this in place there was even less to do so she declared a make-and-mend and left everyone to their own inclinations. Next day they topped the derrick up and piece by piece the equipment which had been so central to their activities was dismantled and swung ashore. Another day and the coal turned up; at least that gave them some direct physical exercise, shovelling it from the lorries onto the deck of the ship and from there into the bunker. With the bunker full a small amount was left over so they stowed that in the aft end of the hold as a reserve, took the rations on board which had been sent from Birnbeck and they were ready for sea. Jane had a final visit to the Boffins to make sure there was nothing else wanted before VIC 5 left. The answer being no she arranged to sail next day on the morning high tide at 1130. Kitbags were tossed on board, Willie and Joe confirmed that all was ready below and they sailed on time. On an overcast but clear day Jane and Punch smiled at each other on the little bridge. "Well, that was a bit different. Were you as scared as I was when we went onto the mine runs after the explosion?"

"Oi didn't like to say anything but I really thought we were pushing our luck with that. So yes, I was scared stiff but bloody determined not to show any weakness. Oi think we managed to impress those boffins."

Which was a major understatement. Commander Goodeve had stood on the pier and watched the latter part of their proving runs, terrified that they were about to be blown up. Goodeve did not lack courage himself and danger was met with a laugh throughout his organisation. But the thought of a group of Wrens being blown up for his benefit troubled him greatly. In his role in charge of the Wheezers and Dodgers, Commander Goodeve had made a point of establishing extremely good connections throughout the Naval world, and beyond that into politics. So when he briefed concerned admirals on the magnetic field project, he emphasised how brave the Wren crew of VIC 5 had been. To go out and make the system work immediately after the other ship had been blown up doing exactly the same thing was, in his estimation, an act of extreme cool courage equal to anything he had seen from men in this war. His briefing note reached Churchill's desk and he was summoned to the presence to explain in more detail what it was all about. "Those girls deserve some sort of recognition for service beyond any call of duty. They were amazingly calm and brave about the whole thing." Churchill said nothing but made a note to set wheels in motion.

Meantime, 'those girls' had set watch and plodded down the north coast of Devon and Cornwall. With Hartland Point and Lundy cleared as dark fell, they sailed on through the night. Jane had seen a weather forecast before she left giving strong southerly winds so made a point of keeping close to the coast for shelter. But by the time they were coming abeam of St Ives Bay it was blowing hard and the prospects for getting round Land's End were not good. With no specific deadlines to meet, Jane and Punch agreed that it was silly to try to bash their way round Land's End into the teeth of a gale, so pulled into St Ives Bay and anchored, finding a snug lie off the harbour pier end. VIC 5 ranged about and did not lie comfortably to her anchor but it held and the crew were able to keep watch easily. Jane and Suki on the middle watch made Kye then settled down in the shelter of the bridge surround. "D'you think we did a decent job there?" queried Suki.

"Oh I'm sure of it. Those boffins seemed really pleased with our results at the end and I think they were a bit surprised that we didn't let any danger put us off. What do you think of being a boat Wren these days?"

"I love it, Jane. I wrote to Dad just before we left and he has been fascinated by the way we were running a proper little ship. Even Algie has been really encouraging despite us challenging his traditional views on women. He's a sweetie really but getting him into the twentieth century has been an uphill task. I see trouble ahead if we ever set up home together."

"Oh, got that far, has it?"

"Well maybe. He's keen enough but unless he stops trying to boss me around there's going to be a limit to it all. What about you? Welcome to the widows' club."

"Thanks. It's strange: I really loved David with a passion but his going has had an unreality to it so it has hardly touched me. I do wonder if I was ever in love with the person or just in love with love."

"It has always seemed to us that you looked forward not back and your commitment to the job was so overwhelming that nothing much else ever got a look in. We took bets on whether you would get to the altar with him or go chasing off after another boat to drive."

CHAPTER EIGHTEEN: Eastward Ho!

"Much good that did me. These past six months have been the worst of my life and even this job we've had now is only a sticking plaster. Bloody Navy. I do wonder at times why I love it so much. Oh well, I suppose life will go on. How about some more kye?"

VIC 5 lay for two days before the deep summer depression moved away and the wind eased off. They picked up the anchor and rolled their way round Land's End in a huge swell left behind by the gale. Once round the Lizard conditions were easier and Vic 5 berthed in Devonport in late evening after a smart passage. There was no-one around so they settled on board and next morning Jane called on the boats officer.

"Ah Beacon, welcome back. You appear to have been a big success with the boffins at Birnbeck, so congratulations. I'm afraid we have no further orders for you yet so just stay on board and we'll let you know what is decided."

"Aye aye sir."

And for a couple of days they waited patiently, apparently ignored by the mighty naval machine. Jane took the opportunity for a night off and visited her father who she found still a bit lost and lacking drive. The death of his life-time partner had hit him hard and Jane suspected that had it not been for the demands of his patients keeping him occupied, he would have been very low. Her brother David had now completed his time at Dartmouth and was eagerly waiting for an appointment. Sister Sarah had come top in her year and was captain of the lacrosse team, but was still talking about joining the Wrens as soon as she was old enough. Jane noted that Eunice was getting ever closer to living openly with her father and seemed to be moving into the role of keeping household and family together rather than just being the cook.

There was mail for VIC 5's crew. Jane's included a letter from the lawyers enclosing a statement showing her finances, and a passionate one from Dora. Wrapped up in the job, Jane had barely thought of Dora in the last weeks and it was a serious jolt to be reminded that her personal life now had complications of a new and different kind. Where the rest of her crew had been in touch one way or another with boyfriends, Jane now had a different sort of girlfriend who clearly expected a similar response from her.

A messenger arrived on board in the middle of day three of their idleness, telling Jane to call at the boats office right away. After the usual formalities, the boats officer said "Right, Beacon, we have orders for your next move. You are to take VIC 5 to Portsmouth and hand it over to the auxiliary service there. There will be further orders for you all when you get there. Are you ready for sea?"

"Not far off, sir. We'll need bunkers again and a bit more food but that should

167

be all. The ship is running very well."

"That's good. You can sail as soon as you are ready."

"Will we be joining a convoy? I would have thought VIC 5 was just big enough to attract the attentions of our German friends so independent running might be inviting trouble."

"Good question. I'll have a word with the routeing people and let you know."

A truckload of coal was alongside the ship the next morning and the usual heavy shovelling saw it all stowed away safely. Bathed and rigged in clean clothes they took a food delivery and were ready for sea. Next, an RNVR lieutenant called on board to hand Jane an envelope with sailing instructions. "You are to sail as soon as you can and proceed independently. We think that so long as you stick close to the coast you are not likely to be troubled. German movements have been low recently and we are not expecting that they will bother expending a torpedo on anything as small as this. Have a nice trip."

"Well thanks. We'll work on it."

It is one hundred and twenty-seven miles from Plymouth to Portsmouth; Jane wanted to round Start Point and to arrive at The Needles in daylight. So she planned to leave Plymouth at 1830, make an overnight passage and arrive in the early morning. Travelling in the dark should also make VIC 5 less visible to any lurking enemy craft. Being high summer meant that the night hours were short but sufficient to allow the most exposed bit of the trip to be in the dark. They slipped from their berth, headed out as planned and ran down to Prawle Point in the gathering dusk. It was hazy with visibility limited to perhaps two miles or so but was sufficient to make a passage.

Overnight they kept watch and plodded on. Jane and Suki had taken the first watch, then relieved Punch and Sparrer again at five in the morning. Slowly the first hint of daylight came creeping. Suki cocked her head. "D'you hear anything Jane? Might be a heavy diesel engine."

Jane listened. "Yes. There might be something there. We'd better keep our eyes open." Suddenly a long low motorboat emerged from the mist, catching up with VIC 5 rapidly. As soon as it was sighted it opened fire, hitting VIC 5 with light calibre shell fire. These blasted holes in her sides and upperworks, sending splinters flying. Suki groaned and fell in a heap. The other girls came rushing out of the foc's'le even as VIC 5 heeled over to the inrushing sea. "Punch" screamed Jane "Boat lashings off."

VIC 5 fell onto her beam ends, the German boat stopped firing, and as suddenly as it started VIC 5 sank in silence other than the roar of outrushing air being expelled from her hull. As the sea rose over them Jane grabbed an unconscious Suki and swam away. But Punch had done her job and released the jolly boat which now

CHAPTER EIGHTEEN: Eastward Ho!

floated peacefully a few feet away, the others clinging to its sides. From there the shocked girls found it was too high to pull themselves in easily. "Punch, hang on to the stern, let the others climb over you and get in." With Sparrer and Evadne in, the next job was to haul the unconscious Suki in. With some difficulty this was done and she was laid on the bottom boards. "Right Punch, your turn next." With both girls in the boat pulling hard, Punch herself using her considerable strength to lever herself up and with Jane pushing from below they succeeded. Immediately Punch turned to take hold of Jane. "Last time I did this was on the Thames and I did my back a serious damage. C'mon girls, take a side." And between them they hauled Jane in. The German E-Boat had lain close by watching this without offering to help. It now hailed them. "Who are you?"

"Just the crew of a little stores boat sailing along the coast. Nothing special."

Jane's voice must have been recognisable. "*Mein Gott.* Are you wimmins?"

Jane wasn't sure if it was a good idea to admit to this but decided there was no point in denying it. "Yes, we are."

"*Gott in Himmel.* Is England so desperate it is sending its wimmin to war?"

"Not really. We were just a little stores boat. Nothing aggressive."

The machine gun which had been pointed at them was put away. "The German Navy does not make war on wimmins. *Auf Wiedersen.*" And with a roar of engines the E-boat shot off leaving them drifting in silence. This whole drama had only taken twenty minutes.

The crew of VIC 5 looked at each other. "Hang on. Where are Willie and Joe?"

"Doesn't look like they got out. It was all so quick they probably never had a chance."

"How sad. They were a nice pair."

"Even sadder that that counts for nothing in a war. What do we do now?"

They were all dripping wet, shivering with cold and shock as they huddled together in the middle of the boat. "Hope to be rescued, I suppose. We can't be far from Portland here."

And within half an hour they heard the sound of engines coming across the water. "Let's hope these are friendly ones." The hope was fulfilled as a harbour gun boat pulled alongside and took them off. A stretcher was passed over and Suki – still unconscious – was strapped into it. Jane went onto the boat's little bridge to introduce herself and ask that the jolly boat be towed in too. The gunboat's skipper was equally startled to discover that he had rescued a crew of women. "Gun fire was heard out to seaward so we were sent to investigate. What on earth are you lot doing out here? It can be dangerous round these parts if Gerry is on the prowl. Did they get you?"

"I'm afraid so. An E-boat just came out of the mist with all guns blazing. Our little ship didn't stand a chance and we were sunk in less than five minutes. I must say I am glad to see you guys."

An hour later they were tied up in Portland, an ambulance had taken a still unconscious Suki off to hospital with the rest of the crew going along for minor patching up. Jane was summoned to explain herself to the duty officer; dripping gently she ran through the morning's events again then made arrangements for her crew to get baths, emergency clothing and breakfast, in that order. Their appearance in the mess caused a minor sensation, with bandages and stitches off-setting their haphazard array of clothing. From there events moved quickly. A day later the whole crew were despatched to Portsmouth, that being where they had been bound; there they were debriefed and kitted out again. Punch had her usual problem with getting any uniform big enough to fit her but the Pompey clothing store managed to dig up enough to make one full uniform. Punch had some entertainment when it came to underwear. She was startled when they produced a box of brassieres and invited her to take as many as she wanted. These had been lying in the store since the Wrens were re-constituted, ordered by some matron who seemed to think that Wrens in general were much bigger than reality. These were all enormous, some even too big for Punch, and she was amused to be invited to take as many as she wanted so the store could get rid of them. While there, they were all provided with one uniform hat. Jane asked if anyone would like a second one and finding that everyone would she happily paid for these, writing out a cheque for four pounds eleven shillings and sevenpence.

While at Portsmouth Merle managed to catch up with them; she had been held up by another serious legal case but managed a day to talk to them all.

"You are all entitled to two weeks survivors' leave, then you will be re-assigned. I presume you would like to stay together as a boat's crew? Beacon will go to some other project and Johnson can take command again. I think you may be assigned to Chatham but that is not final yet." She turned to Evadne. "Do you have anywhere you can go for leave?"

Evadne smiled. "Oh yes, ma'am, I do now. My boyfriend's family have invited me to stay with them on their farm any time and that's where I will go. We're going to get engaged sometime soon."

"Now that is good news. You come from a farm in Rhodesia, don't you?"

"I do indeed. We're both farmers in naval uniform so have a lot in common. My family have invited him to come out to Rhodesia once this wretched war is over and there's correspondence between the two farms about what we could co-operate on to mutual benefit."

Merle then turned to Jane. "I need to talk to you privately but it doesn't have

CHAPTER EIGHTEEN: Eastward Ho!

to be today. Where will you be going?"

"I think I'll come up to Town. I have a fair bit of business to attend to plus needing to replenish my kit and whatever you may want."

"That's fine. I hope you all enjoy your leave then. Do try to take a proper break; you have all been very busy lately and incredibly brave, if the commendations from Commander Goodeve are any guide."

CHAPTER NINETEEN:
Going Close

Jane was startled and had to remind herself of her alternative surname when Dan the chauffeur greeted her at Paddington as Milady. Coming into the flat she had a sense of belonging which had never quite been there before. Lady Ormond cast an appraising eye over her. "Your uniform looks as though it has been having a hard time of it. What have you been up to this time?"

"Oh, just being sunk in the Channel. Nasty things, e-boats."

"So it would seem. Dinner in half an hour."

After a pleasant evening trying not to give away too much about the experimental work she had been doing, Jane nevertheless slept badly despite the softness of her deep feather bed. Shells smashing into her surroundings and the sea coming up to meet her set off her nightmares again and she awoke feeling more tired than when she had gone to bed. So she was up early for a bath and thorough hair wash; somehow a salty stickiness had been clinging to her since the sinking. Jane had little inclination to do anything; a quick phone call to Merle confirmed that there was no urgency for her to go into headquarters right away so Jane surrendered to her lethargy and lay down again. Lying there, tense as a taut wire but utterly exhausted, she kept getting fits of the shakes as visions of VIC 5 breaking up under the hail of shells kept rising up in her mind. Late in the afternoon Lady O swept into Jane's bedroom, looked at the heap on the bed and said "You have been through far too much recently and could do with some medicating. I'm going to ask my doctor to come and see you in the morning."

"Well that's very kind of you but really there's nothing that a bit of peace and relaxation won't deal with."

"Be that as it may, I think we might just help the process along a bit. Seeing you in this state troubles me a lot. No matter how tough we think we are, there are limits to how much any of us can take and you look perilously close to yours. A bit of help might be beneficial."

Just to show that there was really very little wrong with her, Jane stirred herself to dress and join Lady O for dinner but was fairly monosyllabic at the table.

Lady Ormond's doctor was predictably smooth and sympathetic in a Harley Street way. He carried out the usual checks and confirmed that there was nothing physically wrong with her. 'I could have told him that,' thought Jane but kept quiet. He prescribed a strong sedative and recommended a few days bed rest before he

CHAPTER NINETEEN: Going Close

retired for coffee with Lady O.

Emerging from a drugged haze three days later, it occurred to Jane that one week of her survivor's leave was gone already and she had better stir herself to deal with the outside world. Feeling much better she arranged to go and see Merle the following day then set up a meeting with David's lawyers to review her finances. Having got up she called on the tailors to arrange a new tiddly uniform then collected her replacement ration books, finding she had an extra clothing allowance to replace the gear lost with VIC 5. With these practicalities attended to she had had enough and retreated back to the flat's comforts and a better night's sleep.

Sitting across from Merle's desk had a feeling of familiarity about it too. "Good to see you again, Jane. You look a bit peaky. Are you sure you are all right? Being sunk like that must have been pretty horrible."

"Bad enough but I am getting over the nightmares now. What news?"

"Your crew are all well, as far as I know. Did you hear about Suki? It turned out she has a fractured skull: all fixed now and they reckon she will make a full recovery but is likely to be off for a month or so yet. It seems that a shell grazed her head in passing and that did the damage. In a sense she was lucky; a quarter of an inch closer and it would have gone into her with fatal results."

"Oh, poor girl. Was her brain affected?"

"Only in the short term. I spoke to her on the phone yesterday and she seemed pretty bright. The doctors tell me she will make a full recovery so we keep our fingers crossed."

"Where is she now?"

"Still in hospital in Portland. There is talk of her being sent home to convalesce in a fortnight's time so you will be without her for a while yet."

"Does that mean the *Kittiwake* crew are doing another job together?"

"In the short term yes. By arrangement with Superintendent Carpenter at Chatham you will be going to Dover again, but just to pick up a picket boat and take it to Chatham. There you will come out of her and leave Johnson in charge. After that there are several projects the Navy is trying to make its mind up about, and until it does I am afraid we don't know what you will be doing in the longer term. You can be sure it won't be dull."

"After recent happenings, a bit of dull might be quite welcome."

Merle laughed at this. "Yes, Jane I am sure you think so but I bet it wouldn't take long for you to get very bored. Change of topic. We have been sounded out about their awarding you something special for your bravery running over the mines. What do you think?"

"Y'know, we didn't think it was all that dangerous. We'd been over those mines dozens of times before we finished without any trouble and the fact that one rogue blew up the other boat didn't make our mines suddenly more dangerous. But I suppose they will do what they see fit. One thing, though: I'm not having anything unless all the crew get recognised. They were just as much at risk and just as willing to carry on, perhaps even more so than I was. So make sure whoever 'they' are, understand that."

"Yes Jane, we'll fix that. Now, how about some lunch?"

Lunch the next day was grander. David's lawyers, she still couldn't think of them as hers, talked her through her finances then swept her off to lunch. It was Simpson's again, evidently a preferred refreshment place for them. It was some time later before she discovered that the bill for the lunch was quietly charged to her account. Next, it was meeting with Lady Ormond's lawyers to formalise the arrangements for Jane to acquire a quarter interest in the flat and to sign on for her trustee role. This seemed to please Lady O and she took Jane to the Ritz for lunch. Jane quietly reflected that after this fine dining, going back to plain Naval fare was going to be a bit of a come down. The next day a letter from Wren headquarters confirmed the details of her next job and enclosed a travel warrant to Dover. Her survivor's leave was nearly finished.

Coming into the wrennery at Dover had a sense of returning to an old home, the same quarters officer greeting her in friendly fashion. She looked enquiringly at Jane. "Last time I saw you, you were a petty officer. Now you are a plain Wren. What happened."

"You didn't hear about my court martial?"

"No, can't say I did."

"I smacked an officer and they took a dim view of that. Reduced back to ordinary Wren. But I still get used as though I was a petty officer so life is supportable."

"I hope you won't do anything like that here?"

"No, ma'am, there was enormous provocation which is why they kept me in the outfit at all. And we're only here for a few days anyway before we take a boat away."

"Yes, so I gather. The rest of your crew are due later today."

And by evening they had all assembled in the cabin allotted to them while they were in Dover.

Next morning they went to the boat steps, reported to the same old familiar chief in the boats office, and looked at their new charge. Picket boat 171 was one of the later boats, mercifully oil fired so no heavy coaling up to do. A wisp of steam at her brass bound bell mouth funnel suggested someone was on board already so they boarded her and looked around. A petty officer stoker emerged and looked at them. "Do you girls want something?"

CHAPTER NINETEEN: Going Close

"I don't know about want but we're here to take this thing to Chatham. Are you coming with us?"

"You what? You're not saying you are the crew, are you?"

Punch laughed. "Yes, P.O, we are, so get used to the idea."

"Blimey, what's the world coming to? A bunch of girls for a crew. Have you done anything like this before?"

Punch pointed the lanyard across her chest. "See that? It means we are boat crew Wrens and yes, we have done a lot of this before. Don't worry, we know what we are doing."

"I don't like this one little bit. I think I'm going to ask for a transfer."

"Oh don't be silly. We've done longer trips than this perfectly well. Relax, P.O. You are in safe hands."

Jane now chipped in. "Are you ready to go, down below? Got fuel and engine in good order?"

"Don't worry, that part is all ready. She is steaming well and the engine is sweet as a Rolls."

"Good, so we'll make a nice fast passage. It is only round the corner to Chatham, after all. We'll aim to be off day after tomorrow, weather permitting."

But the weather was not encouraging. A stiff Easterly blew up which would make the first part of the trip difficult to say the least. Jane was on board early afternoon, debating with Punch whether to delay sailing by a day, when a Lieutenant-Commander came to the steps and hailed them. "There's a gun boat in trouble round the corner, gone ashore and breaking up. The lifeboat's out on a rescue already and this is the next best boat. Can you go and get her crew off?"

"Good Lord, we can try but it's no day to be messing about inshore. We'll need a little while to get full steam up then we can give it a go."

"That's the spirit. Get going as soon as you can."

Jane's P.O. stoker had been beside her while this conversation went on. She turned to him. "Jimmy, can you get a full head of steam up as quickly as possible? And make sure everything is well tied down. We'll be bouncing about all over the place."

"Righto. This will test whether you lot are any good or not." By 1942 the steam picket boat was an elderly type which had once been the mainstay of boats in the fleet but had been superseded by motorboats. With the pressing needs of wartime those that had survived were kept in service and doing a useful job throughout. They were long and narrow which meant that, although they were good sea boats in general, they rolled heavily if across the swell.

Twenty-five minutes later there was a full head of steam to power the engine and, with their heaviest foul weather gear on, the crew slipped the moorings. Coming through the harbour entrance they got a foretaste of the conditions, bouncing and rolling even as they cleared the breakwater ends. Jane rapidly found that the steering position on these old picket boats was very exposed, a canvas dodger round it giving little protection. A short length of rope was found and she tied herself to the rail just in case.

They made slow progress butting into the heavy seas rolling in, and the ten miles they had to cover seem to take an age, but soon enough they saw the unfortunate gun boat, being pounded on a bank just off the beach. With the cliffs rising behind it, the shore is steep-to around South Foreland which meant that there was plenty depth of water to get in close to the gun boat and it was only a matter of not being overwhelmed by the seas. On those cliffs a crowd of onlookers had gathered to watch the drama. With whipping spray from breaking wave crests and driving rain making it difficult to see much, Jane and Punch surveyed the position. "I think I'll back her in, keeping head to weather and hope to pick them up over the stern. The way those seas are breaking over her we wouldn't last two minutes ourselves if we went beam on."

Punch nodded. "That's as good a bet as any. I'll take charge at the stern and grab them on board. We'll need to get some of them up to the forr'd cabin which might be tricky. I'll rig a lifeline across this gap in the middle."

"Good thinking. As soon as you've done it, I'll turn and back in. That boat isn't going to last much longer."

With the bow into the seas Jane eased the old picket boat astern. She had warned her P.O. stoker that there would a lot of engine movements to keep the boat pointing the right way, and as she backed in frequent corrections were needed. From about fifty yards off the seas were breaking and fierce crests were threatening to come on board but so long as she could keep the boat head into them, it was riding over them. One yard from the gun boat, there was a roaring chaos of wind and sea and the looming remains of the gun boat. Jane gave a burst ahead to make sure she did not fall down onto it too heavily, then let her boat be blown astern until virtually touching. The picket boat was pitching and rolling violently which meant that one moment her stern was up in the air above the wrecked gun boat, the next it plunged down below it. Quite apart from the danger of the picket boat's stern snagging on the gun boat and tipping it up, timing a jump across from one boat to the other was tricky, with a danger of being crushed for anyone who got it wrong and fell in. Punch stood there timing the movement and shouting "jump" as the stern rose each time but the gun boat's crew were competent seamen who understood Punch's calls and managed the gap without difficulty.

Jane rang for minimum ahead revs on the engine just to keep her off. The gun boat's crew was assembled and ready and as the gap closed, they came jumping onto the picket boat to Punch's yelled instructions. Grabbed by Punch, they were directed up the starboard side deck to Evadne amidships then to the little hatch into the fore cabin where Sparrer was stuffing them down into it. After about a dozen had transferred, the picket boat took a sheer which Jane could not control immediately. Wrenching the wheel hard over and giving a burst on the engine she managed to get the old picket boat head to weather again but she had now drifted off the remains of the gun boat. Five minutes of tricky dancing sideways, keeping her head to weather, allowed Jane to ease astern again until virtually touching the remains. Again, the assembled crew came jumping over, one at a time in quick succession. These Punch shoved straight into the after cabin. The last man off insisted on coming to Jane even as she was pulling away from the perilous position. "Thank, you, thank you!" he roared, "My engines failed. This is fantastic seamanship."

"You're welcome, now would you please go below."

He laughed and made a mock bow before retreating to the after cabin.

Once clear of the breaking inshore waves, Jane turned to the west and, running before the weather, covered the distance to Dover in quick time. As they passed the breakwater ends the same man emerged. "Would you please take us to the gun boat berths." And he waved towards the Eastern harbour where other fast attack craft were lying.

It is common for seamen who have endured heavy weather and difficult conditions to sit stupefied, doing very little, once they have tied up safely. So once picket boat 171 had arrived, nothing much happened for a few minutes, before the rescued crew began to emerge and climb onto the MTB Jane had tied up to. One by one they shook hands with Jane and her crew then straggled ashore. A small group of what looked like very senior officers had formed on the quay and greeted the shore-going crew as they landed. With the last of them gone these senior officers climbed over the MTB and boarded 171. A tall lean officer with a bushy moustache had admiral's bars on his shoulders so Jane stood to attention and saluted as he came to her. He shook her hand warmly. "I just wanted to thank you for rescuing my countrymen. That was a remarkable feat of seamanship and will be recognised."

By now the rain had stopped and in the relative shelter of the dock she took her sou'wester off showing her head more clearly; her crew followed. This caused a sensation. "Good God, are you women?"

"Yes sir, boat crew Wrens."

"But that is amazing. I would not have thought it possible for women to do what you have done."

"Well sir, why not? You have just seen that we can."

"I watched you from the cliff top and every moment I thought you were going to be overwhelmed by the seas but somehow you contrived not to be. How did you manage it?"

"Oh, just by keeping her head to sea and close manoeuvring."

"Well that is something special. My country understands seamanship and I have never seen anything like it, particularly by women."

"You are welcome sir. What country are you from?"

"From Norway."

"So the men we've just rescued are all from Norway too?"

"Oh yes." This tall lean admiral seemed agitated. He fished around under his raincoat and produced a medal. "Here, it gives me great pleasure to award this to you." And he stabbed its pin into her oilskin.

"Good heavens. That is very kind sir. Are you sure it is all right to do that?"

The admiral seemed amused by this. "Yes, I am quite sure. I see my flag lieutenant is getting agitated for us to go but I will see you again, young lady."

Once the group had gone ashore a young Royal Naval lieutenant who had been with the party came back to Jane. He smiled, obviously amused. "Do you know who you have just been talking to?"

"Well, some Norwegian admiral."

"Rather more than that. You have just been awarded a medal by King Haakon of Norway."

"Good Lord. Well I never. Did you hear that girls? It seems we are famous in Norway now. I thought perhaps it was someone playing a game with a spoof medal, but it seems it is real."

"Oh it is real all right. I don't know what it is, but I'll find out and let your people know about it."

"The person to speak to is second officer Merle Baker at Wren headquarters. She looks after things like that for me."

"Right, I will do that."

They moved 171 back to the boat steps, and after all that the only thing left to do was to shed their oilskins and have a cup of tea.

CHAPTER TWENTY:
Recognition

After the excitements of the day before, the passage to Chatham was routine. The Easterly gale had blown itself out and with conditions quiet they made good progress. There was an uneasy moment as they passed the remains of the gun boat; stray bits of timber sticking up and the two engines still sitting upright were not much of a marker for what had been a sturdy little craft. Through The Downs, the inshore channel between the Goodwin Sands and the Kent coast, then on round North Foreland saw them tying up outside the dock entrance to Chatham Dockyard fourteen hours after leaving Dover. They found a dockside pub and had a celebratory drink (or two), had fish and chips for a *dinner adieu* then Jane said farewell to her closest shipmates before catching a late train up to London. Dan the chauffeur was patiently waiting and just after midnight Jane was tucked up in what she was coming to regard as her bed.

Lady Ormond caught her at breakfast. "I hear you have had yet another demanding adventure. You really must ease off a bit. No-one can keep up that level of pressure indefinitely and I would hate to see you crack up completely."

"Well thanks Lady O but this one wasn't my idea, y'know. We were ordered to make a rescue and with people's lives at stake, really I couldn't not do it. Fortunately, my little plan worked for if it hadn't, we would probably have needed rescuing as well."

"Which is all very well but if it hadn't worked, I suspect you might have been in deep trouble. It is high time you took a complete break and let the stress drain away and I will have no hesitation about saying so to those who make the decisions."

"This is all very kind of you but I really would prefer it if you didn't do too much interfering on my behalf. My experience of the Navy so far tells me that they take a dim view of people pulling strings and seeking favouritism."

"Jane! This is not favouritism; it is concern for your health when the strain is showing clearly on your face. I happen to have easy access to the higher echelons of the naval world and see no reason why that should not be used to preserve your health. Do not argue with me. Apparently, you have a reputation in the Wrens for arguing and I can see why. You may be quite sure that I know the difference between caring for your interests and interfering and will be careful to watch what I do. Now, what are proposing to do today?"

"Well I'd better phone Wren HQ to see what they have in store for me. Then if I'm not wanted immediately, I have a pile of neglected correspondence which I thought I'd have a go at."

"I hope they do not want you right away. You really must ease off a bit so just go gently at your mail." Responding to her phone call, Merle told Jane to come to HQ the following Monday which gave a few unstructured days. Some minor shopping, topping up on items lost when VIC 5 was sunk, and clearing her correspondence backlog seemed comparatively relaxed and easy-going to Jane. She had dinner with Louise, the nurse she had rescued from Dunkirk, who was as dryly witty as ever once she relaxed, and met Camilla whose cyphering work seemed all-consuming. She was full of excitement as she was listed to go on one of the 'monsters'; the giant passenger liners which ran throughout the war as troopships across the Atlantic, on their own and unescorted, because they were too fast for the U-boats to be able to catch them. Each carried a small unit of Wrens as cypher officers and coding Wrens handling all incoming radio traffic; it was a highly prized appointment and competition among those eligible was politely fierce. "It's such a privilege to get this appointment," she enthused "And after it I might have a little feeling for what your life is like."

"Well I suspect that life on one of the monsters will be a bit different from running around in boats but what an opportunity."

Camilla smiled, happily lost in her own dreams.

Merle was much more business-like and came to the point directly. "A decision has been made to ease the pressure on you for a while. Your next assignment will be to go round those ports that have boat crew Wrens in them, see how they are getting on and then come into headquarters to write a report on your findings, now we are past the experimental stage. We are allowing a week in each port and a fortnight here but that is flexible and it is no problem if you want longer.

Two bits of good news for you: We have decided that you will need a higher rank to do this, so your petty officer status is being restored with immediate effect. This may not be what the court martial intended but we are not going to be dictated to by that and promotions are a Wren matter anyway. So you can put your anchors up again."

"That is good. I kept them tucked away just in case and they are in a drawer back at the flat. And two?"

"Well, you seem to have been a bit of a hit with the Norwegians. We've had them on to us several times already about your rescue efforts off South Foreland and they seem to want to acknowledge them in some way. I gather King Haakon himself happened to be there, ironically to inspect the crew you rescued, and apparently he pinned a medal onto your oilskin in Dover?"

"That's right. I must say I have been wondering what it is and what I should do

CHAPTER TWENTY: Recognition

with it. Do you know any more?"

"It is a genuine medal all right, to add to your collection. I'll make sure you are allowed to put it up. It is Norway's premier decoration so you have been highly rewarded. It is for outstanding bravery and service of any sort and only rarely given to non-Norwegians. Did you know the whole rescue had been filmed?"

"Good heavens no. Why was that?"

"Apparently there was a film unit accompanying the king anyway to record the inspection for sending back home. So they set up on the cliff top and filmed you at it."

"Well, whatever next? One minute a convict, the next a film star. "

"There is talk of some sort of a reception to make your medals more official. I'll keep you posted."

"Oh, fine if that is what they want. Just bear in mind that for me it is the same story: either my crew all get something or I don't want anything. They were just as involved as I was. Any idea when?"

"No, we're not that far on yet. Incidentally, in view of this Norwegian involvement our Director has asked for a report on the incident. Can you have that ready in a few days' time?"

"Yes, I should think so. I jotted some notes at the time and the whole thing is still pretty vivid in my memory. Do you want to see me again or shall I just post it to you?"

"We need to see you once more to discuss your next job in more detail, so arrange to bring it in by the end of the week."

On the train to Plymouth a week later Jane reflected on her abrupt change of fortune again. Armed with her own travel warrant book, introductory letters to everyone from Admirals-in-Command to boats officers and senior Wrens, she was looking forward to seeing how things were going. She tried to keep her visits low key and quietly find out how the Wrens were faring, and largely succeeded. Starting at Plymouth she paid a courtesy call on Superintendent Welby then had a happy couple of hours with the familiar presence of the boats officer. They both seemed amused and impressed in equal measure by her changed status. She took the opportunity to stay with her father and it was good to see him again, perhaps a little brighter than on her last visit, but as with her previous visit Jane noticed that Eunice was now acting as much more than the family cook. The family news was that David had an appointment to a fast minelayer, and so far was loving the whole business of tearing around the seas at high speed. Sarah was blossoming rapidly and the twins were no longer little children.

Leaving Plymouth she thought, 'Well, if every port is like Plymouth this is going to be easy'. But of course, they were not. Calling in to Dartmouth was a challenge.

There the boats officer remained actively antagonistic towards her. He had no choice but to let her go on his boats and talk to the Wrens on them but with ill grace and warned her that if she dared to say a word against him or his crews there would be serious trouble. Fortunately, the girls assigned there were a happy and satisfied group doing a useful job so there was no need to let the personal antagonisms creep into her report.

While there she had a re-union with Dora. This was something she had been trying to avoid, feeling that her future lay with men but Dora's impassioned entreaties could not be ignored and despite her good intentions Jane's nights there were lost in a haze of fierce passion. This felt good at a physical level but Jane suspected that it was a mistake not just to call it off on arrival. Dora's feelings seemed as strong as ever and Jane had to be careful not to seem too casually off-hand in response. She did not want to hurt Dora who had been so good to her, but needed to find a way out of the intimate side of this relationship before it became too settled. The ironic, knowing glances she got from the boat crew girls she had to deal with, seemed to suggest that they knew very well what was going on between her and Dora.

There was a slight sense of relief as she moved on to Portsmouth but there she ran up against a much less friendly atmosphere. Here the Wrens were being restricted to the smallest boats and occasional jobs and were a dispirited group. Jane found that this misogyny ran through the male command from top to bottom and while there was little she could do on the spot with prejudiced admirals she was able to persuade the working levels to take a more accepting view of the girls' abilities. Mercifully, the other ports she had to visit were more positive and it was a pleasure to see her own crew running smoothly at Chatham under Punch's easy but commanding charge.

Six weeks went by before she returned to base calmer, more at ease and sparking again. She reported to Merle and arranged to go into headquarters directly to get her report written. She was summoned to report to the Director in person but this was brief and to the point. Being able to report that overall, boat crew Wrens were doing well and being accepted felt good. Portsmouth's particular problems were passed up to a higher level for action. It took a week to get a first draft of her report ready and shown to Merle. "This is good stuff, Jane. We like your reports; they are clear and concise and lay out the issues unambiguously. Maybe we will get you to do more of this sort of reporting."

Alarm bells rang in Jane's mind. Doing occasional ones was all very well but a life of report writing was much less appealing. 'I want to get back in a boat' was her overriding feeling. Week two saw her report polished and edited and typed up in fair copy. But there was no indication of what she would be doing next and when she asked Merle, she just got a shrug in reply. On the final Friday Jane was summoned

CHAPTER TWENTY: Recognition

to see Lady Cholmondley, the Director being away.

"Well Beacon, or should I say Lady Daubeny Fowkes, it is nice to be seeing you in better times. You have no idea how intense the Board's debate was at times at your Court Martial. But at least Superintendent Currie and I were able to restrain the more prejudiced elements amongst the men on the Board. Now, I have read a copy of your report and am pleased to see it. It is good to see that the role you have worked so hard for, for the Wrens, is now a reality and spreading rapidly. But that isn't the main reason I have asked you to see me. Your various recent exploits have been recognised and I have seen the citations for them. Your demand that your crew should also be recognised raised a few eyebrows but there has been a general sense of 'fair enough' about it and I am pleased to say that every member of your crew will be getting something. Pushed on by the Norwegians, there will be a reception at their legation next Wednesday where recognition of your work with experimental mine clearance will be combined with awards for your efforts rescuing the gun boat crew. So this will be two award ceremonies in one. You are to be there for 1600 so we are arranging cabs from here to Kensington. Please be here at 1500 in your best uniform, and with the medal King Haakon gave you, pinned in place. This will be a further major step for the Wrens; the Director sends her best wishes and regrets she cannot be with us on the day. But alas she is away so I will have to substitute. Discussions are going on with the Norwegians about your doing some work with them but that is not certain yet. In the meantime you will be given more convalescent leave until we decide what you are to do next. Any questions?"

"Do you know what I am being awarded, ma'am?"

"Yes, but that is secret until next Wednesday. Let's just say you will not be disappointed. King Haakon will be there to give out the medals in person; I presume you know your etiquette for appearing before a sovereign, having done it before? We are arranging a few lessons for your crew who have to learn to curtsey and are finding it a strange new act."

"Oh, I know about that sort of thing. Poor old Johnson will find it a bit strange, I rather think."

"Yes indeed but it is all in a good cause."

By the following Wednesday Jane had collected her new tiddly uniform from the tailors who had made a good job of fitting it to her long lean frame. With spare silk stockings in her pocket and the Norwegian medal pinned on she was equipped.

Arriving at the Norwegian legation Jane was startled to find a throng of people in a large hall with a table at the far end, covered in medals. She recognised Commander Goodeve and Lieutenant-Commander Richardson from the Birnbeck group, some faces from the crew she had rescued and the King himself. She was surprised to see General Brownlow further back in the group around the King. When the Wren group, led by Lady Cholmondley, came in there was a pause and an appreciative murmur went round the room. Merle whispered fiercely in Jane's ear, "This is recognition for the Wrens. From your court martial onwards the resistance has just been ebbing away." Which was good, thought Jane, even if the price had been high in her personal terms.

At a nod from Lady Cholmondley an admiral stepped forward and called the throng to attention. "Your Majesty, my Lords and Ladies, gentlemen, it gives me great pleasure to welcome you all today to this unique double ceremony. Making awards to successful seamen is nothing new. When those seamen are women, Wrens from our sister force, we are indeed moving into new territory. This is two ceremonies at the same time as this remarkable group have performed two acts of outstanding gallantry within a few weeks of each other and we are delighted to recognise both today. The first part will deal with their activities on the mine research work, then after a break we will move on to their brilliant rescue of a whole crew from imminent disaster when their ship was breaking up round them. I will invite Commander Goodeve to say a little more, then we are honoured to have His Majesty present the medals."

Commander Goodeve stepped forward and in his Canadian twang said. "When I heard that one of our experimental craft had been blown up with the loss of all but two of its hands, I was deeply distressed. When I heard, then saw, that the other craft, with a crew of Wrens on board, had quite deliberately been taken onto the range by them, operating where the first one had been blown up, to carry out the same experiment, I was utterly horrified. This was calm calculated bravery of the highest order, doubly appreciated as they made the experiments work after weeks of trying. The readings they got that day allowed us to conclude that whole experimental programme. My admiration for the courage they showed that day has no bounds and I was very happy to be able to recommend to the Prime Minister that an extremely high award was due to every one of them. I have heard them say that really, they did nothing special. Do not be deceived by this modesty. At any moment they could have been blown up yet they persisted and made the highly dangerous experiment work. Therefore I am delighted to be able to say that today their skipper, Wren Jane Beacon, is being awarded the George Cross. Her first lieutenant, Petty Officer Violet Johnson, is awarded the George Medal, and the three Wrens on board are each awarded the Distinguished Service Medal. Sadly the two engine room ratings were killed a week later when their ship, the VIC 5, was attacked and sunk by an e-boat. So they both receive a posthumous Distinguished Service Medal. I will now invite them to come forward and receive their medals from King Haakon. Wren Jane Beacon, please."

CHAPTER TWENTY: Recognition

Totally amazed at this turn of events Jane stepped forward, came to attention three steps back from the King, curtsied deeply and stepped forward. The King, smiling broadly, took the medal from its cushion held by a Chief G I, and pinned it on to Jane's uniform. He smiled, "Congratulations, young lady. I will see you again shortly." Jane stepped back and curtsied again, left wheeled and went back to her place with the others. Now it was Punch's turn. Looking utterly terrified she sketched an approximation of a curtsey and stepped forward. Her sheer size was striking as she stood before the King. This was someone as tall as he was. They chatted amicably for a couple of minutes while he pinned on the medal, then on a nod she stepped back, just about managed another curtsey, and escaped. Sparrer and Evadne followed, then General Brownlow stepped forward to collect Suki's medal for her. "May I say a word? My daughter is a member of this crew and it has been a life-changing experience for her to have worked with Wren Beacon. She did not feel able to be here today as she is still recuperating from a serious injury received when their ship, the VIC 5, was sunk by a prowling e-boat. So she asked me to stand in for her and I was delighted to do so as my involvement with Wren Beacon goes back much further. She rescued me from the beaches of Dunkirk, collecting me in her boat at midnight with shells and bullets flying around, none of which seemed to bother her in the least. So I have fond memories of her and am not at all surprised to see her collecting another award for outstanding bravery. Her relationship with the Navy has not always been easy and any time their Lordships decide they don't want her I shall be delighted to see her taken into the ATS. She is one of the outstanding women in this war and it is very good to see that recognised today. Thank you." And with a small bow he stepped back into the throng. The same elderly admiral announced, "That completes the first half of our awards today. We will now break for a cup of tea then move on to the second half." Everyone clustered round the tea urns but Jane noted that people seemed reticent about speaking to her or any of her crew. With tea drunk the Admiral called everyone to attention again. "By chance, the remarkable rescue carried out by our Wren crew was filmed by a unit accompanying his Majesty that day. Before we resume the ceremony, we will have a ten-minute showing of that film which is a dramatic demonstration of rescue at sea under severe conditions." At the far end of the hall a screen flickered into life and then pictures appeared of the picket boat turning to back in to the stricken gun boat. The following ten minutes made the whole rescue appear very dramatic with heavy seas threatening the picket boat but never quite overwhelming it. The movie show over, the curtains were drawn back and King Haakon stepped forward. "This second part of today's ceremonies lies closer to my heart. To watch that small boat rescuing twenty of my countrymen under such conditions is quite outstanding and to discover that it had been a crew of Wrens – young women – who had done it was a revelation. May I say that I suspect that any country that can produce women so capable and so brave, can never be defeated. Your women simply will not allow it. I had the honour of investing Miss Beacon with the Royal Order of St. Olaf on the deck of her boat and I am delighted to see she is wearing it today. But her crew were equally brave and therefore I am investing her first lieutenant, Petty Officer Wren Johnson, with the same order and every one of them receives our Medal for Heroic Deeds." Prodded by Merle, they stepped forward and each in turn curtsied with greater or lesser grace and had their medals pinned on. King Haakon seemed pleased with this, stepping back into the throng afterwards. The admiral took over again. "With these high honours from Norway, the Navy felt it had to respond in kind, and therefore it falls to me to invest Petty Officer Wren Beacon with the Albert Medal in gold." Jane was prodded forward again. Unsure of the protocol she fell back on the little bob of the knee which seemed to serve. Albert Medal pinned in place she stepped back and Punch took her place. The admiral, a short stocky man, was impressed. "By Jove you are a prime specimen. Did you have much experience in boats before joining the Wrens?"

"Yes sir, been in Thames barges all me life."

"Indeed; that would explain it. It is good when such abilities can be recognised. For you, the Albert Medal in silver."

In turn Evadne then Sparrer was invested with the Albert Medal as well. The admiral seemed fascinated by Sparrer's Bermondsey twang and chatted to her for several minutes before letting her go.

"Now we come to the final part of this investiture. As well as the military forces, some civilian organisations give medals for outstanding sea rescues, and some are being awarded today. For this I welcome Sir Grenville Adams from the Board of Trade to present them."

"Thank you, Admiral Seaman. We at the Board of Trade have our own medal for saving life at sea. It is the only one awarded by Act of Parliament and we protect it jealously. But there is no question of our being protective today. The film we saw a short while ago showed these young ladies carrying out the sort of daring and incredibly tough rescue the medal was created for, and it gives me great pleasure in awarding it to each of the crew we have here today." Prodded again by Merle, they all stepped forward, were shaken by the hand, and given their medal. With that done Sir Grenville spoke again. "We are almost finished. The last awards go to Miss Beacon, and are the Royal Humane Society's medal in Silver, and the Corporation of Lloyd's medal in silver, for saving life at sea. They have asked me to present them so if Miss Beacon would step forward again, I have pleasure in giving her these as

CHAPTER TWENTY: Recognition

well. "This duly done, the admiral took over again. "Ladies and gentlemen, three cheers for our heroines." And hip-hip hoorays rang round the hall. Feeling thoroughly embarrassed Jane felt some sort of response was called for. "On behalf of my crew I thank you all for coming here today and for this incredible array of recognition symbols you have given us. My crew and I feel that really, in each case we were only doing our duty and would have done both happily without any recognition at all had that been how it went. But as it is we are now well medalled and I thank you all most deeply for your kind consideration for our efforts. In this country we still have a long way to go but we will come out on top in this beastly war and you may be sure that Britain's women are right there in their determination to see it through. Spare a thought for all those women who toil away without recognition or reward but do their bit towards the day when we can all have a more normal life again. In the meantime thank you so much for what you have given us today, and onwards to victory."

A loud cheer went up in response.

The Admiral spoke once more. "The Norwegian legation has kindly put in a Scandinavian Smorgasbord spread with champagne and Aquavit for the toasts. It is waiting for us next door so I suggest we go to it now."

The throng wasted no time in heading for the door and for the next couple of hours Jane found herself juggling plate and glass as all manner of people claimed her attention. When the King came to talk, she was left alone with him but otherwise there was a queue waiting to speak. It was the same for all her crew members and Sparrer seemed to be having a grand time chatting away to all manner of exalted personages. The King had a few cryptic questions for Jane. Had she ever been to Shetland? Did she work on open seas as much as in harbour? What was her next appointment? What would she think about working with the free Norwegian Navy? She could only shrug and say that as a rating in uniform she went where she was sent. Jane caught Merle's eye and made the introductions, explaining that Merle was her divisional officer and was a first point of contact for any proposals for her deployment. Passing by, Lady Cholmondley remarked "Well Beacon, I think we can safely say your court martial is now ancient history and your future looks bright."

CHAPTER TWENTY-ONE:
Lunch: Trial or Pleasure?

The Norwegians certainly knew how to party: between many toasts and her hosts' enthusiastic willingness to top up her glass Jane was distinctly unsteady by the time a taxi dropped her at the flat. This was the first time Jane had encountered people from an occupied country since the early days after Dunkirk and she was taken aback by the ferocity of the hatred shown towards the German occupiers. The hangover the next morning was brutal and when Lady O swept into her room mid-morning Jane was still in no condition to argue. Lady O looked at Jane's jacket, which must have been picked up by the maid and carefully hung up as Jane's fuzzy memory was of dumping all her clothes in a pile, and asked, "Is that really a George Cross? You have been holding out on me Jane, Lady Daubeny-Fowkes, suggesting that you were just doing a bit of experimental test work."

All Jane could do was croak, "Too much," and clutch her head.

But mercifully, hangovers do not last for ever and by mid-afternoon she was staging a recovery. Even so, staying in the flat seemed like a very attractive option.

A day later she caught a train down to the South coast and called on Suki, now convalescing at her family home. The wounded sailor was well on her way to recovery but clearly, she had difficulty focussing and there were signs of her not being able to concentrate for long. Mrs Brownlow brought in tea and cake, the General being away on his duties, and the three ladies chatted for some time. Suki was full of thanks for Jane saving her but Jane's response was predictable. "I could hardly leave you behind to drown, now could I?" It was clear that it would be some time yet before Suki was ready for duty again. Jane left feeling sad, as Suki had been so helpful to her at a difficult time, and had been such an important part of the *Kittiwake* crew, that losing her was going to leave a big gap.

She then found she had a series of lunches to attend. First was the Corporation of Lloyds, wanting to congratulate the recipient of their medal in person. This proved to be a rather grand affair with a group of very eminent gentlemen from the marine insurance world, held in their private dining room. They were intrigued by her medal collection and listened attentively while she gave them the well-rehearsed twenty-minute version of the Dunkirk story. It was proving difficult to say much about the George Cross because the work had officially been hush-hush but an explanation that her ship had done the same thing as another that got blown up, seemed to satisfy them. They had obtained a copy of the film of the rescue and after watching it again she had to explain in minute detail what had gone on, to this knowledgeable audience.

The Royale Humane Society was rather different, with a number of grand ladies on its board and a sense of social contribution about their interest. Some had been primed already by Lady O so had their questions ready, which gave Jane an opportunity to emphasise how much women were doing in this war, and how it was going to change permanently the social order in Britain. Even this gentlest of feminist suggestions met with some fairly stiff responses, including from a couple of the grand dames, but Jane just smiled sweetly. They apologised for not giving her the Stanhope Medal for the outstanding rescue of the year but Jane took the opportunity to be modest about her own achievements, suggesting that an individual act of bravery was much more deserving. They also had a copy of the film to show, leaving Jane with a slight feeling that although it showed dramatically what she had done, frequent showings of it could get tedious. But in their own polished way they were friendly and Jane left with invitations to see them again sometime.

After that, the lunch with the Board of Trade was rather more prosaic. Although Sir Grenville was there acting as host, they dined in a simple restaurant and had a more direct and practical interest in her doings. There was a good deal of discussion about what women were good for, the fact that Jane's rescue had been with an all-female deck crew being seen as an important pointer to something, although they were not clear about what. This gave Jane good scope to talk about women's role in the postwar world and how their demonstrated abilities meant that there would always be more than mother and housewife open as roles for them. This met with some quite stiff opposition but Jane was learning to smile and let the more vehement responses pass over her. But there were several more open-minded among the half dozen who attended and she managed to have an intelligent and thoughtful debate with them.

After these pleasant excursions, a phone call from Merle brought her down to earth again with a bump. "Hello Jane, are you ready for active service again? When you have finished swanning around having swanky lunches, I'd like you to come in and discuss your next moves. The King of Norway seems greatly taken with you and has also extended an invitation to lunch and discuss possible involvements. This will be official with more than just the King and you in attendance so we need to plan ahead."

"Well, physically I am fine and would love to be back on the deck of a boat. I'm not feeling so drained mentally either so really there is no reason why I shouldn't be back in harness."

"Fine. Can you come in the day after tomorrow then? Make it ten in the morning."

Sitting across from Merle at headquarters was becoming natural, as was being summoned to see the Director who congratulated her on the new medal haul. "You have a highly impressive collection now which has to say something about your strengths."

"Frankly ma'am I think it can all be put down to chance and luck. If my efforts hadn't been noticed I doubt if anything would have been said about them."

"Well, you still had to do those things."

"Yes ma'am, but if Commander Goodeve hadn't been there to see us going up the mine runs, firmly convinced we were about to be blown up when we didn't really think so for a minute. And then if King Haakon hadn't been planning to inspect the Norwegian crew we rescued, and hadn't happen to have a film crew with him so they saw and recorded the whole thing from the clifftops, all we'd have received would have been some thanks from the boffins and perhaps from the skipper of the boat. And the silly thing is we didn't expect anything more than a quiet word of 'well done' from those directly involved. But we were seen and the rest is history."

"Well Beacon, I tend not to regard modesty as your strong suit but there is some truth in what you say." Jane was then given a standard warning not to argue, and a nodded dismissal closed things; the whole meeting had only lasted ten minutes as the Director was clearly very busy. With that out of the way, Merle got down to business. "Have you ever heard of the Shetland Bus, Jane? No, me neither but I have done a bit of enquiring and it seems that the Free Norwegians have a base in Shetland from where they sneak over to Norway in fishing boats pretending to be part of the local fleet. It seems to be fairly hazardous work, but is so regular that it has become known as the Shetland Bus. King Haakon and his officers seem to think there might be some way you could be involved in this. As it is going to be official, he has invited you, a couple of us from Wren HQ and some relevant naval officers all to come for lunch and a discussion about what we can contribute. He seems keen to get on with it so it is planned for the middle of next week. You should be wearing the George Cross and your Norwegian medals for the occasion. Are you ready for that?"

"Oh yes, I think I can withstand one more lunch. And the thought of getting out to sea on a fishing boat which isn't really one, is rather enticing. It'll be bitterly bloody cold up there; In my recent kit re-issue I was given three pairs of blackouts and I rather think I will need them. Wouldn't be seen dead in them otherwise, the way they reach down to the knee."

Merle snorted a laugh. "Yes, not the sexiest garments. Do I presume you don't have a boyfriend or any entanglements like that just now?"

"No, none. It is only eight months since David died and I've barely adjusted

CHAPTER TWENTY-ONE: Lunch: Trial or Pleasure?

to widowhood yet. I can't pretend I am in any rush to get involved again. Doesn't seem right somehow."

"No, I suppose not. If this plan works out you could always keep your eye open for a nice hunky Norwegian."

"Oh come on, Merle, you know that mixing business and pleasure isn't a good idea. Believe me, I will try to be a good girl and keep my focus on the job."

But looking at the Norwegian officers at the lunch, Jane reflected that keeping to any resolution not to mix work and personal affairs might be quite difficult. She was introduced to the Crown Prince and to various tall good-looking officers resplendent in new naval uniforms, then was seated on the right of the King for lunch. Through lunch the conversation was general, largely taken up with the state of the war, and again Jane felt that undercurrent of fierce hatred towards the occupiers. These were not people who would play at war; if she was going to get involved with them, clearly she would also have to bring a level of intensity to her activities which had not always been necessary in recent times. She was quizzed about her family background and how she came to be so expert in boats. That led on to the story of Dunkirk and her time in the Wrens since October 1939. Satisfied, the King remarked that it was a good thing for every enemy of the Boche that everyone should do their bit against them. Britain was particularly blessed in having its women so willing to get involved. That, opined Jane, was the least that could be expected but presumably it would be more difficult for Norwegian women to do much with the oppressors' eyes on them all the time. The King smiled. "You would be surprised at the extent to which all Norwegians are doing what they can against the enemy. Or nearly all. We have lost good people by being betrayed by their fellow Norwegians and an important function of the boats from Shetland is to extract people who are at risk of being seized by the Germans."

Lunch finished, the assembly moved next door to a map and conference room. The King acted as chairman. "It has been our pleasure to welcome Miss Beacon today, to be able to discuss ideas with her and to look into the future a bit. By the way, I only discovered today that Miss Beacon is really Lady Jane Daubeny-Fowkes, the widow of a highly successful Royal Navy officer, so welcome, Lady Jane."

Jane was startled by this but decided to play it down. "Well thank you, Sire, but I am quite happy just to be Petty Officer Wren Jane Beacon. It is not as though I was born to my rather exalted title."

The King laughed and continued, "I will invite Lieutenant-Commander Larsen who leads our work in Shetland to describe the idea we have for Miss Beacon to contribute to our operations in Shetland."

Lieutenant-Commander Larsen, stood and walked over to the large map of the North Sea covering one wall. "Shetland is the closest part of Britain to Norway which makes our operation easier and a logical place to operate from. Also, the Shetlanders have a strong affinity with us which makes our presence there all the more welcome. Together with our brothers operating with SOE, we are doing what we can to make life unpleasant for the Huns. And in some cases rather more than just unpleasant. Our operations from Shetland serve a useful purpose in keeping alive contact between our poor occupied country, and the free world. For some time now we have felt that we should be doing more to involve our women in the struggle, knowing how willing they are to contribute. Therefore we are looking at the possibility of asking Miss Beacon to join us and train some of our women in activities which help our cause while hindering the Boche. We are still exploring what might be done and our first step is to ask Miss Beacon to come to Shetland, look at our operations and see what more can be done. At this stage we don't have a detailed plan for this and are hoping something can be worked out by Miss Beacon joining with us."

The King took the floor again. "Miss Beacon's abilities are well known to us now and we will count ourselves fortunate that we are getting them. We already have a close relationship with the British Navy and it will be a part of our thinking to see if this Wren angle can be developed into something more."

Sleep was hard to come by that night. Jane lay awake, feeling daunted by this latest twist in her life. Whether it was the burning fierceness of the crews she had met, or the thought of the North Sea in winter, or the closeness of an active enemy who it would seem she was going to get closer to, there was no doubt but that she was going to be meeting further challenges before long. These people were going to be demanding at a new level and she could not let them down. It also occurred to her that her whole war so far - give or take an excursion to Dunkirk – had been on and around the South of England. Shetland seemed like an enormous way away. Should she try to back out of this commitment? Find some excuse for staying down South? 'Oh come on, you should be showing more spirit of adventure than this. What are you so afraid of?' But deep doubts lingered in her mind.

These thoughts were pushed out by a summons to come in and see Merle. "Right Jane, everything is set up for you to go North. You will fly from Northolt to Edinburgh, take a train right up to Thurso in the North of Scotland, transfer by ferry to Orkney where you will look in on the Wrens based at Scapa Flow, then take a ferry up to Lerwick, the main town in Shetland. The Norwegian base is at a place called Scalloway on the West coast and you will have to find your own way there. They are arranging quarters for you in some local digs. We are still pretty much in the dark about what you are to do and I suspect they don't have a plan as such either,

CHAPTER TWENTY-ONE: Lunch: Trial or Pleasure?

so there is an opportunity to carve out your own niche in this operation of theirs. There is no specific time limit on this deployment so we will just have to see how it goes. Ask me questions if you like but I don't know any more."

"Will I actually be going afloat and joining them on their trips to Norway? That sounds like fun."

"I don't know. I suspect anything like that will have to come out in what you find when you get there. An interesting but challenging task for you. You will be all on your own in Wren terms, so try to write to us each week with an update on what is happening. We have arranged for you to collect your pay once a month in Lerwick. I presume that will be all right for you?" Merle knew something of Jane's good fortune and that she would not be living hand to mouth from payday to payday. She smiled sweetly at Jane, "So good luck and show us up in the best light you can." Armed with various travel warrants and instructions on her travel arrangements, as well as a crib sheet of information about her latest medals and how to show them, Jane headed back to the flat with her head buzzing. The doubts which had been assailing her faded away as she contemplated what might be ahead, and suddenly a great upsurge of determination ran through her. This was not something to be afraid of, but to look forward to and to try to do her best in. 'Bring it on,' she muttered sufficiently noisily to startle her fellow tube travellers. But getting off at Green Park as usual, London with its noise and bustle seemed very cramped. Wide horizons lay out there and she was going to embrace them.

BIBLIOGRAPHY

TITLE	AUTHOR	PUBLISHER
COURTS-MARTIAL		
Admiralty Memorandum on Naval Court-Martial Procedure, June 1927 (Still the ruling instructions in 1942)		
Sailors in the Dock	Peter C Smith	The History Press
Court Martial	Alistair Mars	Frederick Muller Ltd.
The Law of the Sea	William McCafee	J B Lippiicott Company
The Ancient Laws of Oleron	David Hebden	Thomas Cooper & Stibbard
DEPARTMENT OF MISCELLANEOUS WEAPONS DEVELOPMENT		
The Wheezers and Dodgers	Gerald Pawle	Seaforth Publishing
Churchill's War Lab	Taylor Downing	Little, Brown
WRENS AND WOMEN IN WARTIME		
Blue Tapestry	Vera Laughton Mathews	Hollis & Carter
An intriguing Life	Cynthia Helms with Chris Black	Bowman & Littlefield
Diary of a Wren	Audrey Deacon	The Memoir Club
How a Century of War Changed the lives of Women	Lindsey Gorman	Pluto Press
The Unwomanly Face of War	Svetlana Alexievich	Random House
Train to Nowhere	Anita Leslie	Bloomsbury
The Girl from Station X	Elisa Segrave	Union Books
GENERAL		
February 1942	Adrian Stewart	Pen & Sword

Printed in Great Britain
by Amazon